Called

EJ Pay

ISBN: 978-1-7331202-1-0 (Paperback)

ISBN: 978-1-7331202-0-3 (ebook)

Any references to historical events, real people, or real places are used fictitiously. Names, characters, and places are products of the author's imagination.

Cover design by Mindee Thyrring/PostModernLaundry.com

First printing edition 2019.

www.ej-pay.com

To My Evelyn,
My Chelsea, My Ashleigh
And My Steve.
Look at what
We did!
I love you.

Prologue:
The Nightmare

We all have that dream. The same one we dream over and over throughout our lives. Sometimes details are added. Sometimes details are taken away. I'm no different. I have that dream too. I am convinced that somebody, somewhere, is calling to me while I sleep. "Evelyn, save me," I feel the voice crying. And no matter how hard I try, I can't shake the feeling that there is something I MUST do.

In the dream I am moving through water. I make my way down ruined stone corridors toward something I cannot see. I am in an ancient underwater ruin, but that isn't out of the ordinary to me. I've dreamt about it so many times, it feels like I belong here. Maybe I should be cold or even afraid, but I feel at ease in these murky waters. I know I have to find whatever is calling to me. I'll have no peace otherwise.

I open a coral-covered door to my right, as I always do. A familiar warmth fills my body as I look into the overly-bright room. Stone tables, vases, and remains of furniture line the decayed walls. I enter. And there it is, exactly as I remember, the pearl of light hovering in the open space before me. I want to touch it and yet I am afraid to. I know the consequences if I reach my hand toward that ball.

Suddenly, I hear voices behind me. I don't know why it always surprises me. I have the dream often enough. Some of the voices I recognize, some I don't. I panic. I know what I need to do, but I am afraid. As always, I am left with no time to think. I have to act. I reach my hand forward in a desperate attempt to capture the brilliant stone. As my fingers graze its surface, the ball grows, exploding outward to a hundred times its size. I see familiar faces screaming, but I can no longer hear their voices. Then, as quickly as it expanded, the glowing, burning orb contracts until it is nothing but darkness: a small, black pearl that can fit in the palm of my hand. I reach for it, grasp it, and the familiar dread spreads quickly into my body as I realize, once again – I cannot breathe.

Chapter 1

James brushes my bare arm with the back of his rough fingers and I pull my gaze away from the terminal window, my mind letting go of the remains of my dream. A shiver runs up my spine as I realize how cold it is in this airport. The heat of the Phoenix desert always leaves me unprepared for the frigid, air-conditioned indoors. I give James a small smile and sigh as I dig through my carry-on for my cardigan.

"What were you thinking about, Eves?" James asks as I shrug into my longer sleeves. "I've been trying to get you to come sit with me. That last flight to Vegas finally took off. There are some seats over here."

I pick up my backpack and leave my view of the tarmac and busy freeway to follow my boyfriend to a seat near the check-in counter. I feel the buzz in my pocket of another text from my mom checking to make sure we are still early enough for our flight. My mom isn't happy with my decision to leave Arizona for a college in Florida. Ever since my dad's accident, the ocean has always freaked her out. It's been just the two of us for so long that sometimes her anxiety gets the best of her.

My dad was lost at sea when I was just a little girl. I don't remember much of it. Most of what I know I learned from online articles and from overhearing whispered conversations between my mother's friends when they thought I couldn't hear. As the story goes, he was out looking for an old shipwreck with some rich guy who had a penchant for adventure and wasting money. A crazy summer storm whipped up out of nowhere, the ship's engines busted, and the whole thing capsized. Pieces of the wreckage washed up on shore for weeks and a few of the crew were found – none of them alive. My dad's body never washed up. For years, my mom slept in the same room as me, making sure that I was still there.

I love my mom, but it's time for me to move ahead with my life. I need to find my own answers and make my own peace with my dad's disappearance. That's why I chose a school so close to where my parents met and where my dad went missing. Since I graduated a year early, however, it isn't doing anything to help my mom worry less. Instead, she has to send her 17-year-old daughter off to a school thousands of miles away. She is doing her best to support me, but I know it's killing her to see me go. I pull out my phone so I can respond to her, making sure to not touch anything as I sit in the stain-covered chair by James.

"Is that your mom?" he asks. "She'll come around. She can't stay mad at you forever."

I sigh as I settle into the seat. I tap James on the arm so he'll hold me. He finishes his text and puts his arm on the back of my chair. I nestle my head onto his cotton t-shirt that covers his muscular shoulder, breathing in the scent of his cologne, trying to hold onto the smell as long as I can. We are going to two different schools. Him to Baylor in Texas, me to Florida International. I tried to convince him to come with me and he almost did, but he decided to give Baylor a try. Maybe next year he will change his mind. It will be rough to have a long-distance relationship.

"I hope so," I say in answer to his question. "She's been so freaked out about me going to Florida. I think she's afraid I'll disappear like my dad." James lets out a low sigh that blows through the top of my hair, the familiar smell of cinnamon gum reaches my nose.

"Evelyn," he says, "I know that's how she feels about it, but *you* know that isn't going to happen, right?" He sits up straight and pulls his arm away from me. I turn to look into his hazel eyes and feel the warm familiarity of his gaze while he talks. "Your dad was in a terrible boating accident. That kind of thing just doesn't happen on a daily basis. You aren't going to do anything to put yourself in that kind of danger."

I smile and nod. "I know," I say, and I stretch my arms high in the air, letting out a very satisfying yawn. "I'll be fine."

"Your mom will be fine, too," James says as he looks at his phone again. I nod and take in the smell of his cinnamon gum and play with the hairs on his arm. I think of all the things I will miss about James. From his reddish-brown hair to his tanned freckles and broad smile, he has me – hook, line, and sinker. I've almost said, "I love you," so many times. But I don't want to be the one to say it first. The next few months until winter break will drag on without him. If I didn't feel that dream pulling me to the Atlantic Ocean, I would go to

Baylor in a heartbeat so we could be together. I think of what our lives could be after graduation: marriage, kids, jobs we love. But we've never talked about those things out loud. I keep them locked inside, wishing and hoping that they will happen.

As I settle back into my seat, I let my thoughts drift again to the where they were before – the dream and the forbidden stone. James is scrolling through his phone, listening to music and messaging friends. We sit in silence together, my arms wrapped around me to keep warm, the smell of cinnamon lacing its way into my mind.

We finally arrive in Dallas. This is our parting point – just a two-hour layover for me, but the start of a 90-minute drive for James. I don't want to look weak or needy as I tell him goodbye for months, but I'm not convinced that I can act that well. I'm excited for my new life and answers in Florida. I just wish James was going with me. I take a deep breath as I hold his hand at the car rental counter.

"Well, this is it," I manage to whisper. I squeeze his hand, my thumb stroking the back of his knuckles as he picks up the car keys. "I'll see you in December."

James is silent as we walk toward the airport exit. He will be leaving the terminal, I'll be heading back to my gate. I can feel his palms, cold and sweaty. What is he thinking about? Will he miss me as much as I am going to miss him? Will messaging be enough for us? Surely we don't have to wait until December to see each other.

We can fly out for visits. I'm ready to tell him this idea when a single tear escapes my eye. He stops and turns to face me. I feel a rush of longing as I look into his eyes. Longing for things to remain the same. Longing for safety. Longing for the answers I've never had my entire life. Longing for home. Longing for everything, really.

Those eyes. Why do they have to be so gorgeous? A second tear escapes as James reaches up to wipe away the first.

"Evelyn," he says. I can hear the pain in his voice. He is going to miss me. A warmth presses through my heart and I take a moment to feel completely loved. I give him a little smile, but the pain doesn't leave his eyes. "Evelyn," he says again. "I think we should let this be it for a while."

What?

What does he mean by that? I feel the corners of my smile falter as I search his face for an explanation.

"Look, we've been together for 18 months," he says. "It's been awesome and I've loved the time we've spent together," my mind is swimming. I'm still not able to process what he is saying to me. "But we are both moving in different directions now. I'll be studying at Baylor and you'll be in Florida. It would suck to try to keep up a long-distance relationship."

Is he really trying to break up with me? I feel my own hands go cold in his grasp, my smile falling completely from my face.

"Evelyn," he says as he squeezes my frozen hand. "This is the best thing for both of us."

"James," I begin. I'm trying to figure out how to respond to him, "I don't understand. We have this all worked out. We can text and call and we'll see each other at breaks." He lets go of my hand, adjusts the backpack on his shoulder and shifts his gaze to the floor. He is breaking up with me. He is honestly breaking up with me. I am getting lightheaded as the blood drains from my face, understanding dawning in my sinking heart.

"I know what our plans were," he says, "but honestly, Evelyn, just think about it. We're both going to be drowning in schoolwork. You'll have a job and we'll both be studying. We'll both be meeting new people. It just doesn't make sense to add the strain of a long-distance relationship to all of that."

"Then why were you so willing to get this far with me, James?" My voice has found its way into my throat and I am borderline yelling as I talk to him. How could he let me get my hopes up? Why did he even bother to fly out with me? Anger mixes with shock and disbelief. I have never felt such a confusing set of emotions before.

"Look, we've had a great time together," he says. "You made the last bit of high school awesome for me. We've had a great time. Let's just remember the good stuff and move on."

I cannot believe what I am hearing. A host of counter-arguments and words that would make my mom SO mad are filling my mind. I am ready to pelt him with all of it when we hear my flight being called over the airport speaker. This is it. I have to go, or I run the risk of missing my flight. He knows this. It's why he waited for this moment – he gets to say his bit and take off without time for any real dialogue between us. No arguments. No staying to apologize to the old girlfriend. I am sick at the thought that I am about to be cast off by the guy I thought I loved.

"That's your flight, Evelyn. You've got to go. I'm sorry. I really am, but you'll see – this is the best thing for both of us." He plants a firm kiss on my cold, hard lips. My lips warm to his touch and I feel the familiar sensation of melting when he kisses me. But the kiss is brief, a fun sendoff for our futures apart. It is over in a moment and James is grabbing the rest of his bags to head to his rental car.

The sliding doors let him out and close me in. I stand in silence as I watch my dreams walk away from me. Another stupid tear escapes from my eyes, then another and another. I have no choice. I have to go or be stuck in Dallas. The thought is tempting. The chance to chase after him and tell him all the reasons why he is wrong.

"This is the second call for United Airlines flight F627. All passengers, please report to the ticketing area for check-in."

I am not sure how I am able to shoulder my backpack and turn around. Everything is numb, and I feel like I am watching someone else turning and moving away. I make my way to the gate, hand over my ticket to a tired-looking woman, and board the plane. I find my seat, store my backpack in the overhead bin, and sit down to stare out of the window. I feel sick and the plane hasn't even moved yet. I lean my head back, closing my eyes, giving into the pain of realizing I'm not as loved as I thought I was.

Chapter 2

After a restless flight and stuffy Uber ride with a splitting headache, I finally arrive at the Biscayne Bay campus of FIU. It is early evening and the sun is beginning to set. I have been traveling all day and have been holding back tears through most of it. Reliving my breakup makes everything that much harder to figure out.

The Biscayne campus is a branch from the main FIU campus and is located directly on the Bay. I can see the water in the bay as my driver drops me off at the Bayview Student Housing, my new home for the next few months. It is all I can do to keep from heading straight to the calm bay. I stand and stare for a while with my carry-on dangling from my shoulder. The early August air is warm and humid. I have only been out of the car for a few minutes and I can already feel the sweat rolling down my spine. My hair is sticking to my neck and my clothes are damp. It is a stifling feeling, but all I want to do is breathe it in. I want this fiery ocean air to be a part of me. I can feel it working its way into my lungs and I welcome it.

I reach for my phone to call James and tell him about the view and the heat, but I stop myself. I can't call James and tell him about anything because James is no longer my boyfriend. My vision goes blurry from more tears trying to make their way out of my eyes. I blink quickly, wipe my eyes, and take a deep breath to calm down. I don't need a breakup to ruin my first day in Florida. I'm finally where I belong, with or without James. I can do this.

I pull out my phone and call my mom instead. She laughs at my reaction to the suffocating heat and humidity and asks how my day of travel went. I keep things very general, especially where James is concerned. I'm not ready to have that conversation without crying. Before ending the call, my mom makes me promise to be careful and stay out of the water when it's dark. I won't be going to the water. At least not tonight, anyway.

I also promise to check in with Uncle Russ – the main reason Mom is letting me go to FIU at all. Russell Salvesen is the University president and a longtime friend of my parents. He has promised to keep an eye on me while I'm so far from home and so close to the ocean. His daughter, Celia, is my age and will be one of my roommates. I finish my list of promises to be safe and put her mind at ease.

As I hang up from the call, I hear one last, "Evelyn." I check to see if I missed something, but the phone is off. A few students are lounging on the grass outside the housing complex. I must have misheard, my homesickness playing with my ears. My heart feels heavy as I head to the front entrance of Bayview.

"Evelyn!"

This time there is no mistaking it. I know I heard my name. I take another look around. How many Evelyns can there be? I see no one looking at me, so I hurry inside.

When I finally get to the front desk, security gives me my room key and I head up to my apartment. When I get there, the lock is already undone. I open the door slowly, not sure if someone else is there. I get the door halfway open when it suddenly jerks open and out of my hand. The person standing in front of me has a huge smile spread across her golden-brown skin and dark eyes that carry her smile to the top of her face. I smile back as she opens the door wide for me to come in.

"Hello!" she says cheerfully as I enter the shared living space, "I'm Gwendolyn Mizrahi. And you must be Evelyn. You can call me Gwen." She closes the door behind me and I turn to answer her.

"Hello to you too," I say, "Yes, I'm Evelyn." I set my bag on the small kitchen table and reach for her outstretched hand. Uncle Russ wrote to me about my roommates before I left Arizona. One is Celia, who will be arriving next week. The other is Gwen, a "lovely girl from a rough situation – a scholarship award winner…risen above her upbringing…" His description of Gwen was vague and I wasn't sure what she would be like.

Gwen is warm and friendly, so much different from the person I expected to meet. I thought her difficult life might make her reclusive or guarded, but it seems to have had the opposite effect. She shakes my hand then pulls me in for a quick, friendly hug.

"I hope you don't mind me coming in already," she says, "once I saw that I was the first one here, I wasn't sure which room to take. I figured I would wait to set up my stuff," she points at the tiny couch under the window overlooking the bay. It is overflowing with a small mountain of her belongings. Bedding, books, luggage, school supplies - all of it plain and used.

"Well," I say, "I think Uncle Russ said Celia gets the two rooms on the right, so you'll be in the left rooms with me." I point the way and we head down the hall. I see that the first room has all of my boxes inside already. Uncle Russ made sure they were here for me. That means the room on the end is for Gwen. As she follows me with her grey and worn luggage, I think of the contrast to all the new things I have in my boxes. My mom isn't extravagant, but she always makes sure my needs are met and we did some dorm shopping over the summer. I'm not sure if Gwen has ever had that kind of attention paid to her. I feel a pang of guilt as I compare our situations. I don't know everything about Gwen yet, but I hope she will confide in me. She seems like someone I will like and I need a friend.

Together, Gwen and I unpack and get settled in. The sun is long gone behind the ocean by the time we finish. I am feeling very hungry when Gwen asks, "Want to go check out the bay?"

"Um, wow," I say. My promise to my mom is ringing in my ears. "Isn't it kind of late for that? Aren't you hungry?"

Gwen runs her fingers through her thick curls and smiles. "Yes, I'm hungry. I guess I'm just anxious to get down to the water. I haven't spent much time in the ocean."

"Neither have I."

"Let's go get some food and we can go to the bay tomorrow," Gwen says. "Then we can take as long as we want."

We ended up being the last customers in the campus Chick-fil-A. I felt a little guilty for making them dirty their counters again, but I was so happy to get my market salad and fries that I quickly got over the guilt. Gwen and I talked a lot. She told me about her life – raised by an aunt who didn't like her, she did most of the housework and tending to nieces and nephews. She was regularly excluded from family activities and often told she was a problem. She couldn't wait to get out of there. She knew she was worth more than what she was given. Her own sense of worth and what she wanted from life pushed her to do her best in school. She graduated early like me and applied to several area schools. She got an academic scholarship to FIU and an on-campus job. She left her old life behind.

Gwen was so open, it felt normal and easy for me to open up to her. I told her about my dad and even about my breakup. All the big stuff. She listened and hugged me when I talked about James. I didn't let too many tears out, but the ones I did cry left little circles on Gwen's shirt. We were talking so much, we didn't go to bed until after 1:00. It felt so good to find a friend so quickly.

I slept through my alarm this morning, so I am rushing to my mandatory breakfast meeting with Uncle Russ.

Uncle Russ is a nice man, super tall and thick. Not fat, just a really big guy. He has thinning gray-brown hair, blue eyes and a large smile. He has been sending birthday cards to my mom and me for as long as I can remember and I am looking forward to spending the morning with him.

"So, how do you like the campus Evelyn?" Uncle Russ asks when we are seated in the food court.

"Well, I haven't seen much of it yet," I answer, "but what I have seen so far is beautiful. I can see the ocean from my room. That could be good or bad," I laugh. "I may not be able to focus on my homework."

A shadow crosses Uncle Russ's face for the briefest of moments. But he swiftly pushes it away with one of his broad smiles and answers, "Yes, the ocean is very beautiful, but I'm sure you will find your class work just as exhilarating as what you can find in the bay." The way he says that leads my thoughts straight to the water and I have a sudden urge to run straight for the shoreline. It's all I can do to stay focused on our conversation. I turn to my omelet to help refocus my attention.

"I personally chose your roommates," he continues, "You and Celia used to play together when you were little." He chuckles at some old memory and I smile along, not at all remembering his daughter. "You met Gwen last night. She grew up in a broken situation, you know, but has really risen above it all to make the most of herself. I think you three will have a great year."

I smile at his comment. I hope it will be a great year for my own answers, but if both roommates are friendly and easy going, that will be icing on my cake. As an only child, I've never had to share a room with anyone. Sure, my mom was more into my life than most girls' moms, but when I wanted to deal with something on my own, I just had to close my bedroom door. For the next several months, I am going to have to figure out what to share or not share with my roommates. Things like jerk boyfriends.

I feel the strain of my breakup rising to the surface again, so I find something else to talk about. "Why is Celia living on campus instead of at home?" I ask.

"Well, we felt that Celia would do well to have some space of her own, away from home. I am here so often that it will not be that great of a separation, but she at least will feel that it is."

"And when will she be here?" I ask.

"Celia is in the Bahamas with her mother and will return next week. You and Gwen will have time to settle in before she arrives. Celia has been to our campus so often that she really doesn't need time to adjust.

"Speaking of mothers," Uncle Russ continues, "I talked with yours before we met up this morning. She wants me to remind you to not go into the bay alone and to not go into the bay at night and to not go into the bay when you are doing homework." He smiles and adds, "I'm pretty sure she would be fine if you never stepped a single toe into the water."

"That's about right," I say with a smile. I swallow some orange juice to hide my face. I don't need Uncle Russ to know that I have every intention to spend a lot of time in the bay. I still don't know how much he will tell my mom. "I'm sure I'll be busy with class and homework. I'll go to the bay, but it's not like I'm going to live there."

Uncle Russ's smile fades and he clears his throat. He picks up his own juice and looks around. "Well," he says after taking a drink, "it would be nice if that were an option, don't you think? We kind of have that here."

I know about the school Aquarius Program where participants actually live in an undersea lab. It's an ideal environment for studying sea life and is a world-class facility. But that isn't for me. I want to find answers to my life in the ocean, not answers to sea life in the ocean.

"Maybe for your graduate students," I say, "but I'm not interested in living underneath all that water. I think I would feel claustrophobic."

Uncle Russ smiles and nods. He is quiet and thoughtful for a moment before picking up the conversation again. He asks what classes I am most excited about (MET 4532 Hurricanes – my dad *did* disappear during one and I want to know why), what degree I think I'll settle on (Liberal Arts for now with an emphasis on Humanities and Cultural Traditions – I want to know about the human relationship with the ocean), and what I'll do in my spare time (work – haven't found that job yet – also exploring, which I do not tell him).

Uncle Russ is a friendly man, generally interested in everyone like a teacher/university president should be, but he isn't really to the level of a father figure in my life. I feel comfortable around him and I know I can call on him if I need anything, but for now I am just grateful that our connection got me out to Florida.

We finish our breakfast and he gives me a one shoulder hug as we say goodbye. I'm sure I'll see him around, but I am ready to get going. Gwen and I have a date at the beach and I don't want to miss it. I've been feeling the tugging from the shore all morning long. I don't know how much longer I can resist it.

When I get back to the apartment, Gwen is barely getting out of bed. I've been up and ready for a while, so I wait for her to shower and eat before we head to the beach. As I wait, I look through the small family photo album my mom gave me when I left. It's a book filled with strong women in my family line, supporting me and lifting me up in my journey into adulthood.

The first picture is of my great-grandmother, Ama Awenasa. It's an old black and white photograph from her wedding day. She was full Cherokee and married a smooth talking white boy sometime before the First World War. She is so dark skinned in her wedding dress it is a stunning contrast. Her dress is lightly patterned in the Cherokee tradition and she is wearing some of her traditional Cherokee necklaces – necklaces that have passed down to my mom. The groom, my great-grandfather, is dressed neatly in his army uniform and the couple is wrapped in the traditional white Cherokee wedding blanket. My great-grandfather died a few months later in a battle in France and my great-grandmother gave birth to my grandmother, Ahyoka, and raised her alone – not unlike my own mom.

My grandma Ahyoka married and had two children: Marisol (my mom) and my Uncle Charlie who passed away from alcoholism before I came along. By the time the gene pool was passed down to me, all I got of my Native heritage was my family tree. My eyes are a swirling mix of green and blue. My hair is straight and brown, my skin tans easily, but is otherwise pale. But my mom, she looks amazing. Dark eyes and thick, dark hair. Skin so smooth and brown I used to wish it was mine. She has high cheekbones and stands with the kind of pride you'd expect from the daughter of a great chief. She was raised in Florida like the women of the family had been since my great-grandparents moved here over a hundred years ago. My mom's mom and dad died when I was just little – before my dad disappeared. All the death around her made my mom extra protective of me. Letting me go to Florida is a big step for her. The thought makes me homesick.

But then Gwen comes bounding out of her room calling, "I'm set! Ready to go investigate the bay?" and all my nerves disappear.

"I am so ready."

Chapter 3

Even though the bay is so close to the apartments, there isn't a lot of open sand for lounging in. We will have loads of time all semester to explore the tree-lined bay, but for today, we are heading to Sunny Isles Beach, just a short Uber ride away. Once we arrive at the beach, I am blinded by the sunlight reflecting off the white sand. I remember my mom telling me about some wicked sunburns from that sand, so Gwen and I lather up before laying out.

"This looks like as good a spot as any," Gwen says as she lays out her towel near the pier.

"Agreed," I say and I stretch my towel out next to Gwen's. The beach is filling up with college students eager to get some shore time in before school starts next week. Tanned bodies and pale bodies like mine are laying everywhere. Only a few are actually enjoying the waves. Gwen and I lay out for about an hour before the heat has made resting unbearable.

"Want to head into the water?" Gwen asks.

"Oh my gosh, yes!" I say. Gwen stands up on her towel, her flip flops resting in the sand next to her and heads toward the waves. I stand to follow her, but as soon as my feet hit the sun-heated sand, they are burning up. I hesitate, jumping back onto the towel, but Gwen keeps going. I feel like a little kid at a waterpark. The cool water is so close, but I have to get across the burning concrete first. There's only one way to do this. Run.

I make a mad dash for the waves, passing Gwen who has started the hot-feet-tiptoe-hop toward the water. She starts laughing and so do I and soon we are both running to the ocean. When we finally land, splashing into the water, I am so disappointed that the water isn't colder. I knew the Atlantic Ocean was the warm ocean, but I had still imagined it being refreshing. Even though it isn't as cold as I would like, it is still better than the smoking hot sand we were running in. Gwen and I are still laughing as more and more people enter the water. It is so loud and full of people that I cannot hear the voice that has been calling to me for days. It is quiet and I am happy. All my cares are being washed away by the waves.

"Who is that?" Gwen says wide-eyed, as we stand waist deep in the water.

I turn around to see who she is talking about and see a super-hot guy walking toward us through the water. He is leaving a group of friends to come talk to us and I am trying not to stare so I turn back to Gwen.

"Holy crap," Gwen says again. "Look at his abs!"

"Gwen! I'm not going to turn back around," I say, "It would be way too obvious."

"Okay, then I'll just tell you what I'm seeing." Gwen's eyes are still wide as she describes the guy we are about to talk to. "His abs look like some Calvin Klein model, not too big like one of those huge bodybuilder guys, but more like a gorgeous, gorgeous…"

"A gorgeous what?!" I ask, eager for the details.

"Hi," I hear next to me. The voice is cool and inviting, young and strong. I turn to see the man it is attached to. "My name is Jack," he says, "I saw you two over here and wanted to introduce myself. I work at Oleta River State Park by FIU. Are you two students there?"

My mouth is dry and I can't say a word. Jack is tanned, muscular, and beautiful in every way. His green eyes sparkle under a head full of beach bleached hair. He must be a surfer or something to be so tan.

"Yeah, we're students at FIU. I'm Gwen and this is my roommate, Evelyn." I'm so glad Gwen knows how to talk.

"That's cool," Jack says, "I'm actually a student there myself, getting ready to participate in the Aquarius Program. I'll be living underwater for a few weeks at a time this semester.

"What are you studying?" Oh my gosh. He's talking to me.

"Um, uh,"

"Evelyn is studying liberal arts. She likes the culture stuff," Gwen answers for me.

"That's right," I finally say. I smile at Jack and laugh at my own awkwardness. Goosebumps are raising up my arms despite the heat outside. "I want to know more about people and their relationship to the ocean." Jack looks impressed and my heart flutters in my chest.

"That's awesome. Well, my friends and I are getting ready to play some volleyball. Would you two want to join us?"

"Yes, we would," Gwen answers for both of us and soon we are following Jack up the beach to the shaded volleyball courts. We spend the next several hours playing the game, drinking tons of water,

23

and getting to know some of the other students from FIU. It is such a glorious day.

As the afternoon wears away, everyone gets ready to head home. Gwen and I grab our gear and Jack walks us to the parking lot. He's riding a bike back to his place and has his backpack ready to go.

"Hey, Evelyn," he says, "we are always looking for student help at the Park. If you need a job, I can put a good word in for you."

"I actually do need a job, so that would be awesome," I say.

"Great," Jack says, "Can I have your number and I'll let you know where to come apply and interview?"

"Definitely," I answer with a smile on my face. I give him my number and he puts it in his phone. He gives Gwen and me a handshake before leaving.

"It was nice to meet you and get to know you a bit. I look forward to seeing you again soon," he says. As he rides away, Gwen and I watch him quietly.

He is so good looking.

After several minutes, I get a text on my phone.

"I thought he was into you," Gwen says, "but that was fast, don't you think?"

As I open my phone, my smile fades. "It wasn't Jack texting," I say. "It was James."

"What?! NO!" Gwen says and she takes my phone from my hand. "What the heck does that jerk face want? He doesn't get to dump you then string you along. NO WAY!"

She swipes left and the text is deleted from my phone. Honestly, I'm glad Gwen is here to do that for me. I don't know if I would have been strong enough to do that on my own. I smile and we start talking about Jack as we wait for our Uber. In a moment of silence, I hear a voice again.

"Evelyn," it says. It's so quiet, I turn my head to try to hear better.

"Evelyn," I hear again.

"Did you hear that?" I ask Gwen. "Someone said my name."

"Huh. Nope. I didn't hear anything," she says. "It must have been someone else."

I agree nonchalantly, knowing that it wasn't a mistake. My dreams, the voice, everything is leading me here. I'm here now and I will do all I can to find out what is waiting for me.

Gwen and I spend time at the beach nearly every day. The one day we miss is because I need to nurse a bad sunburn. Jack texts often and I have an interview lined up at the Oleta River State Park in a few days. If I get the job, I will be working with Jack, giving guided paddle tours. Jack came to the beach again with Gwen and me yesterday. Gwen smiled and stared at us while we talked and she gave me lots of winks and nudges when Jack wasn't looking. I've gotten two more texts from James, but I swiped left on my own for those.

Gwen and I are enjoying one of our last beach days before we have to rest up and be ready for school. I am quietly thinking, letting the last rays of the sun bathe my feet. Gwen is fast asleep on her towel, her floppy beach hat providing ample darkness. I take one last look over the horizon before I know we have to head back to our dorm. In the distance I see a large fin splashing far out in the ocean. What kind of fish is it? I don't know. For someone who has been as

25

ocean-driven as I have, you'd think I would know every sea creature alive. So, I let myself follow its path, further and further out to sea.

"Evelyn." I turn my head to see what Gwen needs, but a soft snore is coming from under her hat. "Evelyn." The voice is louder this time and strangely familiar. I can't tell if it's male or female, old or young, just that it *is* a voice and it is calling my name. I stand, turning left and right and trying to figure out where it is coming from. "Evelyn!" once more, louder this time. And coming from the ocean. My head snaps forward, to where the fins have disappeared beyond the waves. Gwen turns over and yawns and I feel a distinct silence. Whatever was calling me has gone.

"Are you ready to go?" Gwen asks. I stay still for a moment longer, knowing it's time to go back. But all I want is to figure out who or what was calling to me and what it wants. What it needs. Gwen gives my leg a tap with the back of her hand, bringing me out of my thoughts. "We'd better get back." I give her a nod and a grunt – it's all I can do to focus on picking up my bag and towel to head back to our apartment. The voice is gone, but the pull remains.

When we get back to our place, Gwen and I are greeted by Uncle Russ and his wife, Cynthia. The front room of our little dorm is overflowing with boxes and bags and luggage. We are exchanging greetings and introductions when I hear a huff from the bedrooms on the right.

"Dang! I forgot my traveling makeup bag. Mom!" She appears before her mom can even formulate a response. She is everything TV tells me is beautiful: tall, thin, blonde, blue eyes and a flawless complexion. She has a light tan and a rested look that I envy after her time away in the Bahamas. I am very aware of the breakout on my chin and sunburn on my cheeks as her eyes meet mine. "Oh, hello," she says in a distracted sort of way – like she's trying to pull her thoughts together. "I'm Celia, but my friends all call me Ceci. Which one are you?" Uncle Russ steps around a tower of packing boxes and moves to his daughter's side.

"Ceci, this is Evelyn Marin," he says as he points my direction, "The two of you used to play together when you were very little. Her parents are lifelong friends of mine." An uncomfortable look crosses his face as he realizes that only one of my parents is still a lifelong friend. The other is gone.

I spare him the discomfort of having to correct himself and step around the same tower of boxes to extend my hand toward the blonde goddess of a girl at his side. "Nice to meet you – or, I guess, to see you again." Uncle Russ gives me a grateful smile as Ceci takes my hand.

"Hello, Evelyn," Ceci says politely as she takes my hand and shakes it. I turn around and gesture toward Gwen who is trapped – boxes on one side, bags in front, and Cynthia Salvesen on the other side.

"This is Gwen. She's our other roommate. We've had the whole week together," I say.

"Well, it's nice to meet you, too, Gwen." Ceci gives a polite smile to Gwen who smiles and waves in return. Ceci returns her attention to her mom. "Mom, I left my traveling makeup bag at home. I think it's in my bathroom. Could you bring it for me next time you come?" Mrs. Salvesen pulls out a notepad and adds to a list she has going there.

Ceci gives her parents quick hugs as they head out of the apartment for the night. Once they leave, she turns to Gwen and me. "So, can you two help me get settled?" We both say that of course we are happy to help her out when Ceci says, "I hope it isn't always as messy in here as it was when I got here." Gwen and I give each other a puzzled look. Sure, the place wasn't pristine, but we'd only had a few things out. Ceci continues, oblivious to our surprise at her rude question, "I really can't stand a messy space. It's so hard to focus properly, you know?" Gwen and I give her a wide-eyed nod of assent, unsure of where this new relationship is headed. Maybe we won't be as happy as Uncle Russ thinks we will be.

We spend the next two hours helping Ceci put her things away in her two rooms and get settled. When we are done, Gwen suggests we watch a movie together. I have Netflix ready to go on my iPad. Gwen and I have enjoyed a few episodes of "Gilmore Girls" (a guilty pleasure) over the past week. Ceci gives us both a sideways glance.

"Actually," she says with a note of displeasure in her voice, "I like to go to bed a little early so I can work out in the mornings. I hope it isn't too loud. I shouldn't hear the movie from my room, though, if you two are watching with earbuds in your room or something." She turns and heads to her own room, yawning along the way. "Thanks for the help, girls. I'll catch you in the morning." She closes the door behind her and in a moment we hear nature sounds coming from her smart speaker.

Gwen gives me an eye-roll and I mouth the word, "Okay…." And I wonder if I really will be friends enough to call her Ceci. Gwen and I may just be stuck with Celia.

Chapter 4

Life with Celia around has turned out to be even worse than what I thought it would be. I am a pretty smart student. I mean I have to work hard at it, but I learn what I need to and do the extra work to make sure I get it right. Celia, however, has the deep pleasure of natural talent (according to her). Her homework takes half the time mine does and she makes sure to check her test grades against mine every time they are released. Really? Must we be so competitive? She never joins in Gwen's and my study sessions, even though she has Spanish as well. She says she doesn't need it. Much as she enjoys our being quiet while she sleeps, she, on the other hand, loves watching Netflix on the couch while Gwen and I study in our room.

The rest of my experience at FIU is actually pretty great, so if I have to put up with Celia along the way, I can't complain. Gwen and I get to enjoy one more trip to the beach before classes start. I don't hear anyone calling my name this time, so I am more focused on my conversation with Gwen and she tells me more about her life growing up.

"My dad died before I was even born," Gwen tells me. "I guess my mom couldn't handle having me on her own, so she dropped me off on my aunt's doorstep when I was a new baby. My aunt wasn't thrilled with the idea of raising me either. I should have a complex or something. She didn't beat me or starve me much or anything, but I knew I wasn't loved."

My heart hurts for my friend. How could someone treat another person so bad? Gwen continues, "Eventually I became the babysitter for my aunt as well as the housekeeper. The whole fam went to the beach every year, but I wasn't allowed to snorkel, surf, or swim. I sat with my cousins on the beach, wiping their butts and noses. But some nights I would sneak out of the hotel we were staying in, just to get a few minutes of quiet at the beach by myself."

"Gwen, I'm so sorry," I say, "You are worth so much more than that."

"Oh, there's nothing to be sorry about, Evelyn," she says. "I know they were wrong. I know I didn't deserve to be treated that way. I chose something different for myself. Earning my way out with good grades and hard work was the best thing I could have done. My aunt will probably miss my work around the house, but it beats her having to feed me and clothe me."

Gwen stands and stretches, taking in a last, deep breath of the ocean air before heading home. I start my job at Oleta River tomorrow. Gwen will be working on campus in the student services complex, I will be working with Jack, giving tours of the bay. Oleta River State Park is adjacent to the school campus. I'll be able to walk or ride a bike to work every day. I haven't told my mom about my job working three days a week on the water. She thinks I'm keeping the park clean. I'll tell her. Eventually.

I grab my bag, deleting another message from James before putting my phone inside. I'm not ready to know what he wants to talk to me about.

Three weeks of college and I have a good routine forming. I am working on how to make it to the beach more often. I discovered a new route to my English Lit class in an attempt to avoid having to walk with Celia. I'm walking it now and as I round the corner of the Student Services building I run right into James.

James.

I am so shocked that I am speechless for a minute. But just one minute.

"James! What the heck are you doing here?" I feel blood rushing up my neck and into my face as my blood pressure reminds me that I am angry at my former boyfriend.

"It's good to see you, too, Eves," He says with a smooth-talking smile. "I actually go to school here now. Of course, you would know that if you would have responded to my texts." He gives me a wink and I want to slap him.

"What?!" I say. "When did that happen and WHY?!" I may not be his girlfriend anymore, but I think he should have tried harder to tell me if he was going to MOVE WHERE I LIVE!!!!! I am angry and hurt all over again as James gives me his explanation.

"Well, I was hanging out with my cousins at Corpus Christi for the couple of weeks before school started. We spent a lot of time at the beach, and I had a…change of heart." He looks at me like I should get what he is saying – like there is some kind of secret we are both in on – and he looks around like he really has something to protect. The only thing he needs to protect is his face because I am about a second away from swinging at it.

"Change of heart?!" I am yelling. "So, you liked the beach and decided to change schools? James, you were going to give Baylor a chance. What kind of chance is a month?" I sound a bit psycho, yelling at my old boyfriend in the middle of campus, but that isn't bothering me at the moment. "What did your parents say?"

James gives me a big, knowing smile and reaches for my hand. "Mom and Dad are actually supportive. I guess they figured that the time in Texas would eventually teach me a thing or two about what I really want, and they are happy that I changed my mind. They say the ocean air will do me good."

They think he's learned what he really wants? What does he really want? Does that mean he wants me? My head is swirling again, just like the last time we were together, and I honestly don't know what to think. I feel like I've been blindsided. I pull my hand away from his, not sure if his grasp is where *I* belong.

"James, I don't understand. This doesn't make any sense. You were so sure you wanted Baylor and now you're HERE at FIU with ME." I look at him with wide, hurt eyes, daring him to make sense of anything he is saying to me. Instead, he sighs, and the familiar scent of cinnamon is on the air again. He puts his hands in his pockets, relaxed and sure of himself.

"Ah, don't worry Evelyn, you'll get it soon enough, I'm sure." I don't have time for this ridiculous conversation. I have a class to get

34

to. James can tell that I want to get moving and says, "Where are you going? Can I walk you to class?"

The last thing I want is to have him walk me to class. He is acting like this was the plan all along and I just forgot. It's such a 180 from where we were a month ago. This is a strange move for him and it's leaving me unsettled and nervous. We walk to class in silence – I have too many angry questions in my head to look him in the eye. We reach the liberal arts building and part ways. James says he is heading for the engineering complex, at least his major has stayed the same. As I enter the building, shoulders slumped and thoughts foggy, I realize I am going to have to find a third route to my English class.

Gwen is my girl and she has my back. When I get back to our apartment, I grab some ice cream from the freezer and two spoons so I can tell her all about seeing James on campus. She freaks out as much as I did.

"Dude, Evelyn," she says with wide eyes and a low voice. "Do you need me to go and lay some smack down on the boy?"

I'm not sure that 'laying the smack down' will be helpful in this situation, but it's nice to know my options.

I smile at her offer and say, "I don't think so, but I definitely don't want to be stuck alone with him."

"Girl, no," Gwen says. "You don't need to be alone with anyone you don't want to be alone with. But I gotta ask: are you really over him?" I sigh and give her a guilty look. The truth is that I have been thinking about James a lot – why he broke up with me, what he was doing at school, had he met anyone new? I let out a sigh that says it all.

"How about this," Gwen says, "on Thursday, I'll walk you to your English class. If you see James, introduce us. I'll let you know what I think."

I am so relieved that I practically jump onto Gwen's lap, praising her for being such a good roommate. My ice cream spoon falls into her hair, a big blob rolling down her cheek. We both start laughing and the worry melts away. Then we hear a noise from Celia's room and she stumbles out of her doorway, her eye mask on her forehead and her hair a crazy mess.

"Oh my gosh, you guys," she says in a groggy tone, "What the heck is going on?" Celia is quite grumpy when she is awakened from a deep sleep. "Can't you take it somewhere else?" She stumbles back into her room and Gwen and I burst out laughing again. Celia slams her door and turns her nature sounds up full volume.

Chapter 5

I am so distracted at work on Wednesday, that I miss things Jack says to me at least three times. "Are you feeling okay?" he finally asks as we are loading up the kayaks. "You're having a hard time holding a conversation."

"Yeah, sorry. I'm fine," I say. "I'm just stuck on a school thing." I'm a terrible liar, but Jack plays along.

"Is it something I can help with," he offers. "I'm pretty good at a lot of that stuff, except maybe the math. You might have to hire out if it's math." I smile at his joke and let the butterflies play around in my stomach. I've enjoyed the time we've had together this past month. We work together 3 or 4 times a week and when we aren't leading tours of the bay, we have extra time to talk and get to know each other. I'm really starting to like Jack. He's funny. He's respectful. I know he likes me, but this thing with James just has me feeling off.

"Just my luck," I say, "It *is* math."

"My loss," he says, "Maybe we could get together another time. You know, outside of work." He is asking me on a date. My attention is suddenly riveted on Jack and Jack only.

"Yeah, that would be great," I say. "What did you have in mind?"

"Well, we've talked a lot about scuba diving. I was thinking it might be time for me to teach you."

Scuba diving? Seriously, I LOVE the idea. And learning from Jack? What could be better? We make plans for several lessons/dates for the next few weeks and I go home feeling much better about my love life.

Two days ago, I was nervous about running into James again. Then I was looking forward to seeing him. Yesterday I forgot completely about him, but today I am back to dreading it. At least I'll have Gwen to meet him and give me her read on the situation. He hasn't messaged me at all and I am starting to wonder if I had a hallucination or something. I meet up with Gwen after avoiding Princess Celia, and together we head to the liberal arts offices. Just like Tuesday, when we round the corner of the Student Services building, I see James. I don't literally run into him this time, but he is on his way to where Gwen and I are standing.

"There he is," I whisper to Gwen. She looks up and I think I see a hint of surprise on her face.

"*That's* James?" she asks. I want to ask her why she is so surprised, but James reaches us first.

"Hey, Eves," he says, moving into that old familiar way of addressing me. He touches my shoulder and says, "I'm glad to see you again. I have something I want to talk to you about. I know it ended awkwardly the other day." James turns to see Gwen at my side, and a look of surprise and recognition crosses his face, he quickly covers it up with a smile. "Who's your friend?"

"My name is Gwen. I'm Evelyn's roommate," she says. James' face is unreadable.

"Well, it was nice to meet you, Gwen," James turns to talk to me but addresses us both. "I'm sorry, I wish I could walk you two to class, but I am a little late for mine. Maybe some other time." And then he is gone. What did he want to talk about? I stand there, speechless, then turn to Gwen. She looks like she is going to be sick. I have no clue what to say. I reach toward her to ask if she's alright and she takes a step back.

"Well, that was weird," she says.

"Yeah…" I agree, but I let my words hang in the air. It looks like there is something more she has to say. She clears her throat like she is ready to let it all out – whatever it is that she saw in James, but instead she adjusts her backpack.

"Let's talk about it later. I'd better be going to my class since there isn't anything more to see here."

"Okay," I respond. Gwen turns and leaves almost as quickly as James did. "See ya," I call to her as she walks away. Without turning around, she gives me a small wave of her hand, and I am left standing alone.

What just happened? My old boyfriend and new roommate actually know each other? They both tried to hide it, but they really aren't good actors. Where did they meet and how? What is going on with them? Why not just say they already know each other? I am super lost, and I have more and more questions in a place where I am supposed to be finding answers.

I arrive at our apartment a little later than usual. I had some studying to do in the library once my classes were done. I'm not ready to ask Gwen why she was so stand-offish today and how she knows James. What if the answers are things I don't want to hear? What if they have a history together? Gwen must have the same kind of feelings because she isn't home yet either. I find a note she left for me saying that she has to work extra hours today. She says I get to eat her leftover cake in the fridge. I roll my eyes and shake my head, irritated that she would assume I need to binge my way through my emotions. I grab the cake anyway. I eat quickly so I can head to work. I love it there. The work is nice, but the environment is exactly why I came to Florida in the first place. It is as close to the open ocean as I can get.

I have had enough of the drama of living. I want the answers I came here seeking. I have hardly slept since moving to Florida. I've just been busy and adjusting to life on my own. I've had ups and downs with boyfriends and roommates. I haven't had my dream once since arriving and I am beginning to miss it. I want my dream to speak to me again. I cannot go to work without feeling the pull of the water beneath my feet. I run out the door, eager to get to my job, and Jack, again.

It's been three weeks since my encounter with James and Gwen. James has sent a few messages, but I continue to delete them. It's become a habit now. When I asked Gwen what she thought of James, she said he seemed like just a normal jerk of a guy. She told me I should just try to avoid him. I have been, but I don't understand why Gwen has been avoiding me. It feels like she is angry with me or hiding something from me or both. She has been closing herself in her room to study alone and finding different routes to her classes. She has picked up a few more hours at work and I have begun to do the same. Life in the apartment is lonely without someone to talk to, two roommates who don't want to be around me, and an ex-boyfriend who won't leave me alone. I don't want my loneliness to lead me back into a relationship with James, so I have been putting in extra hours at work, too.

At least I have Jack to look forward to. Jack's sun-bleached hair is a little fried from a lifetime of being in the ocean, but the result is the messy, care-free style of a surfer. His skin is a deep gold and his eyes a light green. He is tall and muscular and has a way of making me feel like I am suddenly incapable of speech. I love having him as my scuba instructor. My first lesson covers the basics – how to put my gear on and how to use it. We really only have about ten minutes in the water. But the second lesson is better. We talk a lot about diving at work – going over equipment use and hand signals – so I only need minimal help getting ready. This weekend of lessons will be killer hot outside. The heat is sweltering. The ocean is the only place anyone would want to be.

The weather has been rough with several massive storms threatening the Florida coastline, and that ruins some planned scuba diving sessions. But today, I could not have asked for better weather. The temperature is a scorching 95 degrees, there is very little wind, and not a cloud in the sky. The waters are gentle and there is no threat of a storm to be seen. The last tour for the day has just finished up, so Jack and I get in our gear and head out.

The water is glorious today and being out on the open water with Jack, the wind in my face and sun on my skin, is helping me let go of my troubles. We make our way to the best spot (according to Jack) and prepare for the dive. The initial pressure I feel as I dive deeper into the water subsides after only a short time, so I can really enjoy the experience. It's becoming familiar to me to be underwater for a long time. Jack and I swim and dive for what feels like hours. We have about 15 minutes of air left and are ready to head back up to the surface when Jack holds out his hand, fingers close together, palm down, thumb out and begins to rock his hand from side to side. I know immediately that he is telling me something is wrong. I keep my eyes on him as he slowly looks around the water. Fear grips my stomach as Jack grasps his arm and points to my left. The sign for DANGER. Before I can turn to see what is coming, a huge current of water makes its way toward me. I am suddenly caught in the current and cannot break free. The line connecting me to Jack snaps and I am left without my protector and teacher. What am I supposed to do?

I relax my body, hoping that I will be carried to the surface by the raging current. Instead, I slam into something fleshy that literally knocks the wind out of me. My diving regulator is yanked from my mouth. I cannot see where it went and I grasp around, frantically searching for the tubing attached to its end. It feels like an eternity of being tossed in a washing machine. I keep hitting things that I assume are fish as panic settles in. I know I need air and I need it fast. I work like mad to get my regulator back to my mouth, but when I finally succeed, it is no use – the air tank is empty. I frantically work to free myself from my scuba gear, hoping it will help me easily float to the surface, but I am trapped in the current and cannot get out.

I am finally knocked free of the current only to find that my scuba fins have been impaled by coral. I reach for my feet to free myself, but it is too late. My head is pounding, my chest burning, and my vision is blurred. I just need air.

"Evelyn."

As clear as if someone is seated next to me and trying to get my attention, I hear my name.

"Evelyn, breathe."

In an involuntary motion, my mouth opens wide, breathing out the bad air stuck inside of me and I inhale. My lungs quickly fill with water and I wait for the pain of drowning. But it doesn't come. Instead, my headache subsides and my vision clears. In a second involuntary motion, I force the water out of my lungs and inhale again. This time my mind is much clearer. I lunge for my feet again, remove my scuba fins and make my way to the surface. Like a miracle from Heaven, I am only a hundred yards or so away from the diving boat. I can see Jack wildly throwing off his gear as his eyes search the water around him. His eyes catch sight of me and he

43

immediately jumps into the driver's seat of the little boat and heads toward me.

Meanwhile, I am still bobbing in and out of the water and breathing a mixture of water and air. It is uncomfortable, but I'm not in real pain and I still have my wits about me. Jack steers the boat along-side me, kills the engine and pulls me by the shoulders into the boat. I am weak and shaken, so I'm not much help to him. As soon as I can move my body, I get on all fours on deck and spew out the water that remains in my lungs. Jack is kneeling next to me and I could not be more humiliated.

"Evelyn, are you alright? Can you hear me? Can you see me? How many fingers am I holding up?" I can hear Jack, though it sounds muffled. I can see him. Three fingers.

"What happened out there?" I finally get out.

"I've never seen anything like it," is Jack's initial response. Jack's whole life has been spent in the ocean. For him to see something new is disconcerting. "Something inside me didn't feel right," he continues, "I looked around to see if something was wrong and all I could see was a surging wall of water heading toward us. Once it caught you, it turned and headed in a new direction. I got a slap in the face by some fish. I went black for an instant and you were gone. As soon as I came to, I put my regulator back in my mouth and headed to the boat so I could search for you and call for help. I have never been so happy to see anything come out of that water in my life." Jack is holding me tight to him at this point. I am grateful to be alive and very happy to be held by Jack. He gives me a hard kiss on the forehead and all of my thoughts focus on the pressure of his lips

44

on my skin. I have a quick image of how nice it would be to be kissed on the lips by Jack, but I have just as quick a reminder that I just threw up.

"What happened to you?" he asks, a heavy worry in his tone. I relate everything to him…even the part about breathing water – some fluke thing that happens right before somebody drowns, but Jack's face convinces me otherwise.

"No Evelyn. People don't breathe water and feel just fine." He stares into my eyes, trying to read something in them. "Maybe you were unconscious or something." He looks unconvinced, but lets out a sigh and continues, "Either way, I'm glad you're safe. Let's get you to the lifeguard station and have you checked out. We need to see if you need to go to the hospital." I sit back against the side of the boat as Jack starts its engine again and heads to the shore. I feel the coldness of the air against my damp skin, but I am somehow unaffected by it. My teeth don't chatter, and I don't have any goosebumps. My mind is so consumed by the experience that I relive it over and over on our way to shore. The current. The coral. Fish slapping against my face. Breathing without air. My name.

Chapter 6

Thankfully, the trip to the lifeguards is enough to convince Jack and me that I am fine, at least physically. He drives me home and makes sure I have something to eat before heading home himself. My mom would freak if she knew where I'd been and what happened to me. She would be on a plane to Florida so fast. In my text to her tonight, I keep it cool. I tell her about my classes and even about seeing James here. Nothing at all about my job. She thinks I work in the park museum. She is surprised to hear about James, though, and wants to know how I feel about it. I answer honestly. I don't know.

I'm getting in my comfy clothes to watch Netflix until I fall asleep or my roommates get home, but there is a knock at my door. I get up to answer it. It's James.

"James." Disbelief is written all over my face and in my voice. How did he know where to find me? I find my wits enough to ask questions. "What are you doing here? How did you know where I live?"

James looks at me with a sheepish gaze. It's a look I am familiar with. He always used it whenever we argued and he wanted to make up. Even though I am confused and mad, I can't help but be willing to hear him out. "Evelyn, I know you have a lot of questions for me," he's got that right, "and I also know that you need somebody to talk to right now." Somebody to talk to? Does he honestly think I want to talk to *him* about our breakup?!

There's no way he knows anything else that is on my mind.

"James, I'm sorry. You've caught me off guard. I just started studying for tomorrow's biology exam." I'm mad and James knows it. I keep up the lie, both of us knowing I'm making it up as I go. "I can't talk right now. Maybe we can get lunch or something tomorrow."

He lifts his hand and rests it on the door, making his biceps stretch out his shirtsleeve. "Evelyn, this can't wait. I know what happened to you in the water today."

Wait, what? What does he know about what happened to me today? Does he know Jack or something? Maybe he knows one of the lifeguards at the station.

"James, I…" I begin and he takes me by the hand. It's been so long since I laced my fingers through his, and I long for the warmth of it.

"I have to show you something," he says, "We need to go to the beach. It's not that far. We can talk on the way if you want to."

Six hours ago, there was nothing I would want less than to talk with James. But feeling his rough fingers rub against mine, in this moment I want that soothing and familiar relationship again. I agree to go with him and together we head out.

Hand in hand, I walk with James in silence. It takes forever to get to Pier Park and by the time we do, it is well past sunset. There is barely a glimmer of orange on the horizon ahead of us. The air is cooler and the sand is inviting. I take off my flip-flops and let the powdery goodness squeeze through my toes and rub the soles of my feet. There are only a few late day stragglers on the beach. Most of them are couples whose minds are occupied in quiet conversation with each other. Some are kissing. I feel a flush come to my cheeks as I think of the time I've spent kissing James. After all I have felt about him and shared with him, I feel like I should be able to tell him what is on my mind.

"James," I say as I turn to face him, "I am so confused. I can't figure out why you are even here in Florida. It doesn't make any sense to me. And now you're back to holding my hand. Am I supposed to think you want to date again? I have no idea what to think."

James is looking out at the ocean, he does not even turn when I speak to him. His mind is on something far away. "Evelyn, I can answer all of your questions with a long-winded speech, or I can show you something that will help you understand even faster. Can I show you Evelyn?" He turns to face me and his eyes are so intent that I can read his thoughts. He is pulling me in. I nod and he leads me to the water's edge. "Just sit down and wait right here," he says.

As I sit down, I dig my toes into the white, warm sand, comforted by that feeling of heat beneath my feet. When I look up, James is removing his shoes and shirt. I feel a flush of heat rushing through my chest and neck. James has gotten a little tan since I last saw him swimming. He is still muscular as ever and I am finding it difficult to not stare.

Now that he has stripped down to his shorts, he heads straight into the water. He walks out slowly until he is up to his waist in the ocean. He looks like he is playing with the water with his fingertips.

Then he turns to see if I am watching him. He gives me a smile and a wave. I wave back and he dives under the water.

At first, I think he is just dunking his head under to get it wet, but then a minute goes by without him resurfacing. I get up and strain my eyes to see if I can make him out. Two minutes. I'm getting anxious and move my visual search to the surrounding shoreline. Maybe he came up out of the water somewhere else. Three minutes. I start calling out his name, hoping that he will call back. No response. Another thirty seconds. I head into the waves, looking as best as I can into the water to see some sign of James. Five minutes.

I turn around and head back to shore for help. All of a sudden, something grabs my ankle and I go under. Whatever it is, it has a strong hold on me. I didn't take a breath before falling into the water, so I try standing up for air. Something else grabs me just below the knee and pulls me farther into the ocean, still underwater. I am trying to not freak out. I've already had one run-in with the ocean today and I don't want to have another.

I kick my feet at whatever has ahold of me and it lets me go. I swim up and get my head out of the water, taking a huge breath. I'm ready to scream for help when the thing grabs me again, this time around my waist. It drags me very quickly down and away from the shoreline. I kick and hit and scratch as best as I can to get out of its grasp. I can feel that burning need for air coming again. All my fighting is not helping the situation. I cannot see what or who has me, I can only feel it holding tightly to my body. I feel the pounding headache again. Out of instinct, I let out a scream, but I am still underwater. I struggle for breath again and wait for the pain. Once again it does not come. I exhale the water and inhale it again. The headache subsides and the burning in my lungs disappears. It is replaced by a cooling sensation that fills my chest. I relax, stop fighting, and start to breathe.

The iron grasp around my waist loosens and I allow myself to experience this new sensation. My eyes adjust to what is around me. I can see clearly in the dark water. I see tiny little fish swimming to my left and their slightly larger predators to my right. Seashells are scattered on the ocean floor beneath my feet and I realize I am not being held by some*thing* but some*one*. James is smiling at me *UNDERWATER* and has his hands on either side of my waist.

He pulls me closer to him, the heat of his body barely noticeable in the warm Atlantic Sea, and he kisses me softly. It is a new sensation even though I've done it countless times. The feel of his lips on mine, salty water swirling around my mouth, tiny bubbles floating off our skin. I run my fingers up his muscled arms, and nothing else that happened in my day matters anymore. I am underwater in some magical moment, and I am loving it.

After a moment of pleasure, James pulls away and smiles at me.

"Well, what do you think?" I blink to clear my mind. I can *hear* him? We are underwater, but his voice sounds just like it does on land. Nothing is muffled. Everything is clear. None of it makes sense, but that doesn't bother me right now. I'll try talking too.

"I don't know what to think. How did you know this would happen? What is happening anyway?" I pull my eyes away from his face and his lips to take in the scene around us. "Am I dreaming?"

James holds me tighter. "You aren't dreaming at all. You are actually quite special, Evelyn Marin." He kisses me again and I don't have any more questions.

Chapter 7

I stretch lazily in my bed as I think over the last few weeks. James and I spent the rest of that first night sitting with our feet dangling over the edge of the pier, holding hands and talking about what happened to him and what happened to me. James discovered this new water ability while in Corpus Christi. His cousin knocked him off a jet ski and James breathed as soon as his body hit the water. He thought he would drown after inhaling water, but he was fine. He didn't tell anyone about his experience, but every time he went to the ocean with his cousins, he tested out breathing. James knew he couldn't stay in Texas with what he discovered. He needed to find a school on the water. Since I was at FIU, he thought he would try here first and he was accepted. The texts were to try to tell me what was going on. But he also knew he'd been a top-rate jerk and I wouldn't want to talk to him right away. When he finally bumped into me at the school, he had known where I was for a couple of weeks. He wanted to give me space to be ready to see him.

We stayed out all that night, talking about what we can now do and what our relationship can be. We ended the night with a kiss, and when my tired head hit the pillow, I was out.

Since that night, I have been going to school and work and spending time with James. I've had just a few conversations with

Gwen. She has been keeping busy as well and continues to close herself in her room when she's home. I miss the friendship we started at the beginning of the school year. I don't remember whatever it was that came between us in the first place.

Things with Jack have been awkward. I feel so guilty when I am with him now. He doesn't know about me and James. We went snorkeling one more time and I have made excuses ever since. I still like Jack and am so confused. I don't know what to tell him or what I want him to know. I am walking a balance beam between the two of them and I'm beginning to have regular headaches. The strain of holding down two relationships is beginning to wear on me. Part of me wants to walk away from them both and just go spend time with my ocean.

My dreams have started coming back. The faces and voices taunt me regularly, inviting me into their world. "Evelyn! Evelyn! Come! Stop! Help!"

I take every opportunity to slip into the ocean to test how far I can go. Sometimes James comes along, but for the most part, I go out on my own. My head is blurry when he is around and I want it to be clear while I am learning more about myself. I want to find myself on my own.

I haven't had to answer to Gwen or Celia. Celia complains when I get sand on the kitchen floor. Sometimes I leave it there on purpose just to bother her. Jack and I have both been busy working the kayak tours of the bay. Jack says he'll let me do all the talking someday.

For my first few attempts alone in the bay, I am only able to go out as far as I went with James. The pressure on my chest and body are just too great. But gradually, I've been able to make my way farther out and deeper in. By the end of the first week, I reach the end of the pier before I feel the pressure. My ability to transfer between liquid and air breathing is also getting better. I throw up water on my first attempt, but I figure out that a good swallow helps me transfer between breathing methods.

It's been three weeks of going out solo and I feel like I am following the calling from my dream. I haven't heard my name in a while, but I still have that pull in my chest, tugging me out to sea. I'm in the ocean again, alone, and it is dark. I've found it easier to slip away unnoticed at this time of day. My roommates don't ask questions and nobody on shore can see that I have gone underwater without resurfacing.

After an eternity of swimming over the sandy sea floor, I reach the edge of the continental shelf. It really isn't very far from the Florida shoreline, but it is something that I am not prepared to cross. It is a looming blackness and I am unwilling to enter. It is so deep and everything about it so unknown that I can't bring myself to cross that line. I have done all that I can to research the ocean online and in the university library. I have oceanic terms floating in and out of my brain all day long. After all that I have read, there is still no way that I am willing to go into that gigantic abyss.

I stare at the blackness for nearly an hour before I finally turn my back on the empty space and head back to shore. Salty tears from my eyes mix with the salty seawater I am moving through. I feel sick inside – like I am swimming away from my destiny, but I am not ready to head into that space alone. I need to be sure of what I am getting into. I don't want to ask James to go with me either. I am so focused on what I am doing, that we haven't been spending much time together. He wants to go with me, and only me, into the ocean every day. But I'm not the starry-eyed girl he left in a Texas airport anymore. I have a renewed sense of purpose and drive leading me in a new direction. I am stronger now and determined to find my own way.

I stretch my legs and look around the University library as the autumn sun sinks below the horizon. I have been sitting in the same chair for two hours and I am stiff and tired. I've been reading through a dusty and forgotten old book on the Atlantic Ocean, hoping to find something there that I can't find online. My eyes hurt. I don't know what I'm looking for. I need help overcoming the fear that kept me from stepping off the shelf last week.

"Ah, and what is it that you are so intent on studying today Miss Marin?" Uncle Russ is looking over my shoulder as I read. I haven't seen him since he dropped off Celia, but I am happy to see him here now. His face is a nice reminder that life outside of my troubles does exist.

"Oh, um it's a project for biology." I'm proud of that lie. I would have believed it myself.

"That sounds interesting," Uncle Russ says as he takes a seat across from me. What is the topic and how are you coming along?"

"It's just a research paper on local sea life, their feeding habits and migration patterns. It's not due for another month, but it's pretty interesting so far."

"I'm glad to hear that." Uncle Russ picks up one of my post-it covered books. "When I spoke to Ms. Ikenbaum about how you are doing in the class, she had some concerns about your attendance, but it looks like it is all in the interest of individual study." Crap. He talked to my biology teacher? I lied to the University President about my attendance, and I have no quick lies to fill the awkward silence now between us. I settle for looking dumbfounded.

Uncle Russ puts the magazine down and meets my gaze. "Evelyn, I promised your mother that I would take care of you. She called me a few days ago, in a panic because she has not heard from you in three weeks. What have you been doing to keep yourself so occupied that you cannot even call your mother?"

Three weeks?! That can't be right. I'm sure I've texted my mom more recently, haven't I? I can't remember. This is not a good sign.

"I'm sorry, Uncle Russ," I manage to get out, "I've been so busy with school and work that the days have been running together. I had no idea that it's been so long since I talked to my mom. I'll call her today, I promise. I'm sorry. It won't happen again."

"Well, I'm glad to hear that Evelyn. I'm fond of your mother. Our friendship goes back a long time. I have made a promise to keep an eye on you and protect you, and I intend to keep that promise." He stands to leave and looks down at me. "Now, I think you have a biology test to make up."

"Yes I do. I'll go now." I look down at my textbooks and research materials, unwilling to look Uncle Russ in the eye at such a close distance. He looks over the page I am studying: the Continental Shelf. I am embarrassed again by the lie I told. I snatch up the book quickly, run it to its place on the shelf and head out the door toward the natural sciences building. I risk one backward glance toward Uncle Russ. His face is laced with concern and I am sure Mom will be hearing about my behavior today. How could I have skipped calling her or even texting? I know she texted me a few times. My responses must have been absent-minded and distant for her to reach out to Uncle Russ.

I call my mom on the way to class. She doesn't pick up the phone and I let out a guilty sigh of relief. I don't have to explain yet. At least I have the afternoon to arrange my story for her. What do I tell her? How will she react if I tell her what is really going on? She would probably tell Uncle Russ to send me to a school psychologist or demand that I come home. I can't risk that exposure. I can't tell her what is happening. I have to lie. I can't let her know what I have been up to until I know for sure myself.

My palms are sweaty and my hand slips as I open the door to the natural sciences building. I pull harder only to meet with the same result. I cannot get the door open. I look around in confusion and see that I am not at the natural sciences building but the smaller history building next door. My yanking has attracted the attention of somebody inside who is coming to open it for me.

"Hi. I'm not sure why that door was locked. What can I do for you?" I am looking at an older man, probably in his late forties with lightly salted, curly, mousy brown hair. He is wearing tan pants and a tweed coat. Very Indiana Jones. I smile as I answer the stereotypical historian.

"I'm sorry, I wasn't paying attention. I thought I was heading into the natural sciences building."

"Oh, I see. Well, you have a good day."

"Thank you." I turn away but my focus is thrown off by what meets my eyes. James is standing just beside the Natural Sciences building, peeking around the corner like he is looking for somebody, but he isn't alone. Gwen is with him, facing him. They are talking in hushed tones and standing close to each other, too close. James turns his face toward Gwen and leans in close. I can't believe what I am seeing. Is he kissing her? Wait, oh my gosh, he is! Everything that happened the first time I introduced them to each other comes rushing back on me. The awkward conversation, worried looks, and rushed conversation – had they been seeing each other then?

I cannot see straight. What am I doing here? What am I supposed to be doing? Something about a test. This is a test for me. One I don't want to take. I turn on my heels and go to the only place I can think of. I see the history professor looking after me with concern. I don't care what anyone thinks of me in this moment. I know where I have to go and nothing will keep me from stepping into the darkness this time.

I turn so fast that I drop all of my books to the ground. The sound is loud enough for James and Gwen to hear. I stand there, unmoving and unable to meet their gaze. The next thing I know, James is on the ground picking up my books and papers from the ground. I bend to pick them up, still moving with automatic actions. Gwen stays standing by the Natural Sciences building.

"Oh, my gosh, James! I've got it. Go away!" I cannot keep myself from yelling.

"Evelyn, I'm so sorry," he says. Yeah, sorry about the spilled books or sorry about getting caught making out with my roommate?

"Evelyn, can we go somewhere to talk?" he asks. If it weren't for the books and papers in my hand, I would punch him in the face.

"No. I don't need to talk to you."

"Evelyn, just let me explain," he says and I start walking away, loose papers periodically dropping from my arms. James follows.

"Evelyn, I haven't heard from you in weeks." So my silence is an excuse for his cheating face? "I wasn't sure where we stood. And, I have actually known Gwen for a while anyway." I pause at this admission.

"So, you were already seeing her when you kissed me?"

"Evelyn," he rolls his eyes, "not dating her. I've been trying to help her with her transition to the sea."

Gwen can do what James and I can do.

She can breathe underwater. Of course she can. It is some kind of epidemic at the school. I look back at where Gwen is standing, guilt written all over her face. Why hadn't she told me about breathing underwater? And how was knowing that supposed to make anything better? Gwen turns away from my gaze, heading to her next class – escaping an angry confrontation here and now.

"Evelyn, there is so much you don't know about the sea. There is a whole world down there that you can't even imagine." I have no desire to have James tell me about the ocean. "Evelyn," he won't stop talking and I won't stop walking away. "Please listen to me. You would be so amazed. I have met so many others who can do what we can do." I am partially listening as I walk away, wondering if there will ever be a point to his chatter, "There is this woman – it's almost crazy to look at her – she has lived so long underwater that she's started turning into… she has these amazing plans… we could do so much…" I cut him off, tired of being around him.

"James. I have to go. I don't want to listen to you anymore. I don't want anything to do with you anymore. Leave me alone." I drop my bag on the ground and all of my papers and books with it. "If you want to help me," I say, you can put all this stuff back together. Get your girlfriend to take it home with her. She knows where it goes." I walk away as quickly as I can, leaving James with the words he was going to say still stuck in his throat.

Chapter 8

I make my way to Pier Park. I head straight into the water, walking angrily into the waves. I ignore the weight of the water in my jeans. I am going into that abyss. I am going to see what is out there for me. I don't care that other people can do what I can do. I have been called. I've had the dream. I am going to listen to it now. I use the fire within me to propel myself forward. I get to the edge of the continental shelf faster than I ever have before. I don't want to give myself too much time to think. I just have to go.

I step off the edge of the shelf expecting to sink slowly to the ocean floor below. Instead of sinking, I slide onto the back of a large fish. I am startled and fall forward as the fish lurches up so my legs are saddled astride its large body. My hands hit some kind of bridle that has been attached to the fish. I take hold and trust. With all I have been experiencing over these last weeks, I know this is the only option for me. I have to follow where this path leads. This is my choice and this is where I am going to go.

As soon as I grasp the bridle, the fish understands that I am secure. It dives down into the darkness below and I dive with it. At first, my uneasiness in the blackness makes my stomach turn. Then, I think I can make out a light on the distant floor beneath us. As the fish and I draw closer to the bottom of the sea, the light grows brighter and brighter until I can see that it is not just one light, but a multitude of lights. Thousands of lights. I don't believe my eyes as I understand that I am heading straight into an underwater city.

This isn't like any city I have seen before. It looks like ancient ruins that are inhabited. As we approach the ocean floor, we are in the midst of several tall buildings. They look like Greek architecture and yet they have an even more ancient look about them. I see columns and spires and buttresses on both sides of me and my fish transport as we swim deeper into the ocean. The stone is grey and the area we are swimming through is empty of all other life. I start looking less ahead of me and more to the sides and below. I am surprised by what is there.

There are ancient stone traffic ways beneath us and stairs and doorways to the buildings we swim between. The traffic ways are free of the silt I would expect to see in a sunken city. These are still in use. In the doorways hang strips of seaweed that create more privacy within. Some of the windows are lighted by an unseen source that emits a dull yellow glow. That accounts for the thousands of lights. Within these buildings (that look like homes) I can see tools and broken pottery. Inside one dwelling I see an empty table and chairs where it looks like a family has just left their evening meal. Plates of food are left sitting atop the table with utensils nearby.

But these lighted rooms and filled tables are empty of life, nobody is in sight and all is silent. I feel like I am an intruder and all the occupants of this city have fled from me. I want to ask my finned guide where we are and where we are headed when the large fish stops and turns to face a large gate. On the front of the gate is an

64

eroded sign that looks like it might once have been made of precious materials. On it is a curious writing that I cannot at all make out. It looks like Greek, but I don't know for sure. Beneath this ancient inscription is a more recent etching that I can read:

Atlantis: Home of the Ancients

Headquarters for the Modern War

Atlantis? War? What?! I'm not interested in war. I had no idea that my new abilities and lifetime of questions would lead me to such a place. War? No. I want answers. I want peace in my heart, not fighting. What have I been led to? Have James and Gwen already been here? The thought of James and Gwen makes bile rise in my throat. I push them out of my mind and swallow hard.

My companion and I pause only long enough to read the sign when the gates slowly swing open. The gates look so old that I expect to hear a loud grating noise but none comes. I marvel again at my surroundings. Towers and buildings surround me on every side. But instead of the emptiness of the buildings outside the city gates, these streets are teeming with life. People. People are everywhere. Men and women, some walking on the stone pathways, some swimming with webbed feet.

A fully finned woman catches my attention. She looks like the kind of mermaid that fairytales are made of. Her entire upper body is covered by an iridescent shell top, but the lower half of her body is an unmistakable tail. It shines silvery green in the dull glow that emanates from the windows and doorways of the city. She turns her head my direction and I catch her eye. Her eyes are an unbelievable shade of blue, so dark they could be sapphires. Her hair is a long, tangled mess of silver and brown, pulled away from the front of her face with pink coral. Though I can tell she is an older woman, she has aged gracefully. Her few wrinkles are perfectly synchronized on both sides of her face. She looks flawless. That is until I see her left hand. Her last three fingers are missing. I again look to her face. She has stopped completely, my fish has stopped as well. This merwoman looks into my eyes like she is reading my mind. Having found what she wants she looks down and addresses my finned companion.

"Well, Pisces, you have brought to us a most curious specimen today." She says in clear and distinct English. "None of her kind have been seen for many years. What do you know of her?"

How the fish understands her, I have no idea. Then a series of bubbles comes from the mouth of the fish, Pisces, making sounds that I have never heard, but I understand them like it is my own language.

"I read her thoughts quite clearly, Lady Pescara, though I do not think she has yet realized she can read mine. I felt the connection, however. I am certain of it." This fish has heard my thoughts? And he can understand spoken words?!

"And has she exhibited any other abilities?" the merwoman asks. I sit silently as the two continue to talk about me. There is nothing more I can do.

"None that I have yet seen for certain," Pisces responds, "though her waves speak quite strongly to me. I am confident that she has several more of the Complete Seven within her."

The Complete Seven? What does that mean? Are there more abilities than breathing underwater? This is not what I expected when I entered the ocean this evening. I am not sure what I did expect, but heading into a war headquarters with talking fish and mermaids was not a part of it. Lady Pescara, the beautiful merwoman, lifts her sapphire eyes and speaks to me.

"Please forgive my not having first addressed you. It is customary that I first meet with those under my command like Pisces before introducing myself to our new entrants. Since, however, I have met with you on the highway, I have had to deviate a bit from protocol. As I am sure you understand from Pisces, I am Lady Pescara."

I struggle to find my voice and croak out my answer. "I'm Evelyn. Evelyn Marin." Lady Pescara looks at me like my name is not new to her – like she has been waiting for me. I swear I feel a similar emotion from Pisces.

"Of course, Evelyn. We have been expecting you and I can certainly see the family resemblance in your face. Pisces, I will escort Ms. Marin from here." Pisces dips his head in a bow and I release my grip on the handles of his bridle. I swing my leg over his back and slide to the stone pathway beneath my feet. Pisces raises up his head again, faces me and bows once more before swimming back toward the gates. I turn to Lady Pescara. "I'm sure you have many questions for me Evelyn," she says. "Why don't we walk together to the temple and I will do what I can to enlighten you about your new situation."

"Thank you, I would like that very much," I say. I more than like it. I need it.

I can barely move. This evening is more astounding to me than my first encounter with water. I have experienced so many emotions that I feel exhausted as I turn to follow Lady Pescara. She swims gracefully by my side, guiding me by the elbow while I move slowly in my jeans and tennis shoes through the water. The more I look around me, the more I see I am an anomaly. Everyone else here is dressed in clothes made from the ocean. Shells and seaweed make up most of the attire on those around me. I take a closer look and see that shoes are rare, at least my kind of shoes. Many people are barefoot with the beginnings of webbing on their toes. Others, closer to my age, have makeshift webbing made from some kind of sea plant and fitted over their feet. And yet others, have full fins like Lady Pescara. All are headed in the same direction. I do my best to turn my attention to what Lady Pescara is saying to me.

"I have lived full time in Atlantis for over 40 years and have command over several of the brigades here. In my human life, I lived for the sea and her secrets. I studied Marine Biology until I finally realized my own capabilities with the sea. It was shortly thereafter that I chose Atlantis as my home. This is a choice that you will one day have, but you have much to learn before a decision of this magnitude can be made."

"Right now I can't do much more than follow where you are leading me," I say. I am glassy-eyed as I look around. Everything I see is both distinct and blurry. I want to see it all and close my eyes at the same time.

"Yes, I know you will have many questions in the coming weeks," Lady Pescara says. "We will begin your training shortly, but for now, the best place for you to start learning is the war council."

War council? Training? I have no idea where I am headed or what this woman-creature is talking about. I should be scared out of my wits, but I keep following Lady Pescara. I hope my instincts are leading me in the right direction.

Lady Pescara and I stop at what I assume is the temple. It is an ancient-looking building with a large spire over the door. Two more spires are situated on either side of the first and even those loom above me in the darkness. We enter the building with the mass of people. My eyes adjust to the indoor environment quickly. The glowing lights from the rest of the city are ensconced here triple fold. We are in some kind of corridor that loops around the main room. It is circular in shape and wide enough to accommodate the hundreds of people stopping, talking, and swimming in the space. We make our way through the crowd, her hand still on my elbow to help my water-logged jeans move a little faster.

As we make our way through the large, decaying doors of the inner room, Lady Pescara turns her attention from me. She still holds my elbow but isn't speaking to me anymore. Instead, she addresses several men to her left. Again, some are finned, some are not. She directs them where to sit. "The balcony to the left," I hear her say, "I need to take this new recruit to the ground floor. She's a Marin." Surprise crosses the faces of most of the men, the oldest keep their reactions in check. I don't know what is so surprising about my last name, but I am more concerned about being referred to as a new recruit. I haven't agreed to anything. I don't even know why I am here. But I'm willing to bet that Lady Pescara knows a lot. Everyone here must have some kind of answers for me if my name is so recognizable.

"Excuse me Lady Pescara," I interrupt, "I don't have any idea what is going on. I don't know anything about a war. All I want is to find out more about my dad. I'm sorry, but I think I have to go." Lady Pescara looks at me with raised eyebrows and slightly widened eyes.

"Evelyn. I'm surprised you don't already know about your father. I assumed you were here because you were completely aware of his life and talents." I know my father was a good man who gave his life for his family, but my father is dead. What I want to know is why and how. What led him to his death? Did he suffer long? Was he happy to be in the ocean at least? Did he think of me and my mom when he died or was he too afraid?

Lady Pescara interrupts my thoughts. "Evelyn, we will take time to fill you in, but for now, let me take you to where the new recruits are sitting. You can decide later if you want to stay or not, but please just sit and listen through the meeting. You will learn more than you think." She takes me by the elbow again and ushers me away from the group. I follow her silently until we join a group of people my age. Most are wearing a mixture of land clothes and sea clothes. I see a lot of seaweed and several shining shells. I see only one or two wearing denim shorts (better than my long jeans) and some land-use swimwear. Most have very short hair, the rest have their hair in tight buns or braids. Only one or two of the girls have their long hair down, letting it flow in the water. I am suddenly conscious of my heavy clothing. Lady Pescara leaves me with the group and I get a few glances as I move to a seat on the marble bench. The only opening is in the middle so that is where I head. Before I sit, my attention is frozen. I hear a voice I know.

Chapter 9

"Well, it certainly took you long enough to get here. I was beginning to think I was going to have to handle all of this by myself."

I turn to see who is speaking to me, but the churning in my stomach tells me that I already know. I'm not sure how much more of this I can take in a day. I turn around and see, two rows behind me, the brilliant blonde hair I detest most. It is tied neatly in a bun which is good because I am in the kind of reckless mood that would make me pull anything else. Celia Salvesen is looking right at me. She is the last person I expected or wanted to see on this day of days. The smug look on her face is enough to tell me that she has been watching me for a long time and knew this would happen long before I did. Of course she knew.

"Celia!" What is going on?" I say it louder than I mean to. In fact, I yell it. The people around us stop their conversations to observe this new person yelling in their midst. There is so much green seaweed swirling around me that I am getting dizzy. I can tell that Celia has come up with something terribly intelligent and witty as a reply, but when she opens her mouth to speak, everything around me goes black and I am falling.

I see fantastical fish and half-people all around me. Many are ignoring me, but others are openly pointing at me and laughing. I am tied to a pair of cement shoes, trying to walk to a bench. I can only move an inch at a time and all the while more and more people are turning their attention to me. The laughter grows louder until I can't handle the sound anymore. I cover my ears and start screaming to shut them out. I hear my name. "Evelyn!" I stop screaming as awareness fills my mind. I have heard that voice before. It is reaching out to me through my nightmare.

I open my eyes slowly, trying to take in my surroundings. I am in a plain, square room lying on a cot that looks like it has seen better days. The room is quiet and empty except for me. I look to the window above my head. There are seaweed curtains and I know I am still in Atlantis. I feel a wave of nausea warning that I will black out again, so I close my eyes and just focus on my breathing.

I hear someone come in through the doors, but I keep my eyes shut. I'm not sure I can keep from being dizzy again or, even worse, being ill. I can tell that whoever has come in, has done so quietly and is sitting by my bed. I hear lady Pescara's voice from the door.

"Are you sure she's ready for you? She seems to be unable to cope with the events of the day. Maybe you had better try talking to her tomorrow."

"No, I'm sure she needs to see me now," says the soothing, familiar voice.

I am mortified and ready to hide in those hideous seaweed curtains, but I am not a magician.

"Evelyn. Evelyn, can you hear me?" Yes, I hear him, but I'm not ready to open my eyes, so I nod. "Evelyn, everything is going to be okay. I'm here with you. You are okay and I can explain everything."

"You should have explained long before today, Jack." I can't handle this new strain and I turn over to cry, willing myself not to be sick. Jack, my boss and the guy I have been falling for, is here. I think I am having a very, very bad dream this time. There is no way that so many people in my life are actually in the water too and have not bothered to tell me. This is insanity.

"Evelyn. I'm sorry. But it doesn't work that way. You had to find us on your own. That's the only way you would have been ready for everything." I don't feel ready for everything I have seen today. "Evelyn, look at me. Let me talk to you. I can tell you anything you want to know. What can I do to help you right now?"

His hand is on my shoulder now. I know that hand. I have looked at it almost daily for months, and yet it is like I don't even know the man it is attached to. This is a new life. It is like a lie he kept hidden from me. I don't expect Jack to tell me all of his secrets, but I feel betrayed. He could have helped me before today. He could have been the one to answer my questions rather than let me get it via shock. He could have helped me more the first time I breathed water. He could have told me then that he could breathe it too. Why on earth did he not tell me anything? Why did he have to leave it to James to tell me? To let me be broken again by the same person who did it before? I am so uncomfortable with these two people in this close space. There is only one thing I want right now.

"Jack, I just want to go home. I can't do this right now. Please, Jack. Please let me go home."

"You'd better take her. We can reconvene the council tomorrow." Lady Pescara has an air of leadership in her tone. Did they call off a war council just because one *new recruit* passed out? That doesn't make any sense, but really I don't care anymore. I just want to go home. I need to cry and I need my bed. Somewhere inside me, I want my mom, but I know that is out of the question. I am going to be alone this time and that will have to be enough.

Jack puts his arm under my back to lift me up. I refuse to open my eyes when he is so close to my face. I allow him to get me into the upright position and I sit up, swinging my legs over the edge of the bed.

"I'm fine, Jack. You don't have to hold me up." Once I feel Jack's arm leave me, I open my eyes. Lady Pescara is floating in the water in front of me. Her face is largely unreadable since she stands in front of the light, but there is unmistakable disappointment in her voice.

"Given your parentage, I thought you would have been more capable of handling your new situation today. You did step into the open water freely, did you not? Nobody pushed you, did they?"

"No, I wasn't pushed, but I wasn't expecting...well, I'm not sure what I expected. I just wasn't ready for it, that's all. I'm sorry,

Lady Pescara." Even though I don't know this woman, I feel guilty for letting her down. Maybe it's because she is a commander in an army, maybe it's because she is disappointed in me. It isn't anger she expresses. It isn't cruelty. It's the feeling that she knows I can do better but have fallen short of my capabilities. Whatever the reason, I know I want to be in Lady Pescara's good favor.

"If I can just go home and rest and think for a while, I think it would help a lot. I can come back again tomorrow if that's okay. I just need to have some space to myself."

A measure of satisfaction enters Lady Pescara's voice. "I think that is agreeable. I look forward to seeing you tomorrow then." She pauses, assessing me. "Be sure to get plenty of rest, fluids, and good nutrition. I want you to be strong when we next meet. There is much to discuss and much to take care of."

"Yes ma'am. I'll be ready."

"Good. Jack, please help Evelyn get home, then come back here and we will talk about how to proceed."

"Yes, Lady Pescara. Right away," Jack answers. Lady Pescara goes out to the hall and Jack and I are left in the silence. I make my way to my feet, shrugging off his hand when he offers help. I needed him before and he wasn't there. I am determined to not need him now.

"Look Jack, I don't really want your help getting home. My problem is that I have no idea how to get there from here so I am stuck between a rock and a hard place."

Jack smiles and nods, "How about you just let me escort you home and we'll let that be it for today?"

"Agreed."

Jack leads me from the room, but I am slow in my heavy clothing. I allow him to hold me by the elbow and guide me. We make our way through hallways and corridors, some with ceilings, some without. I'm not keeping track of where we are going. I just go where I am led. Eventually, we make our way outside and to the city gates. The life that was missing there when I first arrived has now made its way home. The meeting is over.

Tired as I am, I am still fascinated to see the life that swims outside. People and fish are intermingling in the streets, having conversations and cleaning up for the night. Some turn to look at Jack and me as we make our way to shore, but for the most part, everyone ignores us. I see one or two couples in the crowd, but no children. Just adults. Everyone here is an adult. I want to ask Jack about it, but I still am not ready to be on speaking terms with him.

We make our way to the bottom of the Continental Slope where several large fish are waiting with harnesses on their backs. We are not the only ones leaving for the night. I count at least 12 others who are mounting fish. After only a moment or two, two large fish head toward us. One fish Jack mounts quietly. The other fish I recognize is Pisces.

Pisces comes to my side and turns so I can easily mount his back. I climb into the saddle and am comforted by the silent creature beneath me. I trusted him and he led me to something entirely new and overwhelming. And yet, I cannot help but feel comfortable in his presence. It feels like a great burden falls from my shoulders as I grab the reigns and Pisces swims forward. I swear he is trying to comfort me. I am happy to be with him again.

In 15 minutes, Jack and I are at the edge of the Continental Shelf. Our fish swim about 50 feet forward onto the shelf and stop. I know it is time to dismount. I reluctantly climb down from Pisces and cast a remorseful glance in his direction. Jack's fish has already turned away, but Pisces looks steadily into my eyes. He is telling me something that I can understand. It is reassuring. I need that communication. I need Pisces. I know I will be back.

I touch Pisces just below the strap on his lower mouth to say goodbye. I turn away and am guided by Jack until I can swim with reasonable speed on my own.

Jack is respectful of my need for silence as we venture toward my dorm. I find my apartment door unlocked and head inside. I turn to Jack who stands, waiting, outside my door, a look of concern on his face. I must look like something the cat dragged in.

"I'll be fine Jack. I promise. Thank you for bringing me home. I promised Lady Pescara I would return and I will. I just need to recoup a bit first."

Jack gives me a silent nod and turns to leave. There is more I want to say to him, more I want to ask, but I cannot find the words. I close the door, make my way through the dark to my room, and lay on my bed. I am soaked, but it doesn't matter. I turn my face toward the pillow and let myself cry. I lay like that for hours, but eventually, as the sun begins to make my window light, I fall asleep.

Chapter 10

When I finally open my eyes, a different light penetrates my window pane – the light of evening. I slept the entire day. At first my sleep was barraged with dreams of fantasy. I tossed and turned and even once woke myself up when I yelled out loud. I felt like I was being attacked by something, but my reactions to its grasp were slow and inhibited. Eventually, sleep overcame my hysteria. I felt warmth and comfort again and was able to let go of my frantic thoughts. It was a deep and resounding sleep that allowed me to gain my much needed peace. I stopped dreaming and all was darkness and quiet. It is strange to now open my eyes to an eerie evening light. I feel out of place. Everything feels out of place. I am unwanted by my boyfriend, ignored by my roommates, and I am merely tolerated by some fantastical mermaid.

I make some movement in my bed as I try to get to my feet, but I am unnerved by my appearance. The heavy, wet clothing that clung to me as I fell asleep in the early morning hours is gone. Instead, I am wearing fresh pajamas. Not my pajamas, but Celia's. I am suddenly very aware of how I got this way. As I sit up in bed, Celia enters the room.

"Lady Pescara assigned me to look after you last night. I was sure that you would be fine on your own, but she insisted. It's a good thing too. When I got home you were a shivering mess. I got you dressed into something warm and dry and you finally conked out.

"You should really do some shopping, Evelyn, I couldn't find a decent pair of pajamas in your drawer. I had to put you in mine. Are t-shirts and basketball shorts all you own?" Celia hands me a steaming cup of something warm and a plate with some fruit and a cold sandwich on it. I try to thank her for the food, but she replies, "It's like I said, it was an order from Lady Pescara." Celia leans against the doorframe and raises an angry eyebrow in my direction.

"I don't understand why you did any of this if you are so disgusted by me," I say, feeling self-conscious that my irritating roommate had to help me get dressed in the night.

Celia's face registers frustration and even a little annoyance at my apparent lack of understanding. "I don't ignore orders, Evelyn, no matter how much I may want to. You might want to take a note or two from me on that one."

"I didn't realize that I was under direction to receive orders from anyone," is my quick and exasperated response.

Celia sighs and sits at my desk. A picture of Gwen and me is hanging on the wall behind her. A whole new set of emotions, surrounding Gwen and James, hit my chest. I didn't hear a sound from Gwen all night. Has she even been home in the last 24 hours? Is she with James? This new, anxious flurry of thoughts is interrupted by the blonde sitting across from me.

"I have been asked to fill you in on the necessaries. Lady Pescara wants you to be ready before you come back tonight so you don't have another fainting fit."

"*You're* going to be the one to answer all of my questions?" my tone is as annoyed as hers.

"No, dear," she replies sarcastically, "I am not here to answer all of your questions. I am here to fill you in on the necessaries. Any *un*necessary questions are to be saved for Lady Pescara. I'm not here to help you unlock the key to your soul, Evelyn," she rolls her eyes, "I'm just here to bring you up to speed."

I can tell that this will be a long session of nit-picking if I don't let Celia do her talking. I have to learn something or I will be stuck in this confusion forever. "Fine," I consent at last, "where do we begin?"

"*We* begin at the end of the story, Evelyn. I have to first fill you in on the middle. The beginning, you have to get from Lady Pescara." I sit and let her keep talking. "There is a huge underwater sea war right now. We are under the title of Atlantis while our enemy is gathering an army under her name – Ceto.

"Ceto has been hunting through records and archeological sites underwater for the legendary power source of Atlantis. We don't know why she wants it, but whatever her reasons, we know they must be bad. For years, Ceto has been trying to get our forces to join her in an attempt to overrun the land with the sea. This year, her own sea powers have grown and she has used them to her favor. The active storm season we have been experiencing is a result of Ceto testing out her powers." My eyes widen and I focus more on what Celia is saying. I know we have had crazy weather in Florida lately. I thought it was from global warming.

"We have received intelligence that suggests Ceto is testing what exactly she can do," Celia says. "She has caused increasing damage to mainland America, and it's clear that she is doing it to prepare for a larger scale land attack. It looks like she wants to overrun the land with the ocean, Evelyn."

I take a moment to clear my thoughts, frustrated by Celia's assumption that I will be joining the army. "Obviously, this is bad," I say, "But what are you or I supposed to do about it?"

"*I* have been training under the tutelage of Captain Jack in preparation for battle, Evelyn. *You* have yet to do anything other than faint. If you can get yourself under control, I can only assume that you are meant to join the forces as well."

"You can keep the insults to yourself, Celia, I'm not interested. What I do want to know is how on earth all of this started happening to me. Why have I been turning into something that can breathe and move and communicate in the ocean and why is it so important that I come along?"

"As to your first question, you became a *two-worlder* because that is what you are. It's in your DNA to live underwater or to at least exhibit these traits. The traits won't make themselves manifest until you are ready and *worthy* to receive them. You can breathe underwater, sleep underwater, even live underwater.

"The two-worlders who decide to live underwater full time eventually begin to take on other characteristics of sea life. Most take on the characteristics of finned fish like Lady Pescara. She has become a mermaid because she decided to spend her life in the ocean. Other sea dwellers, take on the characteristics of lesser fish. This happened to Ceto. After deciding to live under the ocean, she began to take on the traits of an octopus. I have never seen her, but I hear she is way creepy looking, all those tentacles. Ugh."

"But why is it so necessary that *I* come now Celia?" I ask.

"Your guess is as good as mine, Evelyn. Lady Pescara insists that you will be an asset to the force. She's had me keeping an eye on you this whole semester. I told her that you were taking too long to come to the ocean, you probably wouldn't ever get into the water. Captain Jack knew you were ready first, of course, but it still took you so LONG to get out into the open water."

Celia is only going to continue insulting me as long as we are here together. I stand up from the bed and head to my dresser, looking for water-appropriate clothing. As I choose my swimwear, Celia walks away to let me dress myself this time. Before leaving the room, she turns to face me again. "You know, *I* have been in the water since I graduated. It only took me a week to get out into the open water. Why did it take you so long?"

I sigh and answer, "I have no idea, Celia. This whole thing is a surprise to me. How did you get into the open water after a week, anyway? Weren't you confused by everything going on around you?"

Celia rolls her eyes like she is trying to teach a total idiot. "I wasn't *surprised*, Evelyn. *I* was *prepared*. My dad and mom talked about it so much that it was natural. Besides, I did grow up in Florida. The ocean is nothing new to me."

I raise my head to meet her eyes. "Hang on. What do you mean your mom and dad talked about it? They know what we can do?" I have to know how she confided all of this craziness to her parents. I realize I will have to tell my mom eventually and I have no idea how to do it.

Celia looks confused. "I didn't tell my mom and dad, Evelyn, they told me. I was raised knowing this could happen someday so my parents prepped me for it."

What the heck?! Uncle Russ?! No wonder he keeps checking on me. He isn't protecting me for my mom's sake, he is just curious to know if I will make the leap. I wonder if he is as irritated by my progress as Celia. How did he know I would turn two-worlder? Do I have it written across my forehead or something? I know Celia is the wrong person to ask all of these questions to. I have to get to Lady Pescara if I want any more information. I'm thinking, but Celia is still talking.

"My dad comes to the open water to assist in the war councils. That's what stopped the meeting last night. Right when you fainted, he came rushing into the room with some kind of important information. He headed straight to the war council leaders and they spoke very quietly for a long time. I don't know what the fuss was about since I had to help you out. Captain Jack saw you faint and had me help him carry you to the hospital. By the time I got back, the war council had dispersed. That's all I know.

"So, if you're finished playing the fainting damsel, we can head back out tonight and see what has been going on. Do you think you are ready yet?"

"Wow, Celia." I slam my drawer shut and start changing into my swimsuit. "I didn't ask for this. I have no idea why I have to be a part of this thing. Trust me, I would love nothing more than to *not* be a part of the *two-worlders*. That's not why I'm here. So let's get this figured out so I can get out of it and you can go back to being the shining star."

I want her off my back and unfortunately, the only way to get that is to go with her, back to the ocean, to meet with Lady Pescara. I know she has the answers I am looking for.

I am ready to go in my favorite, blue one-piece and I pull on my wetsuit. I slip into my flip flops, grab my sandwich, and take a quick sip of the drink Celia brought. "Let's get going Celia. The sooner we get to Lady Pescara, the sooner you can be free of me." With a roll of her eyes and a quick flip of her perfectly blonde hair, Celia leads the way out the door, back to the sea, with me following resolutely behind.

Chapter 11

Pisces is not at the edge of the continental shelf to meet me this time. Another fish, Daria, comes instead. I am disappointed that Pisces is not my guide again. I would be more comfortable to have him at my side. But Daria it is, so Daria I ride. She is smaller than Pisces, but not by much. Her brilliant scales shine pink and orange in the dim light of sunset that barely reach us below. I am surprised to find that I can understand Daria's thoughts as well. It is a little easier to read her as I get used to this new form of telepathy. She understands me and we communicate silently in the water. She reads the needs of my body as she dives quickly after Celia and her fish. Daria's dive is a more gradual slope than Celia's fish. Her mind connects with mine and she warns me when to duck and gives me little pointers on how to make my ride more comfortable.

We make our way to Atlantis and around the temple I saw last night. I stand out much less in my water attire. I am not the only one in a wetsuit, though there are still mostly-seaweed outfits all around, and I get fewer looks from curious eyes than I did yesterday. Daria follows Celia as she leads the way to Lady Pescara. Celia turns around to check on me, then smiles and swims by a group of teenage two-worlders. I recognize several from the meeting last night. I am met with faces trying to stifle a few chuckles. Celia is taking a moment of enjoyment out of her temporary control over me.

Celia and her fish pull up to a building I haven't seen before. It is very near the temple, but not so grand in scale. Celia dismounts and heads inside. I climb down from Daria and head in, whispering a mental 'thank-you' as I leave.

Once inside, I catch up with Celia as she heads up a flight of stairs. A few humans and merpeople linger in the foyer, most of them older and wearing war medals on sashes that run from shoulder to hip. At the top of the stairs is a long, open hall overlooking the floor below. There is no barrier, so out of instinct, I keep closer to the wall. When Celia reaches the end of the hall, she stands before a large door. It shows the signs of having been underwater, but doesn't look nearly as old as the other doors here. After knocking, Celia is admitted to the room and I follow behind. It is an office complete with an executive style desk and maps on the walls, but these maps have markers all over the ocean – none on the land portions. Lady Pescara is floating/standing behind her desk, Uncle Russ by her side, looking over several sheets of wax-coated paper spread out before them.

"Hello Celia! Hello Evelyn!" I nod a small, courteous smile to Uncle Russ's warm greeting. I still feel wounded by his deception. He comes to greet Celia and me with a handshake. "I see you have brought our newest recruit back with you Celia. Well, I'm glad to see she's here and ready to join the ranks."

I know I can't keep my silence. "I'm not sure I want to join the ranks, Mr. Salvesen," I'm not willing to call him *Uncle* yet. "Celia has told me about the war going on in the ocean, but this is the first

I've heard about any of these things. I've only known about my water abilities for a few weeks. I am still confused about what is going on here."

Lady Pescara looks up from her papers to see my face. She is the one person in the room who has been open with me. I am more inclined to trust her.

"Captain, Ms. Salvesen, would the two of you leave Ms. Marin and me alone? I have some things I would like to explain to her. Ms. Salvesen, thank you for your help with Ms. Marin. If you'll both remain just outside the door, I will call you in shortly."

Celia gives a respectful nod to Lady Pescara and heads out the door. Uncle Russ says, "Yes, ma'am" and also gives Lady Pescara a nod of respect before leaving the room and closing the door behind him. I stifle a laugh seeing Uncle Russ in a wet suit; his belly squeezed in a little too tight. It is a brief amusement.

I turn my head to Lady Pescara. She holds out her hand and motions for me to sit in the chair at the front of her desk. She swims over and sits on the desk edge in front of me.

"Ms. Marin. I am sorry that you have had to come to your knowledge of your sea abilities in such a time as this. If you had been brought here in times of peace, there would have been support groups and abilities classes to help you in your discovery of your nature. Unfortunately, this is not a peaceful time. As Ms. Salvesen was directed to tell you, we are fighting against an enemy whose strength is growing. We have had spies out who last night gave us alarming information. Apparently, we have a traitor in our midst. Information about our training camps has been reaching Ceto and she has been using it to her advantage. Her own spy is somewhere among us. That is what ended last night's war council. We must be careful how we proceed in order to root out our traitor."

"Lady Pescara, I'm sorry you have to deal with this, but I still don't understand why I have to be here. Celia said you thought I would be an asset to the force, but why? How did you know that I would even show these abilities?"

Lady Pescara folds her hands in her lap and looks at me silently for a moment before answering. "Evelyn, I have been wanting you here for years." How did she even know I existed years ago? "I knew your parents very well," she says. "You come from a strong heritage of faithful two-worlders who have served Atlantis in times of peace and in times of war. Many have been casualties of this very fight. I have often wondered if your father's disappearance had something to do with Ceto.

"Since your mother moved with you to Arizona, I have thought many times of the strength you could be to our force. Many from your ancestral line have held multiple water skills. It has been my hope that you would hold multiple skills as well. Most of our two-worlders hold one or two of these skills, like Celia. We use those skills to our advantage as we prepare for war. But if I have a person who holds three or more skills at a time, then I am able to use them on more covert missions.

"But understand me Evelyn, I am determined to win this war with or without your help. If you decide to stay, I welcome you whole-heartedly. If, however, you decide that you do not want to join us, you must be escorted out of Atlantis. I will have Celia contact you when the war is over and you can come again to learn about your abilities. That could be years from now, I don't know. It only depends on how quickly we can overpower Ceto."

Lady Pescara sits in momentary silence as she lets me absorb the information. Conflicting emotions fill me from the inside out. War. My father. Lady Pescara wondered if Ceto had been responsible for my father's death. It could be grasping at straws, but the possibility of it makes my stomach turn. What happened to him? I have a line of two-worlders in my ancestry. I had no idea. Did my father hide it from my mom? Did she find out after he disappeared? Is that why we left? I can tell that Lady Pescara is waiting for my decision. I still have a million questions, but I know I can't ask them right now. I have to trust that I will find out the answers, and this is the best place to find them – under the ocean.

I raise my eyes to meet Lady Pescara's solid gaze. She looks like she could be a very beautiful person. She just needs to smile. Is that what war does to you? Makes your smile disappear? I don't have time to follow that line of thought, my answer is ready.

"I will stay Lady Pescara. I thank you for your openness and your information. I still have questions, but they can wait for the right time. Until then, what do I need to do?"

A brief smile of approval crosses Lady Pescara's face. Yes, she is beautiful. But just as soon as that smile came, it goes. Lady Pescara gets up and so do I. "Very well then," she says, "I am pleased. I'm grateful for your willingness to serve even without all of the answers you seek. I do hope you will find what you need while you are with us." We make our way to the door and find Uncle Russ and Celia waiting for us on the other side. "Ms. Salvesen, Ms. Marin will be staying with us. Please take her to Captain Jack and inform him that he has a new recruit. Ms. Marin, I will be in touch with Captain Jack in regards to your progress. Both of you make certain that you are well rested before resuming your day's training. That will be all, ladies."

"Yes ma'am," Celia and I answer, almost in unison. Celia glares at me through narrowed eyes, her nostrils flaring slightly. She nods to Lady Pescara and turns to leave the room. I nod and again I follow Celia.

Chapter 12

I am lost in my thoughts as I follow Celia through the streets of Atlantis. We are swimming now. Without our fish guides. I am so much faster than I was in my jeans and shoes yesterday. But even though my wetsuit is designed for fluid movement, I feel like I am swimming faster than I ever have before. It's like my body was made to do this. The feeling is new and amazing. Even though I am stuck with Celia, I find that this new experience brings a smile to my face. But there are many other things on my mind.

I think about my father and my mind races with questions. Has Ceto done something to him? How could he hide his underwater life from my mom? Is Ceto the reason I have no living grandparents? What are the water skills Lady Pescara talked about, and what skills am I supposed to have? How many other people do I know that have these abilities? I know James is in the ocean somewhere, but who else is here?

James. The craziness I've been experiencing has started to close that wound, but now it is reopening. James. I saw the guy I thought was my boyfriend kissing my roommate and friend. That sucked royally. And I haven't had time to deal with it. He started telling me about life underwater when I decided to learn about it on my own. Had I really ignored him so much it was easy for him to forget we were together? Were we really together or was it just an easy fling? Someone familiar to be with until someone more permanent came along?

After 15 minutes of silent swimming, Celia and I arrive at a large, open area. The field is surrounded by tents. In the center are rows of fenced-off squares. Two squares on the end are filled with equipment – fighting equipment. So, this must be the training area. I see several teams of people battling in the practice arena, armor and all. My stomach sinks about three feet into the ground. I am not a fighter. I haven't wrestled with brothers or even been picked on by bullies. The most fighting I've done was in second grade ballet when little Courtney Lynn took my ribbon wand during free dance. I tackled her and took my wand back. Then we both had to sit on the bench for the rest of the class. I never tackled anyone again: it wasn't worth losing the free dance. War prep is going to be a big learning curve for me.

Celia leads me to a practice area where Jack is standing and giving verbal coaching to the fighters. "Captain Jack, Lady Pescara sent me to escort Ms. Evelyn Marin to you. She is one of your new recruits." Jack turns to face us and I swear I see Celia blush. He is wearing a shorts-wetsuit with the top half folded down, exposing his tanned chest and muscular arms. I am too much a mess in my stomach to have room for butterflies. Then he smiles at me and the butterflies find some space to flutter around. Celia gives me a glare. I guess we both have a thing for Captain Jack.

"Well there, princess. How are you feeling?" he asks, "Are you ready to learn how to fight like a man or would you rather watch today?"

Before I can answer Jack's cheerful teasing, Celia is ready to shine. "Lady Pescara suggested Evelyn and I rest before heading into training sessions for today, but I'm ready to go to work now. I won't speak for Evelyn." Celia looks down her nose at me, taunting me to join the practice when she knows I'm a complete novice.

"No," I respond to Jack, "I'd rather watch today."

"All right, then," says Jack. Then turning to Celia, "Celia, suit up and meet us in training area four."

"Yes, sir," Celia answers as she turns on her heels, swimming straight to the training equipment. She may be a jerk, but I have to admit that Celia is a very beautiful person. I am self-conscious and a little jealous of her muscles while she swims away.

Meanwhile, Jack is facing me again. "We've got a lot of work to do to get you ready. I'll let you watch today, but tomorrow you've got to be ready to work."

I am used to working for Jack. I can do that here too. "I'll be ready," I say.

"Good," he says, "Celia's very good at what she does. You'll learn a lot by watching her." He turns from me and tells the other recruits they can call it quits for the day. Then he returns his attention to me.

"Okay, why don't you come with me and we'll watch Celia in action. I can explain a bit about how things are run here." We swim toward training area 4. I am surprised by how far I can actually go with simple strokes and kicks. It is like there is a little propulsion pack on my back. There is some equipment on the field from the last training session. It looks archaic: two very large, round shields, a sword, a mace, and a pile of armor.

Jack stops by the fence and leans across the framework. I swim up beside him and rest there as well. "I guess I should start by telling you I'm glad you're here, and I *am* sorry that I couldn't tell you about us earlier," he says. "We are at war and I can't risk letting anything out, not even to you. I have to know who is on our side, Evelyn, before I can say anything. It's just the rules of wartime. But I still hope you'll forgive me for not telling you earlier. I wanted to." He rests his hand on my shoulder, and I feel myself relax. It is the first sincere thing I've heard from someone I trust for some time. I am glad to hear it and glad that it came from Jack.

"Thanks," I say, "I appreciate your apology. I get that wartime etiquette doesn't always allow for open communication, I still appreciate the apology though. So, thanks." I give him a half smile, his hand still resting on my shoulder. I feel nerves growing inside me again, so I hurry on, turning toward the training ground to keep myself focused. "I'm here now, so teach me everything I need to know. I guess we'll figure out the rest when this thing is over." I feel suddenly awkward, like I've just told Jack we'd have a relationship when the war ends. The blush runs up my neck and onto my face, burning my ears and heating the water around me.

"Well," Jack says, "we have a fairly large army for underwater battles at this post. There are hundreds of posts along this coast for both American continents. Atlantis is really headquarters for everyone. We get updates from the other posts every few days. It's not like working on land. Can't really use cell phones underwater, it's too deep. A lot of our land-based tech doesn't work with our fish companions. So things are still old-school here. We wait for information and do our best to keep up. Lady Pescara heads the new recruit division, but I think she wants to prove herself here so she can move up in the ranks. She's a good leader. I wouldn't be surprised if she did move up the ranks when the war's done." Jack has moved both of his hands to the top rail of the fence as he continues.

"The new recruits are divided into groups of 50. I am captain of the Delphin 50. I get the recruits who show early signs of the ability to communicate with the sea-life," he gives me a smiling nod, "that would be you. Within each group of 50, there are 5 sub-leaders, each over a group of 10. Celia is one of those and she will be your group leader. She is responsible for making sure recruits are learning their skills well and for aiding me in training. She can be a bit harsh, but she knows her stuff. Just stick with her and you'll do well."

Oh great, I get to spend more time with Celia. Maybe I should have mentioned on my resume that I'm not such a fan. Oh wait, that's right, I didn't have a resume.

Celia swims into the training area. She is wearing her sea armor, made of some kind of metal and fashioned into scales like a fish. The main torso piece is fashioned like a tank top and she wears it over her long wetsuit. Her legs are covered with the same material as the top. Her sleeves, though, are made of chain mail armor and she wears a metal helmet that looks Greek.

"Armor is our first line of defense in battle," says Jack, "but it is heavy and slows us down. You may have noticed that you are able to swim faster than you thought possible, and that helps us in battle, but we are still weighed down by the armor. I have all my recruits practice in battle armor so they can build the necessary strength to perform with greater speed." Jack turns to Celia, "Well, why don't we show Evelyn what a real fight looks like?" He climbs up and over the fence and into the ring. Jack pulls up his wetsuit, much to Celia's dismay I am sure, and grabs the helmet and armor lying on the ground. It doesn't take more than two minutes for the experienced soldier to put on his armor and while he dresses, Celia grabs one of the shields and the mace.

"Battle ready, soldier?" asks Jack.

"Battle ready, Captain," is Celia's reply and the battle begins. Jack is giving me tips from the field.

"You have to be ready to use any weapon on hand, Evelyn," he says. "You won't know what your opponent will use so you have to be prepared for that too." Celia and Jack swim in slow circles around each other, Jack with his sword in his right hand, up and ready to move, his shield in the left hand. Celia also has her shield in her left hand, but her right arm is overhead, swinging the mace in circles above her. Then in a flash, Celia comes down with her mace aiming right for the top of Jack's head. He ducks and covers his head with his shield and swings his sword at Celia's ankles. But she maneuvers out of the way and gets herself settled in a crouch position on the ocean floor, still swinging her mace.

Jack's movement has propelled him upward in the water. He is hovering over Celia now with his shield under his body, slowly settling down to where Celia is crouched. As he gets closer to her, he twists onto his right side, jabbing the sword straight under Celia's shield. But Celia is ready with her mace. She jerks out of the way and comes crashing down with it on Jack's sword. The short chain tangles around the sword as the metal-clad end wraps, swinging around it. She jerks as hard as she can to free the sword from Jack's hand, but he is too strong for her.

Jack jerks back and Celia loses the grip of her mace. Jack now has both weapons and Celia is unarmed. Jack pulls the mace from his sword and tucks it into the back of his armor. "The battle isn't won yet, Evelyn, Celia now has to fight without her weapon. It takes quick thinking and a lot of practice, both of which Celia has, so watch closely."

Celia takes a new confidence and lunges toward Jack. Neither one has their feet on the ocean floor. It is strange to see a floating battle taking place. There are a million angles to use to your advantage as you strike at your opponent. Celia's shield rams against Jack's as she struggles to strike him while keeping out of reach of his sword. Now facing Celia, Jack swings his sword at her back and I hear clanging as his sword hits her armor. The blow looks like it hits full force, and it shows on Celia's body. She arches her back in reaction to his swing and swims backward a few feet. I assume Jack will stop the session, but instead, he crouches down behind his shield with his sword ready, prepared for another attack from Celia. And that attack comes.

Celia's face registers pure anger as she backs away from Jack. She catapults herself into the water overhead, never letting her eyes stray from her target. "Watch how her eyes never leave me," Jack tells me, "she knows exactly where I am, but she must also know her surroundings." Celia's nostrils flare and her face reddens. "Smelling the ocean is a difficult skill to learn. Nobody has it naturally, but if you can master it, it will help you in battle." Smelling the ocean? This must be one of the water skills Lady Pescara told me about. Just as Jack finishes his sentence, Celia plunges down into the water with all the speed she can muster, but she isn't aiming for Jack. Just as she is parallel to him, she hits a large, armored fish, similar to Pisces.

I am shocked to see Celia hit the fish so hard, but even more shocked when I see a second armored fish swim up behind Celia, toward the first fish and it, too, collides. I realize both soldiers have a counterpart lurking in the darker water. Jack swings his sword at Celia's back but gets rammed instead by her fish. Now that the battle has moved closer to the ocean floor, the silt is being kicked up into a blurry cloud of brown. I can't see as much as I want, not that I would be able to take it all in anyway.

The tight group whirls and turns until I see Celia pull herself free from the mayhem. Immediately, she swims behind Jack and grabs her mace from his armor. She lowers her shield to get closer to him and just as she has the mace firmly in hand, she raises it, swinging, overhead. Her movement alerts Jack to her whereabouts and he responds by whipping around. With her shield down Celia is vulnerable and Jack takes advantage by pointing his sword firmly into her abdomen. At first, I am afraid he cut her, then I realize that there is no blood. Still, all four fighters are frozen as if playing a game of freeze tag.

"Do you concede?" Jack asks.

With a look of frustration, Celia lowers her mace and nods. "I concede." All at once, all four participants relax. "What do you think of that Evelyn?" Jack shouts from where he stands. His face is red, but he still wears a look of satisfaction. He had fun.

"I can see I have a lot to learn," is my response.

"And you'll learn most of it from Celia," Jack says. "She's one of our best." Celia straightens and Jack turns to her, "Excellent battle today Ms. Salvesen, I knew you wouldn't let me down."

"Thank you, Captain. I hope to not lose again," she says with a small smile.

"And what could you have done differently in this battle to not have lost, Ms. Salvesen?"

"Keep my shield up," is Celia's short reply as her smile fades.

"Excellent," says Jack, "Go over it tonight and record what could have been done differently in your battle journal. You ladies are dismissed."

I understand that I am to follow Celia, so I swim slowly by her side back to the equipment stalls. She is silent. She is still furious and embarrassed by her loss, despite Jack's praise of her performance. I wait while she removes her armor and places her shield and mace in the proper stalls. When she emerges, she has something to say.

"I will be your group leader from now on. Jack is my superior and I am yours. He is right to say that you have a lot to learn from me: you do. I've tried helping you with your studies at the apartment, but

101

you weren't very receptive nor were you a quick study. Understand that here, you will be expected to work hard and do as I say." I bite back a sarcastic reply.

"I will do my best Celia," I say through gritted teeth.

"Good," she says, "now let's get some food and I'll show you where your bunk is. Tomorrow will be a very long day for you. You'll need the nourishment and rest."

I swim just behind Celia to the outskirts of the training field. I turn to see Jack closing up the training areas. His wetsuit is back down and his fish swims beside him. Celia's fish disappeared after the battle and I wonder if it is a training fish used by all new recruits. Either way, I am looking forward to having an ally in battle.

I follow Celia until we reached the tent area. She points out a tent like all the others; dingy grey with a small light inside. "You'll be bunking there with three other two-worlders whom you'll meet after dinner. Dinner is always served in the main part of the city by the temple. Most of the permanent two-worlders, of course, live and cook for themselves in their own homes. The war has brought a large influx of recruits who don't know how to feed themselves down here yet, so they join with the regular enlisted soldiers in the dining hall."

I have a hard time keeping up with Celia. There is enough on my mind already. All I know is where I am supposed to eat and where I am supposed to sleep. The rest will have to wait for another day.

Chapter 13

The next several days and nights are a blur in my mind. Training battles, trying to figure out how to wear armor and use archaic weaponry, being forced to follow orders from Celia. It is killer stressful. Most of my time is spent with Celia and her group of 10 – I actually make it a group of 11. I catch glimpses of Jack when he gives orders to the group of 50. I begin to recognize faces that I pass by every day. I am sore all over. I'm not used to swimming everywhere I go. Thankfully, nothing in this early training requires that I get bruises to learn the techniques of combat, but I am sure that will come.

We do more than physical training. We have classes in the art of war and battle strategy. We learn about our enemy – Ceto – and her efforts against Atlantis for over a decade. She has been wreaking havoc with storms above the ocean and tidal waves and current changes. Atlantis has fought diligently to bring the natural course of the earth back into play. We learn a few basic survival skills as well: how to cook seaweed and how to use coral to heal wounds. We even have classes to make up for what we are missing onshore. FIU's Aquarius program extends to classes underwater. Teachers from the land join us regularly to help us catch up on our studies.

Near the end of my first two weeks, I learn that we will be given leave for the weekend. Everyone is excited and I am jolted back to reality. Leave? I didn't realize that once I signed up for a soldier position I would be treated like any other army. There are days and times we are expected to be there. I have been too wrapped up in all I have been learning to think about it. I am now very much aware of all I have left behind. Classes have been covered under water and I have even done some work for Oleta River State Park in keeping underwater areas clean, but I have thought nothing of my mom.

My mom. What on earth am I going to tell her? "Hi mom! I live underwater now. Good news: I don't have to pay rent because I'm a soldier!" Will she believe that I have sea skills? Will she be furious that I did these things without her knowledge? Will she demand that I come home to Arizona?

No. That I know I can't do. Too much waits for me here. I can't turn around and go back. I know I am on the right path, I just don't know how I am going to break the news to my mom.

The Friday when everyone heads home resembles Phoenix freeways on the Friday of a three-day weekend. The streets of Atlantis are packed with people. Some are carrying backpacks while they swim, others, like me, are lightly loaded and just ready to head home. I haven't made a home in Atlantis even though I've been sleeping here for almost two weeks. I was given bedding rations and food and the supplies I need, but I haven't made the space my own in any way. I am heading back to land in my same blue one-piece and wetsuit. I am going to have to do some shopping.

Protocols for mass exodus from the sea are that we leave the ocean either when the beach is packed or completely empty. With a packed beach and ocean full of swimmers, it is harder to notice more swimmers coming from the ocean. On the other hand, we can't come swimming out when there are only a few people on the beach because they will notice the influx of swimmers coming from nowhere.

On this Friday, we are leaving before sunrise. Many of the sea dwellers here are big time surfers and know when other surfers will or will not spot them, so we rely on them to give us the go ahead. At the base of the continental shelf a mass of sea dwellers waits for their turn to be given a ride to the top. Some of the stronger swimmers are just swimming up, probably in an effort to show off their strength…or impatience. Either way, I am willing to wait.

I am amazed by the large numbers of people that are actually down here. I have been seeing everything and everyone in blurs, but now that I have a free moment, I can think about and see this new world more clearly. I know that this is not the only take off point for going back to land, but it is the main port to serve the University. Most of the people around me are near my age. There are easily 200 or more waiting for the large fish transports. I spot one or two new recruits by the look of sheer exhaustion on their faces. I am sure my face looks the same. At one point, I think I see James in the crowds. He was trying to tell me about Atlantis, about this new world I am a part of. But his intentions don't matter to me anymore. I make sure to turn away so I won't be easily seen.

My turn finally arrives and I mount my fish. Pisces. Nice. I haven't seen much of him this entire time. I am glad he is helping with the transports. I am more used to my speaking ability with the training fish and I am eager to communicate with Pisces while we swim. His glistening scales and thick body radiate with pleasure when he sees me. He is a beautiful creature with an iridescent sheen on his mermaid-like scales but the elliptical body of a fish born in the sea. His fins are small, but his large body has the power to cut through ocean currents. I mount the intricate Atlantean saddle strapped around his body, taking hold of the reins.

"Evelyn, you stayed," I feel a sense of relief coming from Pisces as he communicates with me. "I am pleased." Little bubbles escape his mouth as he speaks to me in a fish language I innately understand.

"I did stay," I say in return, "I've been working hard and I am super tired, but I'm happy to see you again. You are the first fish I ever spoke to, you know."

"Yes, I do know. I get to bring many new recruits down. Some, like you, are aware when I speak to them. Most are not. You had a stronger sense of my being on that first trip than I am used to. I have been eager to see if you stayed. I wanted to see how your sea communication skills were progressing. I can tell that you are excelling in the art."

Yes, I am excelling. Much to the displeasure of Celia. More than once I was able to communicate with the training fish faster than any of the others in her group. That, of course, leads to me mounting faster, riding faster, and doing many maneuvers faster than the others. It gets me noticed and Celia doesn't like to have the spotlight off her.

"Thank you, Pisces. I am enjoying this new form of communication. It's like a whole body and mind way to talk. I feel like I am able to fully express my desires and thoughts."

"Yes. Those who are able to communicate as you do are more useful in battle. I can already sense that your skills will set you apart. Your sea animal partner will be much better able to work with you. Be prepared to be something special here, Evelyn."

Celia won't like that. That thought makes me smile.

"What other water skills do you have, Evelyn?" Pisces asks. As a part of our training, we have been undergoing several tests to see which water skills we have. I know there are seven, but I have only been tested for two at this point: communication with sea creatures (obviously I have this one) and water temperature control, which I also have. I can manipulate water temperature at will. I'm not sure how that is helpful, but it does keep me comfortable.

"So far I only know of my animal communication skills and my water temperature communication skills. I haven't been tested for anything else yet."

"It is interesting that you would have both communication and temperature skills together. It is an unlikely combination. Most who can communicate with sea creatures have the secondary skill of current control. Those go together nicely when it is time to correct the ocean currents. Then the sea life and sea dwellers can work together to manipulate and move through the current."

"I remember something about that combination. I haven't been tested for current control yet, though."

"Would you mind giving me an example of your temperature control skills?"

"Sure." As I rest on Pisces' back, I call to the warmer water above us. It gathers around me. I have been using this skill to keep warm at night. I let the warmth spread around Pisces as well, being careful to not demand too much temperature from the water. I am learning that water is a living thing too and that it will obey my requests when I am reasonable. I only ask for enough warmth to show Pisces my adeptness with temperature control. I feel like I can speak to the water just as I speak to Pisces, by feeling and thinking at the same time. But I do not speak out loud to the water. The water speaks back to me with images and emotions. The warmth I feel as I share with Pisces is like a blanket wrapped around us.

"Evelyn!" I can feel the surprise coming from the fish's thoughts as I hear his words. "You shared your warmth with me! I expected you to have your warmth just around you. This is remarkable."

Pride swells in my heart. I like compliments just as much as the next guy, but when it comes from someone like Pisces, it feels even better. Unfortunately, I have not learned to control my communication very well and the pride I feel sweeps toward Pisces as well.

"Ah ha," he says, "I see you have not yet learned to control all of your communication. I feel your pride and though you feel you have deserved the praise, I would caution you against getting too caught up in that particular emotion. It can only lead to trouble, Evelyn."

Now I am embarrassed and I quietly close my thoughts. Fortunately we have reached the dismount area.

"Go home and rest my friend," Pisces urges, "there is much still for you to learn. I hope to see you again on Monday, but if I do not, I am sure we will have time in the week."

"Thank you, Pisces. I appreciate your friendship and counsel. I will do my best to follow it," I say with humility. "Enjoy your weekend." How does a fish enjoy his weekend? I sense Pisces smile at that last thought of mine and he turns to swim back for another recruit. I head forward in the dark water and make my way to the beach.

As I reach the end of the pier, I float to the surface and am surprised by how strange it is to switch back to air breathing again. I have gotten used to breathing underwater. I see several other recruits surfacing near me and swimming to the shore where even more are making their way back to Sunny Isles Boulevard and eventually to Highway 826 and on home to the FIU campus. Everyone is moving forward. It is still too early for the surfers. With the sun barely peeking over the horizon behind me, I can see silhouettes on the shoreline. Two stand out against the rest. They aren't moving, just standing and facing the ocean. I think for a moment that we will be in trouble, someone has seen this mass of people leaving the ocean. But then I realize that nobody else is bothered by their presence. Maybe they are lookouts making sure others do not spot us. But if that is the case, why are they facing the ocean instead of the land?

I am intrigued and keep my eyes on the pair as I swim closer to the shore. Finally, my feet hit the sand and I can walk in the waves.

Others are still swimming and I feel the waves pushing me forward, but I feel like I can talk to the water and keep the waves from overpowering me. I finally reach the point where the waves slide back into the sea and I make my way to Sunny Isles Boulevard. My eyes again find the two figures. One raises an arm and points in my direction and they both start making their way toward me. One runs and I slow down. I know that silhouette very well. I freeze and stand still, nervous. The first figure reaches out to me just as the sun's blue rays turn early-morning gold and I find myself wrapped in the arms of my mom.

Chapter 14

My mom is here in my apartment, fully aware of all that has happened, all I have done, all I have kept from her. She is being quiet and contemplative as she listens to me. My mom has rarely ever acted shocked by anything I've said or done. She listens quietly so she can understand a situation before offering judgment or advice. But this is different. I am telling her a story so wild I can barely believe it. But she doesn't need to hide shock or tell me I've been imagining things. She knows I'm telling her the truth because she has lived it before. My mom once lived in Atlantis. I explain everything from the first time I breathed water to the last time I saw Pisces. I leave out James and Gwen. I'm too frustrated and confused to talk about them. The one I would talk to is Gwen, but how could I do that? I get to table that conversation for the time being.

Gwen was not at the apartment when my mom and I arrived and I know Celia is staying in the ocean for the weekend, so my mom and I are alone for now. The teacher from the History building that day I saw James kissing Gwen is the other person who was on the beach with my mom. Mr. Halcyon. It feels like everyone at FIU knows about this two-worlder thing. Mr. Halcyon helped get us to my apartment and then left me and my mom alone. He has been in contact with my mom and is the one who got her here in the first place. How he knows her, I don't know, but now that I have explained myself, I feel like it is time for me to ask some questions of my mom.

"Mom, I don't get it. You are being so calm about this whole thing. What is going on? What do you know that you are not telling me? Please let me know what you know." Maybe I don't have a right to ask these questions. After all, I haven't been honest with her. But now that I am with her and I know she lived this life before, I want to invade her thoughts. I want her to tell me why she has kept all of this from me. I want her to be uncomfortable as she shares what she has kept secret.

My mom rubs my chilled fingers between her warm hands then puts her arm around my wet shoulder.

"Evelyn, I have come with every intention to explain what you need to know. But right now, you are freezing cold and wet. How about you take a nice, warm shower and get dressed in something comfortable? Then we can go to my hotel. I have something there that will help to explain things."

I don't want to move from this spot until she answers me, but I am beginning to shiver in my wetsuit. I reluctantly agree and head to the bathroom. I wash two weeks' worth of salt deposits from my hair and enjoy the feeling of soft water on my skin. When I finish, I brush through my hair and decide to let it dry wavy for the day. I dress in my favorite jeans and FIU t-shirt, slip on my sandals and head out to the living room to go with my mom. When I emerge, I find my mom on the couch talking with Gwen. Anger swells up inside of me as I remember the last time I saw my roommate and friend – in the arms and lips of my boyfriend. I feel my face turn red and I stand

112

motionless, unsure of what to do. I want to confront Gwen, but *my mom* is sitting there and talking to her. I can't figure out how to talk without yelling or move without swinging my fists.

"Ready to go, mom?!" I yell.

"Wow, that was loud," answers my mom, "Yes, I'm ready to go, but I was just getting to know Gwen," she says as she rises from the couch. "She has been telling me about her time at FIU."

Yeah, I am sure Gwen has been very busy with her time. Learning her fun new water skills. Making out with James. Hiding it from me. That must be exhausting. Maybe she has been in Atlantis too. I didn't see her there and I am grateful for that. Of course, maybe she didn't decide to come to the ocean at all. Maybe it's been too fun learning about it from James.

Gwen gives me a smile. She doesn't have anything to say to me. I have nothing to say to her. Has she not even wondered about me for the entire week? I have been trying to keep *her* out of my head. Where was she when I got home this morning? Was she still in classes and enjoying a week with the apartment and James to herself? Maybe she just thought Celia and I were gone for good.

I try to calm my thoughts.

"I'm sure she *has* been busy," I say to my mom. "Hi Gwen. Sorry, I've got to get going. I'm super tired, but I still want to spend time with my mom." I am keeping my anger at bay, trying to leave the apartment as fast as I can. I am at the door with my keys, my mom's purse, and my hand on the doorknob. I need to get out. I am out the door and to the parking lot before my mom reaches me.

"Honey, are you all right?"

"I am, mom, I'm sorry. I'm just exhausted." I can barely look her in the eye. There is too much that I am trying to hide.

"Well, my rental car is over here." Mom leads me to a red, Mustang convertible. I look at the car with confusion. I don't think I have ever pictured my mom in anything other than our beat-up truck. It doesn't feel right. It doesn't feel normal. But then again, what does? I climb into the passenger's seat and buckle up. The seat is warm, even though it is a fall morning. As we pull out of the parking lot, I lean my head against the window and nod off.

When we finally get to the hotel, my mom leads me to her room and I fall onto one of the queen beds and sleep. I wake up around 2:00 in the afternoon because my stomach is actually hurting from hunger. We order room service and have to pay extra to get waffles in the afternoon. My mom sits and lets me stuff myself, getting all the food I need. Once I am satisfied and fully awake, my mom pulls some old notebooks out of her bag.

"Evelyn," she says quietly as she sits by me on the bed, "there is so much for you to know and I feel like the best way to tell you is by letting you read my history for yourself." She sets the books on the white quilt, turning them so I can see the covers. The notebooks are her journals. There are sticky notes poking out from the pages. She has prepared everything I need. Or at least the things she wants me to see. I start with her first journal, a faded black, hardcover volume with blue waves rolling on the cover. I open to the first sticky note. My mom sits quietly on her bed and lets me read:

Dear Diary,

I will be getting married tomorrow. I didn't know that such happiness was possible. I thought my world would always be empty after my mom and dad died, but now I can move ahead and create a family of my own. I have chosen well. Kai Marin is hard working and loyal to the cause. We will be a strong force in the city of Atlantis. I feel like I have found a new home.

Marisol for-the-last-time-ever Barnes

Atlantis. It stings to read about her account in a book she's had my whole life. She could have told me. She could have prepared me. She could have let me know so I could choose. I look up at her, the anger registering in my eyes. It hurts her, I can see, but she nods and encourages me to keep reading. The rest of the story will be there. The black journal has just one sticky note so I pick up the next in the stack. It is glossy and green. It looks like it is covered in seaweed. The pages are coated in wax and the ink has been scratched into them rather than written on them.

Dear Diary,

Contentions are heating up here. Kai's family is not supporting Adrian's engagement to Ceto. Her skin everyday grows more and more sleek. The scaled people are beginning to talk about her water abilities. I know she is different, but if we could only help everyone calm down and understand that just because she is showing different traits, it does not mean that she should be feared. I don't know what to do for her other than continue to be her friend and support.

On a happier note, next week is Kai's and my first wedding anniversary. We are enjoying sea life and loving living here. I haven't developed any scales yet, but Kai is getting a few around his hips. It's kind of funny to see and yet it is wonderful to know we are truly becoming one with the sea. I love him and I love this life we are creating.

Marlsol Marin

Dear Diary,

I am pregnant! Kai and I have been wanting to start our family and I am so excited to tell him. I'm going to tell him tomorrow. Of course, we'll move to the land as soon as the baby comes. We may be there for many years until our child learns to breathe underwater. I didn't discover my ability until I was twenty. Kai was twelve when he came to the water, so we'll see what we get. Once he or she is ready, we can all move back to the sea. There is a cute little beach house that I have my eye on for the time being. Still no scales on me, but Kai's are almost creating a belt below his belly button!

I am so happy!

Marisol

The next journal is a silvery blue. The cover is still sleek and smooth seaweed, but it has retained this false color well. The pages are waxy, like before.

Dear Diary,

Today Ceto told me that she and Adrian wed secretly. She is my best friend and now she is married to Kai's brother. How am I supposed to keep that secret? Certainly, she understands that I will tell Kai, but I don't know how they will break the news to the rest of the family. I am afraid for her. Adrian's upper legs are already beginning to be covered with scales. He is making the change to Merman. Eventually his legs will fuse and he will have a fully functioning fin. But Ceto. Oh Ceto. Her legs are not only shiny but they are changing to a glossy black. I am worried. It can only be eel or octopus at this point. Adrian loves her. He is good to her. Heaven help them both.

Marisol

Dear Diary,

Just another day in Atlantis. I got some seaweed imported from Japan today. I think I'll use it in my sea crisps tonight. Secretly, I kind of want a hamburger, but I have to go on land for that. Oh well, just one more week until the big move. We got the beach house we wanted. Kai said, "Anything for his little mermaid." I will miss this place. I have gotte…

The passage ends and I look up at my mom.

"You've reached the last entry," she says. She looks concerned. She has something to share that worries her. But I need a bit of filling in before I can hear anything more.

"Mom, you're a sea dweller," I say – like it's an accusation.

"I prefer the term two-worlder," is her response, "I can live on land and I can live in the sea, yes."

"Why didn't you tell me? What…What…What…I can't even think straight." I stand and begin to pace the room. "You've known this whole time that this was possible! You've known that I could be and likely would be a two-worlder? Not only was dad a two-worlder, but YOU were a two-worlder! Why didn't you tell me?!" I stand in front of her now, my mouth open with nothing to say. My mom straightens.

"The reason I've never told you until now is because I came to learn the hard way that the sea is dangerous," she says to me. I roll my eyes and sigh as I rub my forehead and pace the room. My mom keeps talking. "Your father was taken by the sea and I knew a similar fate awaited you if you discovered your abilities. Your father's entire family lived in the ocean, Evelyn. I knew they wanted me to raise you with them after his death, but I couldn't do it. There were too many painful memories and there was too much danger. So, I took you as far away from the ocean as I could to protect you."

I stop pacing and whirl to face her. "Wait, you mean we're not alone? I have more family? Why didn't I ever meet them?" My heart is racing and tears fill my eyes. My mom looks like she is swallowing a bitter pill. She has kept this a secret from me my whole life and now she has to come clean. She closes her dark eyes slowly as she exhales. When she opens her eyes again to look at me, I notice the many, many grey hairs growing throughout her brunette waves.

"Your father's family have all lived in the sea for so long they can't come on land any more. They all have scales and fins and are all merpeople. For the most part, your dad's extended family have moved to other parts of the world. Your grandparents passed away a decade ago. You just read about Dad's only brother."

I sit on the edge of the other bed, opposite my mom. "I thought we were the only two people in the world who were a part of our family."

"We were the only two on land, Evelyn."

"What about Grandma and Grandpa Barnes? Do they live in the ocean too?"

My mother stiffens and her eyes glisten with tears. "No, Evelyn. My parents are dead like you were told as a child. They are gone."

Her tears are my warning to calm down. My mom is not big on crying, so I know if I have gotten tears from her, I have pushed too far. I take a deep breath and stare at the speckled pattern of the carpet. As I calm myself down, I look up at her, ready for her to finish. She says nothing for a while. She just looks at me with a thoughtful expression. I know she is trying to figure out where to go from here.

"Evelyn," she says with a sigh at last. "I had to protect you. That last journal entry you read was stopped because of an underwater lava flow. It had started earlier in the day and your father left to help make sure the city would not be harmed." She stands and moves to look out of the window as she continues her story.

"As I was writing in my journal, there was a knock on the door. My neighbor came to tell me that the flow had reached a critical point and we were being asked to evacuate. I swam through the streets as fast as I could, looking for your father. We finally found each other and were headed back to land.

"We found your Uncle Adrian and Aunt Ceto and were all going back together when a cry sprang up behind us. The lava had broken through the city wall and was pouring into the street, creating a huge wall of heat and fire and air. Your father and uncle left to help the other Atlanteans close the breach. Your aunt and I were motionless by the city wall, staring at the lava heading our way." I sit still on the bedside, taking in this new history about my family.

"Your father's mother, your grandmother, came swimming toward us. She was afraid and when she saw your Aunt Ceto, her fear turned to anger. She exploded like the lava behind her. She yelled at Ceto, telling her it was her fault the lava had come through the city. She said the lava was evil and Ceto was evil and the two belonged together. She was out of control and soon other women were stopping to hear what she was screaming about. They were all afraid of what was happening, they were all afraid for their lives and the lives of their husbands and brothers. To hear that the strange person in front of them was the cause of their danger was all they needed to break into a frenzy." My mother sighs deeply and returns to sit on the bed, facing me openly and with an honesty she has kept from me.

"Soon, Ceto and I were surrounded by women, some with fins, some without. They were all yelling and pushing. Some were trying to get at Ceto. I grabbed Ceto by the wrist and we swam ahead as fast as we could. Your father and uncle swam up beside us. They had seen the women and came to protect us. Ceto was crying and we kept swimming. Your grandmother was right behind us, still maniacal in her fear. Still shouting. Still drawing a crowd.

"Your Uncle Adrian stopped and turned to face her. Probably to calm her down. It was his way to be a peacemaker. But I won't ever know what he was going to say or do. Just as he stopped and turned, the lava broke through the wall and it took Adrian with it. We saw the whole thing. Your grandmother started screaming like mad and swam away in another direction shouting that 'Ceto the devil killed her son'. I heard a scream next to me. It was Ceto. She was like a grotesque statue, etched with a scream on her face. I don't think she even knew the sound was coming from her. She started to swim toward the lava flow, trying to get to Adrian's burned body." My mom puts her head in her hands, staring at the floor as she continues.

"Your father grabbed both me and Ceto and dragged us behind him as he swam to safety. I never realized before just how strong he was. He swam with increasing speed, lava breaking through behind us all the way. Huge clouds of boiling water rose upward through the sea with a hiss that almost spoke words. Ceto and I were in shock. He took us a safe distance then kissed me before turning to Ceto. He touched her cheek to show his sympathy. His eyes were full of sadness, but there was still danger to many sea dwellers below. He had to go back to help. So Ceto and I continued to the land on our own." My mom straightens again, but keeps her eyes on something behind me, reliving this memory.

"Finally, Ceto and I reached the surface. I knew I couldn't go back into the ocean. It was madness down there and I had an unborn child to care for. This was going to be my last resurfacing. Ceto was

121

gasping for air next to me. She had changed enough that she couldn't live on land. She looked into my eyes and I knew she could not come with me. She was filled with pain from breathing air and filled with pain from having just lost Adrian. I knew she would leave me. I knew I couldn't follow. I screamed and I screamed. There was nothing more I could do. She dove back into the ocean and I never saw her again. The pain she must have felt that day and at that moment. I am not at all surprised by how much she has done to take revenge. I just wish I could have been with her to help her make sense of it all."

My mother's eyes are streaming with tears, but she isn't sobbing. Her voice is calm and steady. My own eyes are spilling over for this family I never met and the pain they suffered those many years ago. My mother looks at me again as she continues.

"Your father and I lived in the beach house after that. When you were born you brought us so much joy where there had been so much pain and sorrow. We were in love with you from the first moment we saw you. We were very happy." My mom's face is soft for a moment before she continues.

"As your father and I were finishing up school, money was tight. We knew we could lose our little beach house and we were looking everywhere for money. I worked a small job, just part time as a waitress, but it wasn't enough. We didn't want to put you in daycare either, it just wasn't worth leaving you alone. That's about the time that some of our old friends approached your dad about the sunken treasure hunt."

This is the part of the story I know very well. I have asked about it many times. My parents were poor and in need of money when I was barely a year old and they were still in school. My mom was a waitress and my dad worked in a marine salvage yard. They were still a year out from graduation. We were happy, but we were about to be homeless. We were in need with no one to turn to.

Just as things seemed their bleakest, some of my dad's friends from college approached him. They had been studying the Bermuda triangle theories and were sure they could get rich by finding sunken ships. There were tales of gold and treasure going down with their ships and crew, never to be seen again. It was tantalizing and my father couldn't ignore the possibility of financial freedom. My mother protested. She was sure they could figure out some other way to make the money, but my father would not be swayed.

My dad asked the salvage yard owner if he could borrow the boat for a weekend fishing trip, it was early September. He left for his weekend excursion in clear skies. But late the next day as they were getting ready to dive again off the Coast of North Bimini Island, a storm hit. Despite their efforts to pull up anchor, turn around and head to safety, the storm overtook them. Two of the men were swept overboard. By the time my dad and the remaining crewmen on board got the radio working, the two lost hadn't been seen for hours. But my dad and the others wouldn't head to shore without them. They continued to stay at sea and within an hour the boat was lost beneath the waves, the crew on the radio the entire time. Several days later, the body of one of the men washed up on the shore of South Bimini Island.

Another two weeks passed before the air search was called off. My mother, broken-hearted, needed to leave. She took everything she had in the world and we headed to the desert to finish her education. We were poor for a while but we survived. Student loans carried us that first year. Then my mom could teach to support us a little better. Once I entered kindergarten, my mom got her master's degree and later, her PhD in Native American studies. The mystery of the desert and her own heritage had really gotten a hold on her. Either that or she was trying to distance herself (and me) as far from the ocean as she could.

I am beginning to at least understand her chronic aversion to the ocean. It is more than the death of my father, she has seen the ocean at its worst, bubbling in heat and fury as lava – that molten hot land – tries to take over. She's seen the fear and frenzy that accompanies the anger of frightened merpeople. She lost her husband, her only love. She has a horrific fear of the ocean. I do not.

"Evelyn," she says to me, "I've talked with the admissions department at ASU and you can enter in the spring. You don't have to stay here and face all of this. To be honest, I don't know if I can stand to have you face all of this. It has been so long since I've even heard from Ceto. There's no telling what she is capable of or what she is planning. The fact that you are my daughter may not do anything to protect you."

Wow. Ceto. I don't know why it hadn't registered before that my aunt is the enemy Atlantis is fighting against. I don't know if that would be good for others to know. What if they think I am a traitor? But I'm not. I am even closer to the ocean now than I was before. I know I can't leave.

"Oh, Mom. I can't go. I'm just starting to feel comfortable in the ocean. My abilities are getting so strong. Just this morning as I was leaving Pisces, he said that my water temperature control was very impressive. I..."

"Evelyn! Please be rational!" My mother's gentle tones are gone. Her obvious frustration is so strong that it takes me aback. "You have joined an army! You are only 17 years old and you are fighting in an army under the oceans. There is no possible way you can be serious here!"

My pride is hurt at this. I am not a child anymore. I have made some good decisions on my own and it feels empowering. I love my mom very much, but I am not going to live solely to please her. I need to see this thing through, if for nothing other than to find out who I really am. I am determined to make her see that.

"Mom! Wait a minute! You haven't even seen what I can do under the ocean! I haven't even tested all of my abilities!"

She stands. "Abilities! Evelyn! If this was a time of peace, then you would have the chance to test and fully learn about your abilities. All that will happen now is that Lady Pescara will find out what you can do and then she'll line you up with the right minions so you can fight! That is not testing your abilities or learning anything about yourself, Evelyn! That is just playing the part of the pawn!" My mother's face is beet red. Angry tears are welling up in her eyes now. Concern is written all over her face. No, concern isn't the right word. It is desperation.

I should have known this would be the outcome of my mom knowing what I've been up to for all this time. I guess that's why I waited so long to confide in the one person who would love me most. I knew she'd try to protect me and make me change my mind. But I know my mind won't be changed. I push down the fire welling up within me. I know what I have to do. It isn't going to be pleasant, so I want to be as calm as I can to get through it.

"Mom, I love you very much. I'm sorry it has to be this way. I have to go back." I get up from the bed and grab my things. My mom is arguing, pleading with me to stay. I cannot stand the pain of separating myself from her in such an open way. I know I have to leave as soon as I can. As I reach the door, I turn to face her. For the first time in the past few moments, she is complete silence, anxiety fighting its way through her eyes. I go to her and wrap my arms around her, hugging her tightly. She cries softly into my hair, the strength she normally displays completely melting away. I kiss her tear-streaked cheek, pull myself away, and head out the door, the sound of her last desperate, "Please…" bringing stinging tears to my eyes.

Chapter 15

I get an Uber to take me back to my apartment. I remember the driver's smell – very musty. I was silent the entire way. Neither of my roommates are here now. My movements are mechanical. I do everything without thinking. I go to my room, grab my best hiking bag and start filling it with things I will need. I am heading back to the ocean and I want to stay for a long time. Several swimsuits, wetsuits, and even my flippers. I pack up a brush and some hair ties, determined to tame my locks from now on. A toothbrush and toothpaste make up the rest of my supplies. Atlantis takes care of the rest. As I zip up my bag, I see a picture on my dresser. A picture of me and my mom. I need it with me. I put it in a heavy duty Ziploc bag so it will not be ruined by the ocean water, and I add it to my bag.

It has been a long day and I am emotionally exhausted. I want to head back to the sea right now, but I know I want to be well prepared for it. So, I make myself some eggs, bacon, toast, and juice and put on my warm pajamas. Celia's parents are probably spending the weekend in Atlantis with her. Her parents know about her water abilities. They even prepared her for them. She has their support 100%. I don't have my mom's support. I don't have a dad. I am

127

envious of Celia. Warm tears – they will be my last tears – well up in my eyes. I allow myself this last, good cry as I fall asleep. Tomorrow I am going to become new. Tomorrow I am going to begin to discover who I really am. But just for tonight, I am letting go of the old me.

Chapter 16

Early Monday I return to Atlantis. I am one of the first recruits to return and despite Celia's smug look and accusations that I am brown-nosing, I am glad to be back. I keep checking around me to see if my mom has followed me to the ocean. She has water abilities, and I wonder if she will come here to try to stop me. I am relieved as the entire day goes by without seeing her. I am also a little sad. It would be nice to be able to share this with her – with someone who loves me.

Because of my constant tendency to look over my shoulder, Monday drags on far longer than it should. By the time my head hits my sponge pillow and I pull my seagrass blanket up around me, I am sure I won't be seeing my mom here. She had a ticket back to Arizona and she used it.

It's Tuesday now, and I dive head-first into my studies. We train and train day after day, knowing that our lives in battle depend on it. I learn how to use a mace and nun-chucks and a sword. I learn to control my body underwater and how to harness my increased speed and agility. I ache each night in many new places, but I begin to see success as my body learns to fight. My university studies continue here as well. Several teachers from FIU are here, keeping everyone current on their classes. I start working for the Aquarius program, taking information from sea creatures and relaying to those who haven't learned how to speak to them. I am glad for the added work. It gives me somewhere to keep my mind. It brings in more money which helps me keep up on the few land bills that I still have to pay. Captain Jack leaves for a few hours each day to work with the boat tours. I go with him occasionally, usually when I have a day off.

Even though I know my mom is opposed to my being here, I still send her word of how I am doing. A once-weekly post heads to land and I always have a letter in it for her. I receive several letters from her, telling me how much she loves me, begging me to be safe, and offering to come get me if I change my mind and want to come home.

We begin testing our combat skills in mock training battles. For the training battles, we wear bulky armor like Celia and Jack wore when they battled. It is heavy and cumbersome and slows my movement in the water even though I am still moving faster than any man from land could do. I feel so slow by comparison to my unfettered self. But the armor cannot protect us from each other completely. I go back to my tent with bruises and cuts each night.

During all of this training, recruits are being taken out of practice for abilities testing. There are seven known abilities: tide control, water temperature control, wave control, current control, sea creature communications, communications with moisture above water like humidity and rain, and communications with the actual air that lingers over the water. Nature has worked hard to make sure that no one sea dweller can hold all seven skills. So far, I have tested positive for four of the seven skills: tide, water temperature, wave control and sea creature communications. Today, I am with my group of 10 testing communications with the air lingering over the water.

For the test, Jack's group of 50 has been sent south to the ancient, underwater Bimini Wall where we can be disguised as amateur scuba divers checking out the natural rock formation. Each group of 10 has a diving boat, so there are 5 white-sailed boats floating lifelessly out to sea. The Bimini wall is, of course, anything but a natural rock formation. It was anciently a dock for the ships of Tarsus who traded with Atlantis for goods and gold. Like many of the ocean's secrets, however, truth gives way to legend and legend to science. Science hasn't figured out how to measure the ocean's power.

Once our boat floats above the wall, half of my group suits up for a dive. This is so we can look like a real diving group. The remaining half of the group will be undergoing the test.

"Alright recruits," our facilitator says. Our facilitator for the test is ready to give instructions. "Celia will be going down with the diving group while the rest of you stay aboard to test with me. Communications with the air above ocean water is a rare skill that very few possess. When they do, it takes rigorous training to get them ready for anything useful." Celia turns and gives me a smug look. To her, I am anything but useful. I wish I knew why she hates me so much. Maybe she just wants to be the best at everything. "When it is your turn for the test," our facilitator continues, "you will be sitting next to me, facing east over the edge of the boat." He points his left arm out to sea where a two-man sailboat is bobbing lifelessly in the water. "The goal: to fill those sails with wind."

I'm not sure how that is going to work, but I have a while to relax and wait for my turn. Celia and the five who will accompany her are all suited up and ready to dive into the ocean. I envy them. I would much rather have some time in the water with the skills I am already familiar with. I like the dry heat of Arizona and have grown accustomed to the stifling humidity of Florida, but the sea water is much more inviting to me.

I watch as each of my remaining group mates take their turn in the hot seat next to the facilitator. He whispers instructions to them that I cannot hear. After about 10 minutes of frustration, each is excused from the chair and sent to the pile of diving clothes to suit up. Finally, the last girl before me is excused from the chair. Her face is red and I can see a bright blue vein popping out of her neck as she angrily makes her way to the diving gear. "Marin, you're up!" the facilitator is looking bored as he sees me, the last of the first group, heading toward the hot seat. Poor guy. He still has another group left to test after me. I wonder if he ever gets any excitement in this job testing for rare abilities. From the yawn he greets me with, I doubt it. He doesn't expect to find anything out of the ordinary.

"Alright. Evelyn Marin, is it?"

"Yes, sir."

"I once served with a Kai Marin. Any relation to you?"

"Yes, sir. He's my father sir."

"Oh, I see." Embarrassment works its way up on the facilitator's face, "I'm sorry for your loss. I didn't mean to bring up an uncomfortable memory for you." I am quick to reassure him. I don't want to upset the guy giving me a test.

"Not at all sir. I'm happy to meet someone who knew my father." The facilitator straightens up a bit and clears his throat, ready to move on from this moment of discomfort.

"Well then, very good." His eyes are steady on mine in a moment of silence before he continues. "You know, your father was quite good at communications with the elements above water. We used to tease him about being a land-brat at heart." The facilitator chuckles at the memory of his own joke then straightens and becomes more serious. "But truly each one of us in his battalion envied his abilities. What he could do with that power, it was magnificent." After a wistful moment of silence, my facilitator perks up and prepares to tell me what to do. At least he looks more excited than he did for the last four people to occupy this chair. I hope I don't disappoint him.

"Now," he says, "face out over the edge of the boat and focus on the little white sail over there." I do as he says and squint in the brightness of the day.

"Now, Recruit Marin, while you are looking at that sail, I want you to feel the water beneath it." It is easy for me to feel the water, that's all I have been feeling for months. "Are you focused, Evelyn?"

"Yes sir."

"Good. Now shift your feelings from the water to the very top of the ocean's surface. Can you feel the edge?" The feeling of the water's surface tickles my chin as I answer yes. I sense a unity somewhere between the two. Like the space between water and sail is already aware of my presence as I become aware of it.

"Okay," the facilitator takes a slow, steady breath, "I want you to move your feelings from that space upward until they reach the air just above the sea." I reluctantly take my heart away from the water's surface and turn it toward the air above. Suddenly, it is as if 10,000 eyes turn my direction. I feel the molecules of air feel their way toward me. A gentle breeze brushes my cheek. It is filled with questions:

Who are you?

Why are you here?

What do you want from us?

Then, recognition. I can hear their voices swirling around me.

She is a blessed one, a chosen one.

I think I have known one like her before.

Yes, a man. A father.

Indeed, she is the Marin's offspring.

The Marin. So many questions for him.

What do we do with his child?

Do we speak to her?

She hears us already.

A pause. Then a single voice made of the many voices, all female. Speaking in unison.

Hello Marin, child. What is your name?

"Evelyn. Evelyn Marin." I can feel the facilitator holding his breath as I speak to these little molecules around me. Everything else is silent.

We have known your father, Evelyn Marin. It has been a long time since he came to the surface. We have great respect for him. He was never selfish, never greedy. What does his child ask of us?

The whispering voices have a mature way about them. It is like listening to 10,000 whispering mothers, all trying to ask me the same thing.

"Could you send a breeze to the white sail in the East, please?"

Such manners.

Like her father.

Indeed, child, we can do such a simple thing.

The breeze changes directions and heads back to where it came from. Then more wind pushes at my back as it joins the air already on its way to the sail. In just a moment, the wind hits the sail. The once slack, white fabric comes to life as the gentle breeze gains strength. Soon, the sail is full and the sailor aboard is on his feet for the first time all day. He guides the small sailboat in the breeze until he has gone at least half a mile.

Do you wish for us to continue?

"Thank you. No. I believe that will do."

It was our pleasure. The wind stops and the little white sail is lifeless again. *It has been so long since we have spoken so clearly with one of your kind. Please don't be a stranger. We have enjoyed this little piece of intercourse today. We would like to speak with you more often.*

"And I with you. Thank you."

Silence.

I sit in the silence for a moment or two, filled with peace. I have made contact with something other than water. I had no idea such a thing was even possible for me. They spoke of my father. I inherited their respect from him. Thanks, Dad.

I am still relishing this new feeling of closeness when the facilitator reminds me I am not alone.

"Wehell!" his excitement is apparent as he raises his tone far above the whispers he used before. "Looks like you have your father's abilities, that's for sure." Celia and her group of distraction divers are just climbing back into the boat from their dive. She can hear what the facilitator is saying, as can everyone else on the diving boat. "That's right, young lady, we have ourselves a brand new land-brat!"

Chapter 17

The rest of the testing is as quiet as the start. No one else has "the gift" as the facilitator keeps calling it. My group's turn diving with Celia is event free. We are supposed to look like curious divers underwater which is easy. As I swim along the rocky formations of what is left of the Bimini wall, I have plenty of time and space to think about my test. My fellow divers stay together under the diving boat. I swim as far from them as time will permit. I want the time to myself.

My life lately has been dominated by questions and this new interaction gives me a new subject to think about. The air molecules spoke of my father. They felt he was a very talented communicator. I inherited his talent. But more importantly, they respected him, they knew him. And I realize that they would possibly have been the last things to communicate with him while he was alive.

Long before I am ready to return, we head back to Atlantis. News of my air communications test has spread quickly. Jack is one of the first to offer me congratulations.

"Evelyn!" He greets me with a huge hug that makes me warm all over. "I heard about your test. That is awesome! And somebody from my own group of 50, too! Lady Pescara has told me that your training will begin next week. She has great hopes for you and your abilities, Evelyn. Well done." Jack pats my arm. I wanted the hug again.

"Thanks Jack. I have no idea what I can do with it, but I'm excited to learn."

"Air communications help us if the battle goes above the ocean. That is always bad, but it is exactly what Ceto wants. She has already proven that she is well adept at communicating with the water above the ocean, but Lady Pescara suspects she has somebody on her side that also communicates with the air above the sea. It's a dangerous combination. Lady Pescara can communicate with the water above the sea, but her abilities unfortunately don't compare to Ceto's. We've needed somebody, even with modest ability, who can work with the air. Looks like that somebody is going to be you." Jack lets his hand drop to his side as the look on his face becomes somber and unreadable. With this change in his countenance, my stomach sinks a few inches. I am going to have to be used in the heat of the battle and now I know it. Fighting in the fray with everyone else is not going to be my lot. I am going to lead at some point. I know I'll have to prepare.

After a brief pause, Jack continues, "Well, since you won't begin your air communications training until next week, I suggest you stay focused on your other skills and battle preparation. Today's practice combat sessions begin in thirty minutes." He turns and leaves, his shoulders low, the excitement he started with is gone. Is he frustrated to know he will be losing a recruit or is it something more? Could he feel something deeper for me? Concern?

I head to my tent to grab a snack bar before combat practice begins, knowing I will need the extra energy before lunch. Unfortunately, I run into Celia. Literally.

"Watch where you're going, Land-Brat!" She spits out. I mumble some kind of apology, but that isn't enough for the queen of the world. "What did you say to me, Land Brat?!" I really hadn't said anything offensive, but now that Celia is pushing my buttons, she is going to get a

bite back. I pull out my best English accent.

"I'm sorry my generous lady. I had thought myself duly out of your way, but I unfortunately miscalculated your size. The next time I fear I may cross your glorious path, I shall be certain to better measure your wider girth." I give a deep and flourishing bow, rising without a smile.

Celia's eyes are on fire as she stares me down. A moment passes and she says nothing in return. I can see the revenge wheels turning in her mind. She lifts her chin and a single eyebrow and says in a deadly whisper, "Hmmm. I see the land brat is feeling a bit bigger than she should today. Combat training. Fifteen minutes." And she swims away. Whatever plot is developing in her jealous head, I am sure I will find out soon. But I am not afraid. I am tired of being ridiculed by Celia. If she wants to look down on me again, she is going to have to earn it. I grab my sea bar and head out to meet whatever she has waiting for me.

At the training grounds, all of Jack's group of 50 are gathering their gear for the upcoming mock combat battles. I grab the mace. I like the feeling of power it gives me. It has been one of the most effective weapons I've used. We are all donning our heavy armor, helmets, and padding. We are an ominous group and a slightly awkward one. But we have been doing this for several months now so our movements are swift and sure. We know what to do.

For the training, we each battle every member of our group, five pairs working at a time. Celia calls out tips to us. Jack works his way through the whole group of 50. I am not bad at combat; I am beginning to understand my strengths. I am also learning when I am defeated. Two out of my first three battles are against the strongest guys in my group of ten. I know I'll be beaten no matter what I do so I focus on staying calm and save as much energy as I can for the remaining battles. After that, it is like I can't be beaten. I like to use my water temperature skills to super-chill the water around my opponents, making them so cold they have difficulty maneuvering in the sudden change. I also enjoy the mace but can feel the strain in my shoulder from all of the swinging I am doing. By the last battle, I am relying heavily on my shield. But, after winning seven battles in a row, a few of my group begin to offer me congratulations. I get many pats on the back and *atta-girls* from the guys in the group. The first two want to battle against me again – sure that I threw the match their way. Unfortunately, the praise gets Celia's attention.

As we start heading toward the gear stalls and dinner, Celia calls out to her group. "My group stays," she says, "I want to give you one more lesson before dinner." There is a general grumbling through our group as we reluctantly head back to our group leader for the *extra training* she has in store. I'm pretty sure it has to do with me and I'm sorry to make everyone else wait for dinner.

Once we all arrive at the training stall where Celia is dressed for combat, she addresses the group. "You've all fought well today. I'm impressed with the progress you've made. But your progress isn't going to be enough when the real battles begin. You won't always have the leisure of rest when you're tired or food when you're hungry or in meeting an opponent whose skills are equal to or lesser than your own.

"You are much more likely to be awakened in the dead of night after a long day of training here. If the battle is a long one, you'll be exhausted as you are now. But you will still need to fight!" A tinge of uneasiness in me warns as I see what is coming.

"Evelyn," yep, it is coming, "you've fought well today. Do you consider yourself ready for battle?"

"No, Celia. I know I need more preparation." I know she wants to humiliate me.

"Good. I'm glad to see you're so willing to get better. Climb into the ring. You'll be battling *me* now." A few in the group begin whispering to the people next to them. Most of them know Celia doesn't like me. It makes some uncomfortable to watch her humiliate me. But the rest are just glad it isn't them.

I make my way into the ring, carrying my shield and my mace slackly by my side. Celia hasn't been battling all afternoon. She is rested and fed. She is taller than me, stronger than me, has been in the ocean longer than me, and has both a mace and a sword at her disposal. There is no way it is going to be a fair fight. Now I know what my snarky comments to her earlier earned me. I still feel the same. If she wants to look down on me, she is going to have to earn it.

141

I am not going down without a fight. I am going to give her all I have left.

As I swim into the small battling ground, Pisces enters my view. My devoted fish companion must have sensed my need and has come to be by me, at least for moral support. Celia spots him, arches her eyebrow in a look of dismay, and in just a moment, her own companion arrives. Hers is an over-sized stingray named Zeus. We are becoming a little more even now.

With a swift movement from her head, Celia motions for the training battle bell to signal our start. At the sound of the bell, I crouch down on the ocean floor with my shield on my left arm, raised to cover me while my mace, clutched in my right hand, sinks to the sand behind me. Celia shoots upward in the water and pulls out her own mace with her left hand, holding her shield to her side. She looks down on me, that familiar look I have come to recognize. I brace myself for her attack.

With super speed in her well-trained body, she dives toward me, mace held high above her head. With my shield in my left hand, I maneuver my body around so her blow will not strike me. She slams her mace into my shield and raises her arm to do it again. I can tell she is angry and I hope I can use that to my benefit. Three times she strikes my shield with her mace, anger and disgust written all over her face and her blows. Having gotten a bit of that immediate anger out, she backs away from me until her feet are just above the ocean floor ten feet away from where I am crouched.

I stand and straighten my body, feeling the achiness from the previous ten battles. This is going to hurt, but I know it will be worth it. I lunge at her, shield first, mace raised high. Our shields collide mid-water and we both swing hard at each other. My mace skids off her helmet while her mace strikes my armor in the middle of my back. It is a strong blow and I arch my back in an attempt to absorb the shock. A small grunt of pain escapes my lips and Celia takes advantage of my moment of weakness.

Using her shield against mine, she shoves me into the sand, pushing and pushing me into the loose silt beneath me. The cloud it creates makes it difficult for me to see what to do next and makes it difficult to breathe. I swing with all my might, pain searing through my shoulder as I feel the strain of the day rip through. It ends up being a good move, the mace hits Celia in the back and she moves away in an attempt to regain her breath. I struggle to get up for a better vantage point when a huge surge of water hits me in the face. Celia has current control skills, I do not. I stumble in a cloud of water and debris as I fight to see my surroundings. Finally, I catch a glimpse of Celia in a corner of the ring, shield down, arms spread wide as she pushes the current toward me. I slam into a wooden barrier with my back and focus on Celia.

Reaching into the depths of my soul, I pour all I can into the water surrounding Celia, begging it to cool down so that she will be distracted. To my surprise, the water chills faster than it ever has before. The current pinning me to the wall slackens as Celia is surrounded by tiny crystals of ice. I can tell the water is getting too cold, so I ask it to relax a little before Celia freezes. No sooner have I thought the request than Celia's stingray slams into my head. I forgot that he was there, I was so focused on my battle with Celia. I call out to Pisces to take over the battle with Zeus. The two push at and around one another until they are caught in their own whirlpool of dust and debris on the left side of the ring.

As I turn to face Celia, I realize I have taken too much time with Pisces' battle. She is bearing down on me from above with her sword drawn, tiny crystals of ice still stuck to her armor. She is still cold and it has slowed her down. I raise my shield just in time for her blow to glance off. She raises her sword again, and I raise my mace and swing with everything I have. My mace wraps mercilessly around Celia's frozen sword, snapping it in two. Just then, she swings her shield in so that it catches the chain of my mace and knocks it out of my hand. In a flash, her mace is drawn and overhead. I call for Pisces just as I raise my shield to protect my head from her strike. She hits my shield and raises her mace again. Pisces hears my cry and rushes from the stingray, slamming into Celia's right side. Her stingray companion is not far behind and pushes Pisces into the wall of the ring while he is distracted. Pisces is knocked momentarily unconscious by the blow and I push myself up from the ground with my feet so I can reach him. I leave my shield behind in the sand.

Before I can make it to Pisces, Celia is standing over me, mace raised. "Do you concede land-brat?"

"Celia. I have to see to Pisces, he's hurt."

"Fish will be hurt in battle and you'll be killed too if you lose your focus to care for them." Celia's stingray swims up behind her and floats silently at her side. I can feel him echoing her sentiments.

My body is screaming at me for all I have put it through and my mind can only scream to Pisces. I feel his consciousness returning, though he lay still on the ocean floor.

"I repeat, Land Brat. Do you concede?" I feel Pisces reach out to my mind.

You must concede, Evelyn. If this were battle, you'd be dead by now. Shame fills me as I realize I have been foolish.

"Yes, Celia, I concede. The battle is yours."

Celia removes her helmet, shakes out her hair and looks down at me again. The ice crystals that covered her before, are swiftly disappearing from the heat of the battle. She raises her head again in a triumphant glare. Turning to the group, she says, "Let this be a lesson to each of you. Lose your focus for even a moment and you will lose as Evelyn just did. Dismissed." The other recruits watch for a second or two, waiting to see if Celia will leave me alone or if I am going to make a move against her.

Normally, following a training battle, the winner is supposed to help the loser from the ocean floor and see that their needs are met. Celia just turns from me and swims out of the training ring with her stingray by her side. In a moment, a conscious, but groggy Pisces is by my side and my group mates make their way slowly to the mess hall.

Are you okay, Evelyn? Are you critically injured?

No, Pisces. I am sore but I am well. How are you? Any injury you cannot heal from?

A cool chuckle rises from the consciousness of the large fish.

I may be old, but I am still able to recover from a fight with a slippery stingray.

I'm hungry, let's go to the mess hall and see if there's any food left.

I pull myself off the ground and Pisces and I head to the armor stalls. Just as we reach the long row of stalls, a reverberating sound echoes throughout the chamber and throughout all of Atlantis. It is deep and ominous and low. It strikes again. Though I have never heard it before, I know what that sound is. It is the war gong. We are going to battle for real now. Training is over.

Chapter 18

Chaos is everywhere. I am nearly over-run as thousands of my people, the two-worlders, flock to the battle equipment stalls. I recognize many of the faces that swim around me. Haven't I been swimming with them for months? But something is different in each face – in the expression each bears. I see fear. I see determination. I see strength. Several of my comrades are like robots, going through the motions of putting on their armor and strapping on their weapons. I am exhausted from the training battles of the day, but I feel a new surge of energy within me as the anticipation of all I have trained for approaches. Like everyone else, I strap land lights to my back. Whatever it is that powers Atlantis does not extend beyond the edge of the city.

I make my way through the mayhem with Pisces. We are on our way to our battle stations. At the edge of the training field is the ancient Atlantean wall. It once ringed the edge of Atlantis several stories high, but over the years the sand of the ocean has buried the wall and surrounding area so that now its height is only a single story. The training field lies shore side of the wall, on the other side is… well, there is nothing. It is open, empty ocean on the other side of that wall. Just a few hundred yards downslope is where the new armies of Atlantis gather in their battalions to receive further instruction.

I move into position and am soon joined by the rest of Celia's group of 10 within Jack's group of 50. The leader of each group of 50 stands at the forefront of his or her band. The formation takes shape as groups of 50 become groups of 250 then groups of 1,000. Each group of 10,000 has its own chief captain. Uncle Russ is ours.

Soon, the field is covered with two-worlders. Pisces follows me to my position and then leaves for his own. The fish of the sea are in two groups in the center of the formation on the field, legged recruits on the right, finned two-worlders on the left. There are over 40,000 fighters in Atlantis' army. Uncle Russ stands with the other three chief captains at the head of the army. Lady Pescara, General of the Army of Atlantis, faces her novice followers.

"We have received word that the army of Ceto has just crossed the Eastern border of the Atlantic sea. She and her army are moving with ferocious speed. They will be here by week's end. But I ask you, army of Atlantis, will we sit here and wait for their arrival?"

With a thunderous noise, the entire army shouts their response, "NO!" Shields are waved and weapons are pounded on them. The noise is deafening. My heart races at what is taking place all around me. Lady Pescara raises her arm into the air and the crowd is silenced.

"Will you follow me in a flight of our own to meet this unworthy foe in battle?"

"Yes!" is the thunderous reply.

"We will not be defeated! Atlantis must remain unscathed! We will protect our home! We will protect the sea!"

The entire army erupts into cheers and yells. Again, weapons hammer against the shields of soldiers as they cheer for their general. I join in the action, the moment is so exhilarating.

"Remember your training, my people. Remember your home. Follow me and we will see ourselves conquerors!" With her battle sword raised high in the air, Lady Pescara turns to face the dark sea before us. Uncle Russ comes to stand before his group of 10,000. He raises both hands high into the air and draws from us a fearful shout. The other chief captains do the same and soon the entire army is again a mass of shouts and yells. In this formation, we swim forward, following our fearless leaders. Celia swims just to the left of me as the leader of our group. I am feeling such camaraderie that even her nearness cannot bother me. Her face is exultant as she leads us toward the battle. This is what she has been training for and she is ready. I take confidence in this, my foe of only a few hours ago. We may have our differences, but Celia and I are now united in cause. And that cause is Atlantis. Our joint enemy is Ceto, an octopus woman. My aunt.

My armor is light as I swim with all my might in this Atlantean army. We race toward our foe with increased speed as those with power to control currents propel us forward from behind. In the space of an hour, we have crossed over hundreds of miles of ocean terrain. One hour becomes two and two becomes four. At first, the excitement of the upcoming battle is buzzing throughout the troops. Then as the journey continues late into the night, a hush spreads over our ranks. The efforts I expended during the day creep up on me. I am tired, very tired. I see weariness on the faces of my companions. We are going to be heading into this battle fatigued.

Countless hours later, with only one stop for rest, I am wearily considering our situation. Jack swims up next to me and addresses me. "Evelyn, Lady Pescara has issued an order that you are to remain in the rear, on the right flank." Celia is at our sides in an instant.

"What is this, Captain Jack? Is there an order from Lady Pescara for me?" she asks.

"Not for your entire group, Celia. Just for Evelyn. She is to remain in the rear for the duration of the battle."

"Why should she be separated from her group of 10? We have trained together. This can only weaken my group." The fatigue Celia is battling shows in her willingness to question a direct order. I know it is gut wrenching for her to have to express a need for me in any way.

Jack stretches taller until his head is higher than both Celia and me. "Leader Celia. You have heard orders that you are to obey. We are heading into battle, not into a diplomatic conference. Here, you obey first and ask questions later. Do you understand?"

Celia's eyes narrow ever so slightly and resignation creeps onto her face. "I understand, Captain."

"Good," says Jack. "Return to the head of your group. Evelyn, come with me." Celia swims back, her posture stiff and her head high, to the front of her band of 10. Jack turns from me and swims to the outer right of the formation. Since I am under orders to go with him, I follow. I am tired, but this change in events has awakened my senses and I feel myself more alert.

Beneath our collective feet and fins, I see nothing but blackness. The ocean floor is nowhere to be seen. Even so, we are at least two hundred feet below the surface of the sea. I feel strangely cold as I realized that, other than our massive army, there is no life around us. Apprehension fills me. The creatures of the sea must be in hiding. Nobody wants to be seen.

A few minutes later, very near the back of the entire army, Jack pauses and turns to me. As the army continues on, we are dropping back even farther. I am anxious to rejoin the safety of the larger group and anxious to learn why I am so far separated from them. Allowing us to fall behind, Jack comes close to my face so that my eyes cannot be turned from him. He speaks in tones so low, I have to lean in to hear him.

"Evelyn, I did not allow Celia to ask any questions, but I will answer some that I am sure you must have right now. You know that you have talents in speaking with the air that lingers above the water. You cannot possibly understand what that means in the history of our people and what it means in the war we have now entered. It is a rare talent that can be developed into a powerful skill. You have not had time to learn those skills. Your comrades will be at the front lines. We cannot risk sending you there. Your talents are needed too much. For this battle, you are being ordered to sit in the back. You are not to engage in battle."

Shock and revulsion fill me. How can I not fight? How can I let my group go into battle with everyone else and I not be a part of it? I will be branded a coward and will lose their trust. My emotions register on my face and Jack raises his chin into the air in an act of authority. He continues, "Ceto will have spies and they will be on the lookout for someone with special skills. Even if you only display the remaining four skills you have, it will be enough to make you a prime target." His expression softens for a moment. Just long enough for him to say, "You are too valuable. We cannot lose you."

I know I need to respond now and think later. "Yes, sir," I say in as confident an air as I can intone. I raise my chin as Jack did and look him boldly in the eye.

Jack grabs both of my shoulders with his hands. We were already close, but this movement brings us even closer. "*I* don't want to see you get hurt, Evelyn. You have become too valuable to *me*." He pulls me close and presses his lips against my forehead as he did when I first breathed water. I melt into the kiss and forget everything around me. I know no battle. I know no war. I only know that a burning is growing within me for this person.

As I lean into his body, Jack releases my arms and swims away to his band of 50. I am still for a moment, relishing the warmth of his touch. But I am brought back to reality when that cold, empty ocean water swirls around me as the last of the recruits passes by. I am at the rear and it is time to get moving. I pull myself into place at the back of the army, trying to figure out what I am supposed to do if I am not going to fight.

Suddenly, an explosion of water, light, and sound stun me. The commotion is maybe 500 yards in front of our army. No doubt, we have finally come face to face with Ceto's army. The battle is about to begin.

Chapter 19

Without me. The battle is beginning without me. My entire body is on edge and ready to go. This is what I have been training for. This is what I am prepared to do. With Jack's orders still fresh in my mind, my heart tears away from the thoughts of his warmth. My left hand grips my shield, and with my right hand I pull my mace free from my belt. I swim forward and am instantly thrust to the side by Pisces.

"Pisces! What are you doing here?!" I yell at my friend and battle companion, "We should be engaged in the battle, not sitting aside watching our companions do the work for us!" I feel rage filling me, almost to the point of overflow. I am determined to get into that fight and defeat Ceto. I will do it alone if I have to. I can't sit back and watch everyone else do my part.

Pisces swims close enough for me to mount him, but I sense enough tenseness in his body, that I know I will not be welcome on his back. He, too, would rather be in the fight.

"Young one," he says in a firm and clipped voice, "I am here to protect you and make sure you remain in the rear as directed. I will not be moved from my orders and resolve. Too high a prize is at stake!"

I know he means that my talents are too valuable to our army. That somehow it is okay for everyone else to be hurt. I am too special for that. I have to be kept safe. I have to be protected. I have to be held in the back like a defenseless baby until everyone else has proven themselves worthy. Lady Pescara must have known that a new recruit who trained for battle would be reluctant to obey orders to stand down. Pisces was sent here to enforce the order I'd been given.

With anger and frustration toward all those who want to control every move I make – Lady Pescara, my mother, Celia, Jack, and now Pisces – I strike forward, determined to barrel into the gargantuan fish. This is a mistake. Before I can make it, Pisces swivels his gigantic body sideways, blocking my path. I swim full force into his decorated armor. The water is temporarily knocked out of me and I float backward several feet.

"Young one, I will not let you pass."

Infuriated by his obstinacy in forcing me to stay put, I pull up my shield and charge again, this time faking my forward motion and diving downward at the last minute. This also proves to be a useless effort. Pisces merely dives on top of me and slams me further down. Pain shoots through my back, just under the place he hits my armor. I let out an audible gasp and cry from the injury.

"Young one. We can go all day and all night in this manner or you can obey the orders you have been given. As for me, I will obey my orders. I will not let you pass."

I feel the tenseness and determination in all of Pisces' thoughts. I know he will not give up. Many hundred feet ahead of us now, the battle is growing. Ceto's army is nearly as large as the army of Atlantis. Those in the back of the formation are not yet engaged in the fight, but I know it will be that way for only a few more minutes. I know I will have to watch them engage, every last one of them, and I can do nothing to help. Nothing to do in behalf of my new-found people. In complete mental defeat, I turn my face up to Pisces.

"I submit, Pisces. I will not fight." Hot tears fill my eyes as my oldest sea friend swims beneath me so I can mount him.

"I am glad for your willingness, my young friend. I feel your anguish at not being able to fight when you have trained so well. But trust me, Evelyn, you will live now to fight for another day and be a far greater asset to this great sea home we share." I mount his back slowly, feeling the swelling begin beneath my armor from the blows I received from my protector. Pisces is more gentle than usual as he waits and even aids me in climbing onto his saddle. "We cannot remain far behind or we draw attention to ourselves," he says. My eyes sweep the sea before us. Three hundred yards or more now separate us from the Army of Atlantis. We are like sitting ducks. I hold tightly to Pisces' reins and lean down toward his head as he shoots through the water. I am going to have to be so near the fight I can be disguised as a fighter, but I will not be able to do anything. Dread fills my stomach as we approach the fray.

When are only ten yards from the last battalion of two-worlders, I look up to the back of the line and see Gwen. There is no mistaking that dark hair and her confident posture as she turns from

155

the battle toward Pisces and me. In my months beneath the sea, I have never seen her face. I am shaken and confused. The world around me swirls again as my mind races to understand what I cannot yet see.

With our mental link still close and strong, Pisces feels my surprise register within him. He is caught off guard and looks to see where the source of my perplexity is. Just as his eyes raise to see Gwen, she raises her hand and a huge smile spreads across her face. She looks happy to see me. Happy to have finally found me. How long has she been waiting to find me here? How long has she been in Atlantis without my noticing? She was kissing James the last time I saw her.

Out of nowhere, a swarm of Octopi swims from beneath the battle. They congregate quickly and head in our direction. Pisces senses the bent of their course and turns to swim in the opposite direction. I was lost in my thoughts at seeing Gwen and have to re-grasp the rein. I nearly slip from the fish twice as he creates a zig-zag pathway in the ocean, darting right, left, up, down, and even diagonally to avoid the oncoming enemy. His general course has altered and he is leading us closer to the Army of Atlantis even as he is darting away from the sleek, bulging heads. Inky, blinding blots shoot around my head more than once as Pisces avoids their sloppy aim.

I turn to see how close they are. 100 yards, 95 yards, 85 yards. The mammoth creatures with their inky weapons are gaining on us fast. Again, I spot Gwen. She sees the octopi, and is swimming with all her might toward me and Pisces. But can she get to us in time to help? Do I even want her too? I am not sure how I feel about Gwen right now, but I know I am not ready to let her sacrifice herself for me. I let go of the reins with one hand to wave her off and try to shout amid the furious noises all around me. Pisces makes another zag, this time even closer to the safety of the Army of Atlantis. I am not prepared for the move and I pay for it. I am flung out of the saddle just as Pisces changes direction. The rein in my left hand breaks and I am tangled in a leathery mess, trying to free myself and swim away.

Pisces turns and swims straight for my sinking figure. But in his haste, he is struck directly in the right eye with a slimy black ink blot. I feel his pain as he flies backward several feet. In desperation, I reach for the small knife in my waistband and cut at the leather strap that is binding my arm to my leg. An ink blot hits my arm, and a steamy mess raises up from my armor. I dropped my knife as pain hits me. Somewhere behind me I hear a cry. I turn my body to face the familiar voice and see Gwen racing toward me. Can she possibly get to me? I feel Pisces doing all he can to locate me with his one good eye and our mental connection. I am not sure which way to turn. Gwen has gained ground and is still able bodied. If she can get me out of this ridiculous leather strap, together we can help Pisces and make it back to the Army. It is a long shot, but it is all I have. I swim toward Gwen as best as I can. In less than two minutes, Gwen reaches me, mace in hand, ready to fight. "I am here for you Evelyn. I am here for you," she manages to say between heaving gasps for breath. Relief sweeps through me as she reaches for the leather strap that twists around me. Ink blots spray at us through the water. Gwen turns and yells at the enemy octopi, her useless words muffled by the barrage of noise all around us.

I feel panic sweeping through Pisces behind me. I turn around in time to see an over-sized, great white shark rocketing upward toward my faithful friend. I open my mouth to scream, but cannot get a sound out before Pisces has been catapulted upward by the terrific beast. I wriggle with super-human strength until I am free from the leather strap. I shoot through the water, leaving Gwen holding the strap behind me. She swims after me as fast as she can, the swarm of octopi gaining ground.

I reach the great white just as he and Pisces initiate a battle. But Pisces is wounded. The ink blot that hit his eye has left him blind on that side. He needs me to see for him.

Pisces, I am here. I reach out to his mind with mine so he knows he can fight with me. I am instantly repulsed by an inward feeling emanating from the fish.

NO! Evelyn, stand down!

The great white barrels into Pisces' left side and underbelly as my friend is distracted by my presence. By now, we are above the main noise and confusion of the battle against Ceto. Pisces swings around and plants his side armor directly on the right side of the shark's head. The great white shakes it off and turns to go at Pisces again. How can I not help him? Rare abilities or no, I am not about to let him die. I make my decision.

I crunch my body into a ball and hold my shield above my head. Just below the strength of my shield, I hold my mace, the ball trailing along my back. I hear the scuffle moving above me. I wait until I sense Pisces' position. Gwen is within two arm's lengths behind me. I propel my body upward, straightening my body as I do so. My shield moves powerfully above me as I stretch out my left arm. I ready my right hand with my mace, elbow bent and raised with my clenched fist ready to spring from behind my shoulder.

When I feel Pisces near enough, I move the shield aside and swing with all my might at the great white shark directly above my head. The heavy, spiked ball makes powerful contact with the shark just behind his right fin, grazing the fin on its way to its mark. Blood from the shark fills the water. In the blinding red that surrounds me, I lose sight of Pisces. I reach out to him mentally, but he is blocking my communication – still trying to keep me from the battle. I feel the water above me swirling as the two injured fish again resume their fight.

I swim downward to get out of the blood and get a better view of the battle above. I am met by Gwen who has her mace up and ready to fight. She drops her shield as she reaches me and takes hold of my right arm. "What are you doing?" I ask her, pulling away. I am too concerned about Pisces to worry about running for my life with Gwen.

"The shield is too heavy. I'm faster without it," she answers. I looked wide-eyed over her shoulder as I see the swarm of octopi upon us. We have just a few yards left until we will be overtaken. I drop my shield for greater speed. Gwen still has ahold of my arm. She is frozen with fear and incapable of letting go.

"Gwen," I yell, "let me go to Pisces!" Then I see the look of determination on her face.

"I'm sorry, Evelyn, I can't let you do that. You are too important" is her calm and firm response. Is she in on the plan to keep me from fighting? Can nobody let me help in any way? Gwen drops her mace and I am amazed at her foolishness. How can she fight without a weapon? In an instant, she wraps herself around my body, swimming around from behind, never letting go of my right arm. Her right arm crosses the front of my body until it reaches my left arm and holds on tight. I am trapped. Even her legs are entwined around mine. I fight against her grip, reaching out to Pisces instinctively for his help. But Pisces is silent. Soon, the octopi are on us. Gwen refuses to let me fight. I am certain the octopi are on their way to help the shark with Pisces. A seasoned battle fish such as Pisces is a great trophy. Why can't I even help *him*?

In complete aggravation I send a mental, raging scream out to the octopi to stop! To my surprise, they all stop – around Gwen and me. What have I done? The next thing I know, the octopi close in around us and everything goes black.

Chapter 20

We are moving quickly through the water and have been for several hours. Gwen's arms and legs are still wrapped around me, their strength all but gone. Her protective posture is like a blanket in the blackness. I am wrapped by Gwen and she is wrapped by several octopi. Two or three at least. Neither of us has spoken since we were captured. We each have an octopus tentacle firmly clasped over our mouths. At times I even find it difficult to breathe.

Finally, I feel that we are moving downward. The water around us is getting colder and darker. We come to a stop. I hear voices and sense sea creatures talking to one another. Like the consciousness of the octopi, the sea creatures' minds are new to me. Maybe sharks, maybe eels. Definitely not sea creatures found in Atlantis.

The pressure around my body relaxes as the octopi release Gwen and me. I fall to a stone floor of a cave. Poor Gwen. She has been holding onto me for so long that her limbs are completely limp. An octopus picks her up and carries her in its many tentacles. Fingers grow grotesquely from the ends of each tentacle. He is a two-worlder. His transformation is almost complete. Gwen is unconscious and the octopus two-worlder swims with her through a door at the back of the cave. My own arms and legs tingle like mad as I lie on the stone floor.

I feel its unyielding cold, even in these frigid waters. My voice is hoarse and cracked when I finally speak to our captors.

"Where are we? Why have you brought us here? We cannot possibly be worth anything to you."

"Oh, you are worth much more than you know, Dearie," I recognize that voice. No, I recognize that consciousness. It is the shark who attacked Pisces. As my eyes adjust to the greenish light of the small cave we are in, I turn my face upward toward the great white shark. His eyes are glossy black and his nose large and pointed. I see rows upon rows of sharp teeth in his massive jaws. His tremendous, scar-covered body hovers in front of me as I speak to him. From where I sit, I cannot see his right flank – the one I hit with my mace. The memory of it still brings me some satisfaction. A smile creeps onto my face.

"What do you smile at, child?" the shark communicates angrily down into my eyes. Those eyes on that body I saw attacking my protector. My entire body goes from cold to hot in a matter of seconds and I feel the water around me heating up with my anger.

"What have you done to Pisces?!" I shout. It is the shark's turn to smile now. A low, rumbling chuckle starts from deep within his throat and grows and grows until a full bodied laugh erupts from his massive jaws. "Pisces?! Pisces?! What have *I* done to Pisces?! Let me tell you, little child, that Pisces friend of yours has been a thorn in my side my entire life! I only gave him what he deserved!"

"Did you leave him there alone with no one to help him? Was he alive when you left?" The questions are moving beyond my unwilling lips without my permission. Having seen the first strikes of

162

this behemoth of a shark, I can only imagine the worst for my friend and guard.

The rumbling chuckle of the shark remains within his throat this time. He is working hard to restrain himself. "You don't need to worry about Pisces. He didn't suffer long."

That is all the answer I need. I know it is over for Pisces. He is dead. He is dead. He is dead because he tried to protect me. Why would the Army of Atlantis make such a trade, allowing a warrior like Pisces to protect a new recruit? I feel bile rising in my throat, the taste bitter and burning in my mouth. I vomit into the heated water around me. One of the octopi behind me pulls me back so I will not be swimming in my own filth. As the cooler water swirls around my face again, the pain in my heart awakens. From somewhere behind me, a voice, a man's voice, calls out to the shark in front of me.

"Tertius, you are wanted in her majesty's chambers. She desires a report from you on your success and your prisoner."

"PrisonerS," I can't help correcting the error. I won't forget about Gwen. With Pisces gone, she is all I have left from our battle. She is all I have left of my life on land. We are likely to die in this cold, dark, and murky place, she is all I have left at all.

Tertius, the great white shark, makes an acquiescent grunt and heads toward the opening of the cave. He is better at obeying orders than I am.

"Can I at least be in the same cell as Gwen?" I ask. I know she is passed out, but I need to see her to know she is okay. Tertius opens his mouth to answer me but is interrupted by the voice from the man I cannot see.

"You are under strict orders not to communicate with the prisoner further, Tertius." Tertius closes his mouth and leaves the room. The giant octopus that is holding me moves forward into the cave. We enter a door on the left and make our way through long, twisting tunnels in the naturally created cave-dungeon. No matter how many times I protest or ask where we are headed, all three of the octopi remain mute. After a while I realize they aren't two-worlders. They are octopi recruited by Ceto to work as dumb minions. I try reaching out to the octopus that is holding me. I briefly touch his consciousness. It is murky and clouded – not as easy as communicating with Pisces, but I am able to communicate slowly. I decide to work on them one at a time, trying out each to see who might be susceptible to persuasive conversation.

Where are you taking me? I ask. Surprise registers through the sea creature as he senses my question, still he remains unresponsive. I try again. *Where are we going? Where are we?* I feel the creature stiffen. He is struggling to not answer my questions. *I'm sure your leaders would be fine with answering such simple questions,* I communicate. Finally, a slow and quiet response fills my mind.

I am not to speak to prisoner. Excellent. I got through and have the brute speaking to me.

It's not talking if you don't open your mouth. I say, wondering if he will buy my explanation. He remains thoughtful for a moment and I don't push him. I wait for him to make up his mind to speak to me.

I guess so, He finally says. *I never thought of it that way.* Of course he hadn't. He hasn't thought about much at all. I will use that to my advantage.

So, why don't we start with more civilized conversation? What is your name? From the way this slow-of-speech octopus straightens his body, I can tell the thought of being called civilized is a new concept to him and one he wants very much.

Gus, He replies. *What name you?* He asks.

I'm Evelyn, but my friends call me Evie. Not true, but entering the word 'friend' into the conversation is a good idea.

Evie pretty name. I call Evie you.

Oh, no, Gus. Only friends call me Evie. We haven't really known each other long enough to be friends.

Maybe soon we be friends.

If circumstances allow it, Gus. At present, you are taking me to my jail cell. It's hard to be friends that way.

I try harder.

Thank you, Gus. After ten minutes, we reach the cell. It is a shallow opening in the wall of the cave that indents only three feet or so. A thick wall of ice covers most of the opening. Since I can control water temperature, I know that will work to my advantage, but I have to make sure my timing is right. *Gus, where is my friend you also captured? Her name is Gwen and I am concerned for her.*

She girl you friend?

Yes, Gus.

Oh, she fine now. She in good room. At least I have some form of comfort there. I don't think Gus is capable of lying. It would use up too many brain cells.

The giant octopus sets me down gently in the jail cell.

My watch not now, he says. *Murphy not talk too much. Even to me!* I sense a hint of humor in Gus' mind. I can't see where his mouth is to find his smile, so I give him a smile of my own.

Goodbye, Gus.

Goodbye Evelyn-soon-friend. This is going nicely.

As two of the octopi slide away back through the cave's hallway, nobody put a door on my cell. At first, I think this is neglect on their part and very good luck for me. However, the third octopus, Murphy, remains at his post next to my cave entrance. With a one-on-one guard system, I am not sure who would ever need a door. But I do wonder what they would do if they ever had more prisoners than octopi. I try valiantly to reach out to Murphy despite Gus' encouragement to the contrary. I find, however, that Gus was right. Murphy isn't big into communication. I touch his consciousness but he gruffly pushes my efforts away.

I settle in for a long night but my body has had enough. From the battle with Celia to the trek across the ocean to this new dungeon, my body has given all it can. I lay down on my jail cell floor, hunger pains tearing through my stomach, and settle in for a very fitful sleep.

I have been searching forever. Finally, I find what I am looking for. As I enter the room, the now familiar warmth greets me like an old friend. The fear that I have been holding onto dissipates. I know I am in the right place.

Just as it always does, the glowing orb pulsates warmth and brightness in the space before me. But this time there is something different. This time I can hear it speaking to me. Yes, yes it is speaking to me. But what is it saying? It is more of a feeling than actual words. I strain to listen.

Then, just as they always do, voices come screaming into the room. I recognize more of them, some I still do not know. The voice of the orb grows faint. I reach for it, knowing the entire time what the consequence of this action will be. I sense someone near me. Someone familiar. They are reaching out too. Panic grips me again and I know I have to be the first to reach out to the stone. I stretch out my arm, my fingers barely skimming the surface of the ball in front of me. I see flashes of light. Images shoot through my mind. Images that I do not understand and cannot entirely see. Suddenly, the orb bursts into a giant, glowing ball, pushing me backward with the thrust of its growth. Just as suddenly, it contracts again, this time into a size that can fit into the palm of my hand. Its glow is gone as is its brilliance. Instead, it falls to the floor as a heavy black ball. I lunge forward and grasp it desperately with my hand. My fingers curve around the fist-sized ball in a grip that cannot be broken.

Once again, I realize with dread that I can no longer breathe.

Chapter 21

Evelyn-soon-friend. Evelyn-soon-friend. You up now. You meet majesty.

Gus? Is that you? I shake myself from the terrifying paralysis of my dream.

Yes, Evelyn-soon-friend. I Gus. I take you now meet majesty.

Gus, where is my friend, Gwen? The one you said was in a nice room? Is she okay? Is she strong this morning? Can she talk? Can I see her?

Many question, Evelyn-soon-friend. I know she good. You Gwen friend good. Now come. Now you see majesty.

Gus, I want to see my friend, Gwen.

You see majesty. Maybe majesty take you see Gwen.

Reluctantly, I peel my body off of the jail cell floor. My entire body is stiff and sore. In my stomach, I feel intense pressure. I am sure it is hunger, like my body is trying to force its way to some source of food since I am not going to provide it. Instinctively, I press my hand to my abdomen to stifle the hunger pains. As I push, I feel a little pop. A tickle. The corners of my mouth twitch upward in a humored expression.

You think Gus funny, Evelyn-soon-friend? I not try be funny.

Oh, no, Gus. It wasn't you. I felt a little tickle when I was getting up, that's all.

Oh. Okay, now, Evelyn-soon-friend. You come me and majesty give you good food.

That piques my interest. I pull myself up to full height and prepare to follow Gus to meet this majesty person – probably Ceto. As I leave, he reaches two of his tentacled arms out to me, wrapping them securely around my mid-section. The little spot on my stomach that felt the pop, feels another. This, coupled with the giant arms wrapped around me, forces out a small giggle.

Okay, Gus. This time, you tickled me. I feel Gus's pleasure, and we head down the hallway to my next destination, exchanging small talk on our way. I learn all about life for Gus and his interaction with the two-worlders. His feelings are neutral as to war and which side he is working for. He is merely following the orders of the first to ask him. I wonder how many other species of sea creatures live in this way. Following the opposition solely because they have never been given a different choice. Would he follow Atlantis if given the option? Would others?

I am forming more and more of these questions when Gus comes to a stop in front of a large, circular stone leaning against a wall. Two more octopi stand by the stone and greet Gus with a nod. This time Gus addresses them out loud in an octopus language I can understand, "Majesty ask see prisoner. Prisoner here now." The other two octopi nod their heads. The one on the left joins his companion on the right and with some of their tentacles pushing the stone and the remaining tentacles keeping them upright on the ledge, they roll the stone out of the doorway. First a crack of light gleams from the edge of the exposed entrance, then the light grows brighter as its covering is moved out of the way. Gus and I enter the room and the soldiers roll the giant stone back into place.

I blink to adjust my eyes to the brightness of the room. It is nearly all white – white walls, white floor, even a white ceiling. I see gold elements here and there. A large chandelier hangs directly in front of me in the center of the long, oval room. Its crystals, rather than a teardrop or Fleur de lis or other typical chandelier shape, has oval centers with long, spindly arms coming out of them. I counted the little arms on one of the crystals – eight. Just like the eight tentacle legs of my octopus enemy. The walls have sconces with the same unique crystals hanging from their bases. Under the glowing white light of the distinctive chandelier, is a long, white, oval table. A thin gold border caresses its edges all the way around. The table is surrounded by chairs, solid in construction, made with a material I have never seen before. It is some kind of stone. The chairs provide the only color in the room. They are green and carved with scrollwork with a Middle Eastern flair. These, too, are trimmed in gold.

Even though my attention is absorbed by these bright and elegant surroundings, I still feel a tugging from somewhere in my stomach. But this time it isn't from hunger. I am being watched as I hang suspended in the space above the floor, held there by Gus' tentacles. I move my eyes and face to my left – the direction the tugging feeling is coming from. There, seated at the end of the oval table is Ceto.

Chapter 22

I have never seen her before, but I know who she is. She sits in a chair, arms spread wide, hands resting on the white surface before her. Her skin is green, the shade of kelp in mid-day light. Her torso and lower half of her body have made a full transformation. One or two black, shiny tentacles move in the space by her sides, belaying the remaining legs which are beneath the table. The shiny, black skin of those tentacles covers almost her entire torso. Her features have changed so much from that of a human, that clothing is unnecessary. There is nothing left to cover. For the most part, the octopus skin is below her shoulders. However, one strand of black, like a curious tentacle, is growing its way up her green neck like it is going to strangle her. Her hair is twisted into hundreds of dark brown dreadlocks that slither ominously around her face. Her face is her one redeeming quality. It is beautiful. Her skin is youthful, no laugh lines or crow's feet or wrinkles. Her nose is long and straight. Her jawline is square and sharp. Her lips, set in a soft smile, are the one bright area of color on her entire body. They are painted in a bold red lipstick. Except for the movement of her hair and tentacles, she remains a statue.

Ceto lets me stare at her without reservation. She understands that I need a few moments to take her in. She is definitely one-of-a-kind. Once I have proven that I am not going to scream or fight, she addresses Gus.

"I think you can set her down now, Gus. I don't think she is going anywhere. You can leave us alone." Gus sets me on my feet on the cold, white stony floor. He bids me a farewell that only I can hear, and I return his silent goodbye with one of my own.

Once we are alone, Ceto rises from her chair and speaks to me. "Well. Evelyn Marin. I finally have the opportunity and honor of addressing you. As I am sure you know by now, I am your aunt, Ceto." She moves to the side of the table so her entire body is in full view. Six tentacles caress the ground like the ruffled edges of a skirt. Ceto rests her hands on the chair next to her own, "Please, come sit with me. I will be eating lunch shortly and I would love to have you join me. I'm sure you are famished after such a long night." Her voice is gentle, soothing, and though she is my enemy, I acknowledge her respectfully.

"Thank you. I will," I reply, moving slowly toward the chair.

"It has been such a long time since I have seen any of my old friends. Your mother and I were very close. May I give you a hug?" A hug? Why on earth would someone who wants to destroy my way of life ask for a hug? I am wary of her actions and intentions. I cringe, thinking of her arms around my shoulders, but I am her prisoner. Can I really refuse?

I nod in response and she wraps her arms around mine. I return her embrace with both of my arms and hands lightly touching her back. Though her cheek on mine is soft and warm, the skin of her back is anything but. It is cold and smooth and firm. It reminds me of when I once touched a sting-ray at the Monterey Bay Aquarium. It is the same feeling of strong muscle and tissue beneath the tough exterior.

As she pulls away, Ceto looks thoughtfully into my face. "I am surprised at just how grown you are. I'm not sure what I expected but it wasn't such a mature and lovely young lady." She motions to a chair and I sit down, confused by the attention I am receiving. She sits again at the head of the table and at the same moment a side door opens and two stingrays enter carrying large plates of food on their backs. They swim just above the table then each arches upward right in front of us, sliding the plates of food from their backs as they do so. I look at my plate and my stomach growls. I am so hungry. My plate is covered with prawns and clams and even a bit of seaweed. I am not accustomed to eating seafood. I have never liked it and since I entered Atlantis for the first time, I find it a bit unsettling to eat anyway. I decide to try the seaweed first. Fortunately, it is cooked so it isn't rubbery as I expected it to be. I have no idea what it is seasoned with, but it is delicious. Different from what I eat in Atlantis, but delicious.

I am halfway through my portion when the idea of poison enters my brain. I have no idea how this food was prepared. It is possible that Ceto is luring me to my death. I sit up and place my hands in my lap, evaluating each part of my body with my mind. My stomach is feeling better, nothing aches anymore. I don't feel dizzy or lightheaded and I can see fine. I decide I am not being poisoned and return to the meal.

A soft chuckle comes from Ceto. "Were you checking to make sure I wasn't trying to sneak something into your food?" I stop chewing and look down at my plate. "Don't worry, Evelyn, I would be surprised if you didn't check. But the food is fine. You are safe in my care. You are my niece, dear. I have no desire to kill you." I feel calm and I meet Ceto's gaze. "You and I have so much to discuss, so much to catch up on," she says, "I'm sure you have many questions for me."

That is true. I do have many questions for her. I have been trying to find the answers to questions about my life, my family, and my abilities for months, but now I can only speak of one person. "Where is Gwen?" I ask, "How is she? Has she eaten? Can I see her?"

Ceto looks surprised but answers in a calm tone, "Your friend is fine, my dear. Rest assured she has eaten and slept well. She is recovering from the arduous journey the two of you made last night. You will see each other soon enough. You are a good friend to her to be so concerned about her well-being."

I feel a tinge of guilt at being called Gwen's friend. The truth is, I have hardly spoken to her in weeks. Since seeing her with James, I have only felt anger toward her. We haven't had a chance to talk about that day. I threw myself so fully into my life in Atlantis that I kept myself from having time with Gwen. But seeing her coming to my rescue last night (even though it was a failed attempt) brought back the feelings of friendship we once shared. But Ceto isn't ready to take me to Gwen. She has other things on her mind.

"It has been so long since I have lived or even visited the land," she says. "What is life like now above the sea? What is it like for you?"

I am not interested in small talk. I have larger concerns, so all I can think to say is, "Life on land is pretty good, I guess. I haven't really spent a lot of time there lately."

A smile creeps into the corners of Ceto's mouth. She is pleased with my response and continues with her questions.

"And how did you come to know that you were a two-worlder, my dear? Was it your mother who told you? She was so proud to be a two-worlder you know."

How many conflicting emotions can I possibly feel at one time? Yes, I was angry with my mom for keeping my two-worlder status away from me, but now I am missing her. I don't want to talk about her with Ceto.

"No, my mother didn't tell me. I found the ocean on my own."

A crease pinches itself in Ceto's brow. "I see," she says, "I thought your mother would have trained you from birth. But people are not as steady as we would have them be."

A spark of defense shoots through me, "My mom was protecting me," I answer too hotly, "it may not be what you expected, or even what I wanted, but she did what she felt was the best for me. She was the steadiest thing in my world." I am so agitated that I grip my hand around my fork like it is a weapon. Ceto tilts her head to one side as concern crosses her face.

"My dear niece, I had no intention of demeaning your mother. When I knew her she was a faithful friend and supporter. I remember her with fondness." She reaches out and pats my hand, "I was merely surprised." I relax and Ceto continues, "But now that you are here, in the sea I mean, how do you like it? Isn't it beyond your wildest dreams?"

Ceto knows nothing about my wildest dreams, and I am not about to let her know. I have enough sense to not let her in that far. My glowing orb nightmares are mine and mine alone. I am getting too caught up in Ceto's warm reception and gentle tones. I have shared enough about me. It is her turn to tell me about her life and circumstances. I assume I will eventually be killed by Ceto, but there is still a possibility that I can escape. If I do that, I want any information that I can take with me back to Atlantis.

"I'm not sure what my expectations could have been about living in the ocean," I reply, "but what I have found has been both overwhelming and amazing at the same time." I allow Ceto to rest her hand on mine for several seconds and now I squeeze her fingers softly as I speak. We are going to pretend to be friends. "What is it that brought you to live in the ocean?"

Ceto lets go of my hand, resting her own in her lap. She leans back in her chair and regards me with narrowed and saddened eyes. She doesn't like divulging her past either. Whatever her thoughts, she decides it is fine to share her story with me. She inhales the sea water around her and lets out a long sigh.

"My upbringing was very different from yours. My own mother was a woman I never knew and from whom I never felt an ounce of affection. My father always said she had seduced him unwittingly while he was on an excursion in Jaffa. He had nothing but disdain for her. Once he learned of her abilities and history with water, he abandoned her completely. Ran back to the safety of his books." Ceto grows tense as she continues. She interlaces her fingers and plays with them absentmindedly. Her eyes are hard as she stares at a point somewhere beyond me. "My mother contacted my father once she realized she was pregnant. It is rare for children of the sea to be raised in the sea itself. For the most part their proclivity for water has not yet shown itself so they are raised in houses along the shore until they are ready for life here.

"And so, my mother sent me to my father to live until I was grown enough to return to her. Still completely rife with anger, he did not raise me by the ocean as he ought to have done. He kept me far from my mother out of contempt for her. Of course, she never reached out, not even when I finally entered the sea, so I was left solely with my father to raise me as he saw fit." Ceto spits out these words through clenched teeth.

"Though my father told me about the two-worlder history I was from," Ceto continues, "he did not encourage me to test my abilities. Instead, everything I did was met with disapproval from him. He married and had children with my stepmother. She treated me with as much disdain as my father did. I was little loved, even by my half-siblings. Only rarely did we share in the fun that most siblings on land seem to share." A small tear leaks out from Ceto's eye and I feel sorry for her. What kind of person would I have grown to be with that kind of life?

Ceto straightens and returns her eyes to mine. "When I was old enough, I ran to the ocean as fast as I could. I knew what abilities

I had inherited and I was certain life in the sea would be far better than anything I had seen on land. My father completely disowned me at that point and I disowned him. I heard from my half-sister that he died within a year of my leaving. I haven't spoken about him to anyone in years."

Ceto's stingray servants enter the room. Swooping low over my place at the table, and with a little flick of his wing, one flicks my plate of half-eaten food onto his back, swimming back out of the room. Within moments, both sting-rays are back, carrying our second course. Ceto brightens and sits up in her chair with a look of anticipation on her face. The sad, tense atmosphere that filled the water between us is pushed away with Ceto's new tone.

"Oh how nice," she says, "I love seafoam pudding. It is meant to be a dessert, but I always insist on having it after my first course. It does such lovely things in cleansing the palette from the aftertaste of prawns." Wartime talks with a prisoner are not the time to get excited about a dessert. I am witnessing the signs of delusion that sets in for two-worlders like Ceto. She is turning into the octopus two-worlder she inherited and is losing her mind as well. That makes her more dangerous than ever, but it also gives me the conviction that I can manipulate this woman into letting me go. I ask more about her life, trying to bring her back to the conversation.

"What was life like for you once you came to live in the ocean?" I ask, but Ceto is not ready to let go of her seafoam pudding yet.

"No, no, my dear," she replies, "I insist that we take a break from this heavy conversation and enjoy our food."

I look at my plate. A little bowl rests on top with a seafoam green substance inside. It looks like the frog-eye salad my mom used to make when I was a kid. It is creamy but filled with colorful bits of sea plants I cannot identify. I start with a small bite, eating slowly and watching for signs that something might be amiss with the food. I feel no burning or stinging as I eat the first bite. No poison. Besides, Ceto is not in the mood to let me skip eating her favorite food. I take another bite, determined to finish quickly and get back to our conversation. The pudding is sweet and light. It bubbles in my mouth and feels like eating air.

"So, how do you like it?" Ceto asks with a beaming look in her eyes.

"It's very good. I like it a lot. Thank you."

"Oh I'm so glad you like it. It is such a favorite of mine."

As we finished our pudding, the sting-rays return for our plates and bowls. It is a good time to revisit our conversation. I turn to face Ceto, but she has risen from her chair and is waiting next to me.

"Well, my dear. I would normally love to continue to sit with you, but I have many things to do. Why don't you come with me? I have someone I would like for you to see."

The large stone door to the room rolls open again and Gus, Murphy, and a third octopus come into the room. Ceto faces them and I stand, disappointed and confused by the change.

"Thank you, men (I'm not sure I would have called octopi men). Evelyn and I will be visiting the treasury. I would appreciate an escort." She turns to me and with a smile adds, "You are my niece, my dear, but you are also my prisoner. I certainly couldn't let you head to the treasury on your own, now could I?"

A sinking feeling fills my stomach as I realize Ceto is paying attention. Not completely crazy yet, she may not be so easy to escape from. Then I turn toward Gus and feel a dose of confidence. I still have one option left to cultivate.

I follow Ceto to the doorway and am surrounded by the three octopi. Though none of them put their tentacles around me, I know I am trapped in their midst. Ceto leads the way out of the room and into the cold, dark ocean water outside. Her tentacles roll along beside her like a billowing skirt. We move into the open water and swim downward. I expect the water to grow even darker as we go deeper into it, but instead I see a faint, orange glow beneath us. The closer we get to what lies below, the brighter the murky water becomes. After only a few minutes of swimming, I can make out several rows of lights. As we drew nearer, I see that we are headed into an underwater city, one much larger and more modern than Atlantis.

The lights here are man-made and bright. I don't know how Ceto has electricity down here, but it has happened. The walls of her city are golden-white. They reflect the lit sconces on their exteriors so buildings glow in the dark water. The architecture of the walls is Roman, with columns and marble facades. Arched openings lead into long passageways and various rooms. In some of the rooms I see stone benches and tables. Some look like offices, others like dwellings. In a few, I see other two-worlders, some mostly human, most years deep into change.

We receive a lot of attention as we swim behind Ceto. Several two-worlders stop their activities to look at us, many sharks and stingrays out in the open water pause to see us pass by. To each who catches her eye, Ceto gives a warm greeting. Not everyone responds, however. Many keep their gaze on me, their examining eyes flint-like and wary.

We swim deeper until the lights of the city shrink away. We swim even further, beyond the reach of the orange-gold light until we are once again in cold water, much darker than I have been in before. Ceto slows her pace and draws near to a cave opening. Just like the palace, there is a large stone guarding the entrance to the cave's opening. Without a word being uttered, the octopi swimming around me push toward the stone door. I feel Gus' tentacle wrap around my waist (just one tentacle this time) as he works with his fellow octopi to roll the stone out of the way.

"Thank you, men," Ceto says, "I shall only need one to escort us through the tunnels. I don't think Ms. Marin is much of a flight risk at this point." She enters the tunnel. I realize I am meant to follow behind and so I do. Though my mind reaches out to Gus to beg him to come with us, he says he is outranked by General Sampson who will be guarding us through the treasury. I send my regret to my ally and am followed by the largest of the octopi. Together, we swim through the darkness.

Even though the tunnel entrance is completely masked in shadow, my eyes adjust to the black water. Soon the faint glowing green that I saw when I first entered my prison creeps into my vision. It grows brighter and lighter as we swim further into the tunnel. I am unsurprised to notice notches and caves of creatures from other times as we swim through the murky corridor. The walls are far from the smooth stone of the alabaster city above. Instead, they are pocketed and bumpy. No tools were used to create this passageway. Ceto has been talking to General Sampson about his octopus family as we swim. I am not paying attention to their conversation so I nearly bump into Ceto as she slows. She stops in front of yet another stone doorway on our right. This door, however, is sitting on hinges so Ceto can open it herself.

She moves to the side, and with one hand on the door and another extended to me, she says, "Alright Evelyn, my dear, I have someone I would like for you to meet."

"Who is it?" I ask.

"Oh, you'll see. I think you will be pleased. Go in."

I hesitate, not sure if I am being set up for a trap. But what other choices do I have? Besides, I have a cell waiting for me higher up. There would be no point in abandoning me here in a dungeon. So, with gentle strokes, I swim cautiously into the new corridor.

"I'll be right outside the door, dear. Do let me know if you need anything. You have just a few minutes as I really do need to get back to my work for the day."

As I turn my back on Ceto and toward the hall, I see a warm glow, not unlike the city above, coming from an opening at the end. I swim toward the light, assuming that this is the way to go. As I draw near, I can hardly believe what I see. It looks like every sea treasure ever written about or mapped or pirated in all of history is here in these deep, stone walls. From where I float, I see piles and piles of gold coins, speckled throughout with jewels, necklaces, goblets, gold bars, chests of treasure, and even fine armor. I am stunned by the sight. It is like a glittering dream. I enter the room and reach my hand out to run my fingers through a pile of coins when I am grabbed by the wrist.

Looking at this enormous treasury, I forgot where I am, who I am, and why I am here. And now I have allowed myself to be captured without even a fight. That lesson was taught in Soldier 101. I try to twist my arm away from the creature, but his grip is vice-like and unrelenting. All I can see of him is his grey-skinned hand as he holds me tight. He is cloaked in a robe with a hood that veils his features in a darkness that I cannot see through. The robe is long, almost to the treasury floor. Floating just beneath the robe, I see two feet, nearly human, with webbed toes and scales growing just above. So, this is a two-worlder. And not just any two-worlder. This is an Atlantean.

"Who are you? What are you doing here? Who sent you into my treasury? Nobody steals on my watch – and I am always watching!" I know I should be afraid of this stranger, but I am not. There is something in his voice that touches something deep within me. I know I can never fear him.

"My name is Evelyn Marin. I was sent here by Ceto to meet someone. Is anyone else here or are you the one I am meant to meet?"

I have stopped trying to twist away. I want to see my guard, if that is who he is. But as I speak, his hand goes slack. Slowly his fingers let go of my wrist and his arm returns to his side.

"What did you say your name is?" he asks. His voice is at once so deep and soothing that I feel like I can melt into it.

"Evelyn. Evelyn Marin is my name. Who are you?"

The two-worlder lifts his hand to his hood and pulls back. He is tall and handsome. His hair is dark with many strands of grey about his temple and starting on the top. It moves about freely in the water. He is a merman. His nose is straight and strong, his jawline equally as strong and angular. His skin is greying like his hair, an effect from too many years without seeing the sun. But the most striking things about him are his eyes. His eyes are the color of the sea before a storm, the churning greenish blue that warns of what is coming. They are vast and piercing at the same time. I have seen eyes like that before. Every time I look into a mirror.

"Evelyn. Evelyn could that possibly be you?" He reaches his greying hand to my face and I back away. He pulls back like he was pricked by a thorn, then with emotion filling his eyes, he speaks again, "Evelyn. Evelyn. I had no idea what time could be erased so instantly and so thoroughly by seeing your face again. How I have missed you." His voice cracks with suppressed tears and I stand silently in front of him. He swallows hard then addresses me again, "Evelyn, it's me. I'm your father."

Chapter 23

*My father? You are my father? How can that possibly be? I
don't believe you. My father was lost at sea during a hurricane when
I was just a little girl. You can't possibly be my father. If you are my
father, how is it possible that you could have been here for so long?
Why didn't you contact us? Why wouldn't you come home? We
needed you! We needed you! You can't possibly be my father!*

All of this runs through my mind like a flaming current of
ocean water, boiling from a lava flow – bursting into my mind and
heart like boiling hot steam. But I can't utter a single word. I stand
there, completely frozen. My icy exterior a complete mask over the
flame I feel inside. All I can do is stare. I hear him reaching out to me,
making excuses for his absence from my life. He was lost in a
hurricane, but Ceto saved him from the wreckage of his cheap old
boat. She cared for him while his body healed and he stayed one year
when she promised him treasure for his family. In that time he came
to understand what she is like, her cause is not the evil he once
thought it to be. She really isn't as horrible as I have been taught. I
hear all of it, but all I can do is stare.

Eventually, this man in front of me, who claims to be my long lost father, realizes that I am in shock. He calls out to someone for help then puts his arms around me and swims to the outer corridor, back to Ceto. I am scooped up into the arms of General Sampson and we swim back out to the open water. Once there, Gus tries to reach out to me to speak, but I am too frozen to respond. All I can do is manage a brief, but pained glance in his direction. It is enough to communicate my distress to him and I know he feels my suffering.

"Oh Kai," I hear Ceto say with warmth, "I thought she was a stronger girl and up to the meeting. Come, let's get her back to the palace."

We ascend back the way we came. Though Ceto again leads the way, that man is right beside her, whispering in hurried and anxious tones, constantly making furtive and concerned looks in my direction. Up we go through the dark until we again pass through the glowing city. This time even more of its inhabitants stop what they are doing to see the procession.

As we rise alongside the brilliant stone walls, we swim by a window where I hear two women arguing. I don't know what in all of seadom they are arguing about, but their yelling is enough to bring me to my senses. I am a soldier being carted around by my captors. Not some baby girl in need of tending. If these two-worlders and sea creatures think there is something to look at now, they have no idea what is coming.

I am fully aware of every one of my sea elements: tide, water temperature, sea creature, and wave. The air above water can do nothing for me so far beneath the ocean's surface, I will leave that for another day and another battle. I scream out mentally to Gus who is just behind General Sampson. He urges me to do nothing so I will be safe, but I can't and I won't. I let go of my connection to Gus and focus on my water temperature skills. I approach the water around me and ask its favor on my behalf. The water thinks this is a funny ruse, something to add some entertainment to its dull life. It will comply with anything I ask of it. Within a matter of seconds, General Sampson lets out a small groan of pain as his tentacles freeze. He is distracted enough that I push out of his freezing tentacles and into the open water. He yells but is caught mid-breath by the icy water that clings to his head. A few seconds later, he is frozen solid and sinks slowly to the ocean floor, hundreds of feet below.

None of this goes unnoticed by those around me. While Gus hangs back in surprise at what is happening, Murphy reaches toward me with four of his tentacles, determined to hold me and keep me in check. But I am not easy to hold. As he reaches out, his own tentacles begin to freeze. Disbelief registers within him, and I am blown to the side by a tremendous current of water. My connection to the water temperature is broken and I am sent flailing through the water, toward the city walls. Ceto has current control abilities.

She comes toward me with a deranged look of anger on her face, arms raised to send a wall of water straight at me. Our family connection is not going to keep me out of trouble with the reigning queen of sea evil.

I brace myself for a serious impact with a wall, but Ceto is nudged to the side herself. Just as quickly as she came after me, she turns her attention to my would-be father. He has reached out with a current of his own to protect me. Though his skills are limited from years of disuse, it is enough to keep me from slamming my head and body into the edifice behind me.

Then, this man, who claims to be my father, starts to freeze. First his hands, then his arms. I can see his feet writhing in pain from under the hem of his cloak. Ceto is not going to be countered by one of her underlings. Pain fills his face as the freeze creeps higher. I reach out with my own water temperature abilities when Gus' conscious prickles mine.

Please stop, Evelyn soon-be friend! Ceto has many skill and very strong! She kill you if you try cross her! Please stop!

As the freeze grows higher on her victim, I realize that either this man or I will die if I don't end this.

"STOP!!" I shout. "Please stop!! Please don't hurt him. It was my fault!"

Ceto stops mid-freeze and turns to look at me. I am powerless before her. She has incredible skill that I cannot match and I know it. I have learned from my interactions with Celia when I am outranked. I am going to have to find another way to fight these battles.

"Ah, Evelyn," her voice is soft and tender and scarier than anything I have ever heard before. "Are you saying you surrender?"

Bile rises into my throat as I let out the wretched answer, "Yes, Ceto. I surrender."

"Good. Gus, take her. Miss Marin is going to have new quarters." She lets Kai go and swims ahead. Gus takes me in his tentacles and swims after his queen. We pass Kai whose arms have been unfrozen. He looks after me with so much concern that I cannot help but feel bad for the pain I just caused him. I am not ready to accept him as my dad, but I can at least acknowledge that he reached out to help me. Murphy recovers and reaches Kai as Gus and I pass. He wraps four of his tentacles around Kai, who is limp from his ordeal. I know he will be joining me in Ceto's prison.

Chapter 24

Since I displayed my water temperature abilities, I am not led back to my original cell of stone and ice. Instead, I am taken to a cell deeper in the vault of the prison, this time with bars as the fourth wall. I am quiet as Gus swims with me back to the cave. He tries several times to reach my mind, but I am too depressed to respond. I am foolish. I could have used this time to learn important information and find a way out of this place. Instead, I allowed my embarrassment, frustration, and temper to rule the day. And I gave away a piece of my identity in the process, forcing my enemies to put me in even more guarded accommodations.

With no daylight reaching me in my cell, it is impossible to keep track of time. I am given food periodically – uncooked seaweed and decomposing shrimp – but the timing is so irregular that it is difficult for me to count the days by it. I cannot bring myself to eat the monotonous and unappetizing meals at first. But over time, my hunger gets the best of me. I won't touch the shrimp, I have too many reasons to not want to eat it. But eventually the seaweed courses diminish and disappear altogether until shrimp is all I am left with. Ceto is determined to bend me to her will.

My guards change regularly, though I see Gus only once. The one time I do see him is very early in my incarceration. He does all he can to console me, to bring me out of my depression, but I am too deep to allow for his attempts at kindness. I don't bother trying to reach out to any of my other guards.

Night after night I dream of Atlantis, of finding my sea abilities, of the people I left behind. Sometimes I have vivid dreams of James, holding his hand and laughing. Then in an instant I see Gwen by his side, holding his other hand, talking and laughing. I let go of his hand and he breaks out into even louder laughter. He and Gwen laugh at me for my stupidity. "You can't even escape from a dim-witted octopus," they say, "What kind of two-worlder are you? Fish eater!" Each time, I awake feeling embarrassed and ashamed, sad and lonely.

I spend some of my awake hours thinking of Jack, dreaming about the time on his boat, taking people on tours, and the many little instances where he smiled at me and I would go all weak inside. I imagine following his orders and doing all I can to please him as a soldier, determined to make him proud. I imagine that in some way he cares about me. What is he thinking now? How did he react when he heard I was gone? Was he angry with me because Pisces was lost? Would he try to rescue me?

These hours of thought are followed by fitful sleep and disturbing nightmares. I dream that I am training under Celia. I follow her on diving expeditions, always searching for something that is not there. Sometimes I talk to the air around our little boat, but Celia punishes me with slaps to the face. In one dream, she makes me the

194

example of training failure. "Look at her well, recruits. Evelyn Marin is the perfect example of how to get caught. Follow her path and you will all end in ruin. Associate with her at all and you will still end up in ruin." I come at her with my mace over my head, ready to fight her and show my strengths, but she blows me back with her current control. Just as I use the water to freeze her to the point of death, her face changes into my mom, pained and confused. Why would her daughter do this to her?

My mom. That same woman whom I barely spoke to on our last day together, whom I left behind pleading for my safety. How can I ever face her again? What can I say to her when she loved me so much but I abandoned her? What would *she* do now that I am gone?

Weeks pass in this stupor of inner emotional abuse. Then one night a new dream enters my sleep. It is a dream I know well – like a memory.

A familiar yearning creeps into my heart, pulling me and pushing me forward. My body follows the motions that I have no control over. Instinct is making me adhere to a path I am meant to pursue. I am in the ocean and I feel completely at ease, even at home. I am in a cold and lightless hallway, heading toward my doorway. Then, instinct is gone, choice taking its place. I don't need that yearning to pull me forward, I am going to take myself to face my destiny.

As I near the door, I feel a familiar warmth pulsating behind it. The water which has been so frigid is now comfortable and inviting. I open the door and blink to help my eyes adjust to the brightness inside. This time, though, I see more than I have ever seen before. Despite the cold and deteriorating exterior hallway, this room is warm and lavishly furnished. It is round with a pearlescent patterned finish on the walls. Gold and jewel gilt frames surround crystal clear paintings of a time long past. Men and women, wrapped in ancient white robes cover every painting. Some are laughing and singing, their ringleting hair forever captured in a happy bounce. Others are praising a god, dropping jewels and fruit on the top of an ornate altar. Still more are weeping over a great loss, perhaps the death of a child or a king, draping their scarlet capes over a casket, covering their heads in sackcloth. I am moved by their grief and my own heart reaches out to theirs in pity.

As I move around to view the pictures in the room, I watch myself to keep from swimming into furniture. Incredible ottomans and lounging couches sit beneath each painting. Every item is different. Some are covered in a pure white satin, others are encrusted with jewels on the arms and legs. A few have very decorative and ornate pillows to lounge on, some have decorative tables to the side, covered with books. I bend down to look at one of the titles and am stunned by what I read. Tinnaeus by Plato. This is a relic of ancient literature containing a partial account of the fall of Atlantis. It is a book I have learned about but never seen. It was lost when Atlantis first sank into the sea. Beneath it is its cousin work, Critias, also by Plato. Both books are bound in scarlet-shaded leather and embossed with gold letters. But lying next to these ancient works is a far more modern book on the same subject. The Sunken Kingdom: The Atlantis Mystery Solved, by Peter James.

I turn from admiring these works and face the center of the room. And there it is, just as it always is in my dreams. That ball of spherical perfection, glowing with radiating light. Swirling designs of light and dark liquid, pale yellow and gold, move about within the ball. It is nearly half my size but floats midair at the level of my eyes. I feel the ball reaching out to me, calling me to it and telling me who it is. It is like a living soul is reaching out to me, seeking to shake my hand in greeting. I am being offered an introduction. Am I going to take it? The fear that normally seizes me when I find this globe is not present. Only curiosity fills me now. Yet, I still know what awaits me if I touch that glasslike orb.

A movement to my right draws my attention to another person in the room. There stands Kai, still wearing his robe, his eyes more awake this time. He is saying something to me. I cannot understand his words but their meaning is unmistakable. He is encouraging me to take hold of the sphere. I am uneasy and unsure why this man is encouraging me to do something that will lead to my death. Then I hear them. The voices I always hear. Kai's voice is mixed with theirs. The others are outside the room, far down the hallway, but they are fighting, and not just with words. I hear the dull clinking of metal hitting metal in water. I know a battle has reached this place.

Then they burst into the room and this time I can see their faces: Celia, my mother, General Samson and others I have seen in the glowing city Ceto leads. I am filled with the need to act. I panic. I know what I have to do, but it frightens me. There is no time to think. I have to act now. I reach my hand forward in a desperate attempt to capture the brilliant stone. At the same time, Kai reaches for it as well. I look into his face to understand what he is doing and as I do,

he is no longer Kai. He is Gwen.

Chapter 25

I wake with a start. Gwen. How on earth could I lay around and wallow in my own sorrows when Gwen is still here, somewhere in these walls. I know I have to make an attempt to find her. I have to know that she is alright.

When my guard changes, I try to reach out to his mind. He turns to face me for a brief moment, but does nothing else to return the conversation. When I try using my voice to speak, it comes out raspy and gargled. It's been too long since I have used my voice. This croaking draws a shudder of laughter from my octopus guard, but no other response. He is not going to engage in any kind of conversation with me. So, when my meal comes, I decide to make the most of it. I eat the unappetizing shrimp and its raw, kelp garnish knowing that I will need strength if I am going to do anything for my situation. I instantly regret eating the food as I feel nausea washing over me. But after sitting still, the feeling passes and I begin to feel more energy. I decide to come up with plans as I sit in silence near my guard.

Maybe three days drag on this way. I try talking to each new guard, both mentally and vocally, but none of them are willing to speak to me. I eat all that is brought to me and think of my possibilities for escape. It is possible that I can find a way to create a distraction during the changing of my guards. Maybe there is a weakness I can exploit to my advantage. But with none of my guards willing to talk to me, it is difficult to find their vulnerabilities. Periodically, I hear the sounds of other prisoners moving about or calling from their cells. I strain to see through my bars and get a better idea of how the cell block is arranged, but each time my guard moves in front of my face to impede my view. For the most part, the entire hallway is silent. I don't know how my guards stay awake. I would have been asleep so many times if I weren't so focused on trying to plan my escape. I try to watch for patterns in their behavior, something that gives away a blind spot or a flaw in their routine, but I have not yet found anything useful. So many of my own sea talents are only useful at or near the surface: tide control, wave control, the air above water. There is little I can use them for so far down. Finally, after days of eating rancid food and regaining strength, I have an incredible stroke of luck. Gus is back as my guard. He brings a heaping plate of cooked seaweed, just like I ate with Ceto. It looks so good I could cry.

Ceto hear you eating your food and much better prisoner, Gus says with his mind.

Oh, Gus. I am trying. I am so happy to see you.

I happy you acting better. You scare Gus when you no talk me. Ceto say you act better, you eat better. He places the food into my cell. I eat ravenously at first, just thrilled to have something other than old shrimp to eat. Once my stomach starts feeling better, I eat slowly and take time to savor each bite. I am aware of Gus watching me. He says nothing while I eat, letting me enjoy my food. I know he was sent to watch and report back to Ceto on how I am doing. This is going to be where I will create a plan. Be a model and repentant prisoner. Try to get back into Ceto's good graces. And find a way out.

Thank you so much, Gus, I say as I finish the last of the food. *Please tell Ceto that I appreciate her kindness.* I feel Gus brighten.

Oh Ceto be so glad hear you say so, he says. *I sure I see you again soon.* He takes my plate and goes, leaving a new guard in his place.

Ceto is keeping tabs on me even in the dungeon. My link to my family (and hers) has some kind of value to her. I cannot imagine any other reason why she would check on me. Maybe it is for Kai. Maybe not. Maybe she thinks I know something I don't. Why else would she have reached out to me in the beginning? I am sure she will see me again if I behave.

For what feels like several days, I continue my pattern of good behavior. I eat everything I am given, and I make sure to be up and active each day. Although my cell is small, I know laying around in a depressed state won't garner any favor with my captors. I swim, maneuvering the tricky stances and movements I learned while in battle training. I even play with water temperature control – careful to do nothing that can be seen or felt by my guards. Today, my food is a little too cool for my taste and I use the water to heat it up. I get a little carried away and end up burning some of my seaweed. I eat it quickly, hoping my guard won't notice. It tastes good, with that burned, smoky flavor added to it. Smoky is something rarely tasted or smelled in my sea quarters. Fire and smoke are obvious land qualities and I find myself missing my home on land, my mom, school, even my roommates.

As I finish my last bite, a new plate is placed in my cell. A little bowl sits on top and inside is seafoam pudding. When I look up to thank my guard, I see Gus standing in the doorway of my cell.

You big treat now, Evelyn. Ceto send and say ask if Evelyn friend to Ceto again.

So, Ceto sent a message. She heard that my behavior has improved and wants to reach out to me. Maybe she thinks I will be more pliable this time. Spending weeks in this watery dungeon should have been enough to break me. But Ceto doesn't know me well enough. I am going to use this opportunity to my advantage. I have a friend to rescue and a home to return to.

Yes, Gus, I reply. *I am ready and willing to be Ceto's friend again. Please tell her I am grateful for her generosity.*

Gus' eyes squint at that last word.

You tell Ceto yourself, he says, *She say you eat pudding, then I can take you to her.*

I am satisfied with how things are working out. I say a little inward prayer of gratitude and eat my pudding like a good prisoner. When I finish, Gus moves out of the doorway so I can follow him. I haven't been out of that little room for so long, I am surprised by how good it feels to enter a hallway. Finally, a change of scenery. No wonder Ceto thinks I have broken. As Gus scoops me in two of his tentacles, my thoughts turn to Gwen. I can't help but wonder what her accommodations are. Where has she been this entire time? Is she still alive? Why haven't I seen her? Has she been turned to Ceto's side? Maybe Gus knows where she is being held.

Gus, what has happened with my friend Gwen? Do you know where she is being kept? Has she been taken care of and fed? Is she okay? Is she alone in her cell or with other prisoners? I overwhelm my poor guard with so many questions at once, but I can't help it. I am concerned for my friend.

I feel a warm smile and sense of satisfaction coming from Gus. *You no need worry,* he says, *You friend Gwen good girl. She eat good and sleep good.*

That is a relief to me. At least I know she is alive and isn't being harmed. *Thank you, Gus. But where is she being kept? Is she down here where I have been or is she where I was at first or is she somewhere else?* If I am going to stage a successful rescue operation, I need to know where she is. But before Gus can answer, we are leaving the lower levels of the prison and are headed toward my first prison block. I see several more two-worlders this time. Perhaps they were also captured in the battle. Perhaps they are from another battle or operation of Ceto's. At least they are still in the nicer area of the prison. I search faces for anyone I recognize. Then I see *him.*

I turn my gaze ahead again when I see his eyes. My mouth goes dry and my stomach does a strange flip and my heart gets soft and I threaten tears. And yet, when I do look straight into his hazel eyes, I feel embarrassment and anger. I entrusted so much to him and he betrayed me. He was supposed to be my boyfriend and how well had that worked out? But I cannot deny that seeing James, my James, in this prison setting is so unsettling that I can no longer think clearly. How did he get here? I didn't see him in the battle. I thought I saw him once on my way home for leave. But during my months of

203

training I worked myself to pieces to avoid both him and Gwen completely. He must have been in another group of 50. That is why I never saw him. But why is he here? Was he captured in the same battle I was? My head is swimming. He catches my gaze and is stunned. He is surrounded by a group of guards. Maybe he was recently captured. Maybe he is being transported to a darker cell for misbehavior. I want to call to him and tell him to play along, to bide his time patiently until the right opportunity for force comes along, but the only thing I can do is droop heavily into Gus' tentacles as he takes me to our Captor.

Chapter 26

When we make it to the palace, Gus lays me on an ottoman in the same room I was in when I first met Ceto. A prickly sensation tickles my arms as they lean against the gold embroidery of the pillows. I open my eyes slowly to find Gus hovering near my head, at attention, two eels twisted together at my side. They are doctor and nurse and are talking together about me. They speak to someone else in the room using zaps of electricity shot into the water. I have never heard an eel speak before, but I think they are announcing that I am awake. Gus looks down at me. When he sees that everything is alright, he goes back to attention. I sense someone coming to my side and look to see Ceto advancing from behind the eels. "Ah, so I see," she says. "Thank you so much for your care, doctors. We shall watch over her from here." The two eels zap a reply and slide back to the floor. They exit through another doorway, nearer to the entrance to the kitchen. Ceto turns her attention fully to me.

"You gave us quite a scare, my dear. Here I thought I would be welcoming a friend to my table again and instead you were brought here no more alert than the swordfish on my plate."

I wonder about the fish on her plate. Maybe her subjects are punished that way. The thought makes me ill and I turn my attention back to Ceto.

"Are you feeling alright, dear? Should I call the doctors back in?" she asks.

"Thank you, no," I reply as I try to sit myself up. "The feeling is passing now." Ceto reaches her hand behind my head to help me sit up, her tentacles rearranging the pillows I am leaning on. "I really feel okay," I try to assure her, "I don't know what came over me. Maybe I was moving too fast." Ceto gives Gus a reproving look and he shrinks lower.

"Well, you're here with us now and that is all that matters," Ceto says. I don't understand what she means by 'us.' Is there someone else whom I am to meet? Maybe it is just Kai again. As I sit up on the ottoman, I stop. There, seated at the table, is Gwen.

My eyes bulge when I see her and I cry out, "Gwen!" Ceto turns with a smile from me to face my roommate and friend. Gwen rises from the table and makes her way to the ottoman where I lie. Her color looks good, though her eyes have black circles beneath them. She is strong and able bodied, not thin and wasted away as I had feared. There is so much I want to say to her, so much to ask, but we aren't alone. We are in the castle of the enemy – prisoners to both her kindness and insanity.

Ceto moves to the head of the ottoman, her hand resting on my shoulder. Gwen sits by my legs. "Evelyn. I am so happy to see you," Gwen says. She is smiling from ear to ear and I see real happiness shining in her eyes. A wave of relief floods over me as I take her hand. Gwen is alive and she is well.

Ceto allows us this moment to embrace, watching us with satisfaction. I don't understand her ulterior motives for treating us this way. But I know I have to play her game until I can find a way out of here. After a few minutes, our meal is brought out.

"Do you think you are well enough to make it to the table, my dear, or do you prefer eating here at the couch?" Ceto asks.

"I think I am fine now, thank you," I reply.

"Very well then. Gus, will you please help Miss Marin to the table?"

Gus holds out a tentacle for me and I pushed myself up from the ottoman. He doesn't wrap a tentacle around me this time. There is nowhere for me to go. I use his tentacle instead as a floating crutch to make my way to where Ceto motions for me to sit. This time I am on her left side, facing both Gwen across the table and the large stone door across the room. Gus stands guard while we eat. Ceto doesn't trust me fully yet.

"Thank you for inviting me here and thank you so much for inviting Gwen," I begin, but Ceto interrupts me.

"My dear, it was always my intention to take care of you and have you stay with me. Until your unfortunate display, I had thought we were going to be good friends." I look duly ashamed of my behavior. I know my plans depend on it.

"I am so sorry for acting like that," I say. "I think it was just the shock of the day and that particular meeting. So much has changed for me since I moved to Florida." I keep my eyes on the plate in front of me and do my best to show remorse. I want her to buy into every bit of it. I have a chance to help the war. Maybe I am young and naïve, but I am going to give it everything I have.

Ceto regards me with wary, but gentle eyes. She is silent for a moment, her hands laced just below her chin. "Yes," she finally says as she lowers her green and greying hands, "I'm sure it has been a very confusing time for you, my dear. It has been an unlucky few weeks. Shall we let bygones be bygones?"

A few weeks?! Is that how long I have been in the dungeon? What happened during that time? How is the Atlantean army? How is my mother? These thoughts and questions race through my mind as I calmly answer. "Yes, please let's let bygones be bygones. Thank you for your understanding."

Ceto places her hand on mine and gives it a squeeze. "Now, I'm sure you would like to talk with Gwen. How about you two catch up during the meal and you and I can talk after?" I love the idea until I realize that Ceto plans to stay seated at the table with Gwen and me. We can talk, but we will be heard.

"Thank you, Ceto," I say.

"Aunt Ceto, my dear. Remember, we are relations."

"Of course," I smile, "Aunt Ceto." She is pleased and turns her attention to her meal, her ears open, listening eagerly. I look across the table to face Gwen.

"Gwen, I am so happy to see you. I have been so worried about you." Gwen's face is placid as she hides her emotions from Ceto.

"I am okay, Evelyn," She says with confidence. "I have been taken care of. I am so happy to have you here with us this evening." But she makes it sound so casual, as if this were not the first time she has dined with Ceto. Maybe Ceto has been grooming Gwen for my return, eating lavish meals together, making sure she is well cared for. She wants Gwen on her side – any Atlantean on her side in dealing with me – whatever it is she wants me for.

"I'm glad too," I keep away from asking about her stay in Ceto's prison. That conversation would get the wrong kind of attention from Ceto. So, I to stick to the several weeks beforehand where we hardly saw each other. "How are your classes going?" Gwen gives a chuckle and shakes her head like she is trying to clear something out of it; trying to think back that far.

"They are going well enough, I suppose. I spent a lot of time at the library, studying. My history class was pretty boring. Mr. Halcyon took a leave of absence so we were stuck with a fill-in teacher who is barely older than I am." Mr. Halcyon was the merman I saw with mom the day I came out of the ocean and found her at the water's edge. He has been teaching in Atlantis. Gwen should know that's why he had a land replacement. Wasn't she taking the classes in Atlantis? Something prickles in my stomach as I look at Gwen. Something isn't right. Maybe Ceto has turned her after all. We continue to make small talk about classes until we finish our meal. Seafoam pudding is brought out for dessert. I wonder if Ceto eats it at all of her meals.

"Well, ladies," she says with satisfaction, "I have enjoyed listening to the two of you get acquainted again. I hope I'm not being too insufferable by reinserting myself into the conversation."

"No, of course not," I say.

"Not at all," Gwen says.

"Well, that pleases me," Ceto says with a smile. "Gwen, you are welcome to stay if that is preferable to Evelyn."

"I would love to have Gwen with us," I say. I don't want to lose Gwen again.

"I thought as much," is Ceto's reply. "Shall we adjourn to a more comfortable seating area?"

We leave our seats and follow Ceto to the couches. Her six tentacles roll along the floor as they propel her forward. It looks like the movement of a lavish skirt.

The couches are all white. The same octopus chandelier sconces by the table line the walls where we sit down. I wondered if Ceto revels in her future as an octopus or if it frightens her. Is she using this décor as a show to mask her fear? Ceto sits first in a large, white chair with golden armrests and legs and motions for Gwen and me to sit. Gwen takes the ottoman and I take the couch on the other side of Ceto.

"You know, I envy you girls," Ceto says. "You are just starting out your life in the sea. And you have such good relationships with those about you. You have me, of course, and I am here to lead you and guide you in this new life. I think we are going to get along so nicely." This is my opening to get Ceto talking about herself and her plans again.

"Yes, Aunt, you were telling me about when you first decided to enter into life in the ocean." I want to keep her happy, so I skip over her life with her father. "What was it like for you then?"

Ceto sits back and gets comfortable in her chair, ready for a long story. Gwen relaxes and pulls her legs onto the ottoman. I rest against the arm of the couch, but I am still leaning forward with complete attention given to Ceto.

"In the sea, I felt like I belonged – finally," Ceto begins. "I was surrounded by two-worlders just like me. People who were drawn to the sea. So many had long lines of family history that dated back thousands of years in the ocean. But there were just as many who had no past ties to the sea at all. Some came from wonderful families who had loved them their entire lives. Others were complete outcasts like me. But none of that mattered in the sea. We were all joined together in our likeness and abilities. We all had incredible talents and skills which we were working to improve and grow. Oh, I made so many friends. I was so happy." Ceto takes a deep breath and lets out a long sigh as the water swirls around her face.

"Eventually I met Adrian – your father's brother," she says as she turns to me and I glance at Gwen. This is the first time she has heard the details about my relationship to Ceto. She keeps her eyes steady on our enemy. "There wasn't a kinder or more wonderful man in all of the sea," Ceto continues. "He was strong and handsome. So many girls fell madly head-over-heels for him. But I had never been taught how to love properly. I assumed I was worthless. Yes, I was accepted by the friends I made and the other two-worlders, but I didn't think it would be possible to actually find something to *love* about me," Ceto rests back in her chair, gazing ahead and remembering another time. "But Adrian found something in me that he thought was wonderful. We spent so many hours together after our training, just talking and swimming and enjoying our abilities.

"Then one day, he confessed his feelings for me. He loved me and wanted me to be his wife. *Me.* I had been so in love with him for so long, but hadn't even imagined that he could feel the same things for me. I was very happy.

"His family welcomed me into their arms at first," Ceto's happy smile fades slowly and a darker expression enters her eyes, a sadness that looks more a part of her than the smile.

"But then I started to change. For most sea people, their sea skin wouldn't begin to show until they had been in the water for a decade or more. I had only been living in the ocean for 12 or 13 months. But my skin, of course, wasn't the shiny, scaled version I assumed would come to me," her voice grows angry and I see a reddish color creeping up her neck and into her face as she speaks.

"No, I was destined to be undesirable from the day I was born. I hadn't inherited anything that was lovely or wonderful or acceptable. I was born to be an outcast," her voice is low and rumbling as she continues, "The skin on my legs was the first to show the change. A slick and shiny black started at my toes and worked its way up to my knees with a greenish tint affecting the rest of the skin on my legs. At first I was frightened, I thought I had contracted some kind of disease in the sea that my body just couldn't handle.

"Adrian was so gentle. He knew what it was that was happening to me and he reassured me that everything would be fine, that *we* would be fine. I was just taking on a form that we hadn't expected. That was all. We could still be happy together. Everything would be okay. But his family didn't feel the same way." The reddening of her face disappears as ashy grey/green once again takes over her face. She looks so much older. I pity her for the disappointments in her life.

"Adrian's mother, in particular, was a very superstitious woman. She was more than happy to welcome me into the family when I was sweet, adored, and normal Ceto. But when my skin changed, so did her opinion of me. She was certain that my changing had been a sign, a warning against my marriage to her son. Nothing he could say would change her mind. And his father was so controlled by her, that he dare not oppose her. 'Don't worry about this one, Adrian,' he said, 'there are plenty of other women in the sea. You will soon forget her.' Adrian was appalled and I was frightened. I didn't want to lose the one person who had ever shown me real love. I had grown such hopes that we could raise a real and loving family. All of those hopes were tumbling down on top of me, crushed by his vile mother and family." Ceto twists her hands as she remembers her youth.

"I want you to understand that your father and mother were on our side, Evelyn. They wanted Adrian's mother to accept me and assured her as best they could that all would be well, that we could be happily married and have a normal family. Your own parents had been married for just over a year and were expecting their first child – you. But nothing could dissuade that woman. She refused to give her blessing and Adrian's father refused to give his, too afraid to do anything different." Ceto straightens in her chair, looking faraway as she continues her story.

"Adrian convinced me that we should run away together, that we could elope and move back to the land before my transformation

213

took me too far. Once that happened, I wouldn't be able to survive on land. It took me an entire month to agree. I had so hoped we could find a way to convince his family to accept our union. By the time I said yes, the black and green changes had fully engulfed both of my feet. We were married secretly and made plans to leave as soon as we could find a home and make a living on land. Six grueling weeks went by and the day finally came that we were ready to leave our life in the sea behind." Ceto looks back to Gwen and me as she continues.

"On the day we were to leave Atlantis, I entered the kelp forest that we had determined as our meeting place. Every sound and movement made me shudder with fear. Where could he be? Had our secret been discovered? But just as the afternoon light was beginning to fade to gold, he found me. He wrapped me in his arms and held me so close that every fear and every worry I had been harboring in my heart just melted away. He kissed my face all over and buried his head into my hair. But, just as I relaxed my head into the hollow of his neck, he pulled me away from him.

"'Ceto,' he said, 'I am so happy that you are still here. There has been a lava breach near Atlantis and I have been fighting to hold it back all day.' He held me close again and continued, saying, 'I was worried sick, hoping and praying that you were safely here, waiting for me.'" A single tear floated from Ceto's eye and into the water. It started as a glistening drop but faded as it became one with all around it. Ceto continued.

"I would have waited forever for him. My heart was so happy. I had the man I loved, loving me in return. We were married and starting our life out together. The lava flow had been subdued enough

214

that Adrian knew it was in safe hands, so we picked up right where we had planned to and headed for the shore.

"As we rushed on our way, we swam into your mother and father. Your mother was so fully pregnant with you that it was difficult for her to move quickly through the water. We all understood that it was time for her to move ahead to shore. Adrian and I were so happy to be going with them. But then it happened."

I am familiar with this part of the story. I read it in my mother's journal. Ceto continues on with her version of the events of that day as Gwen and I listen quietly. Ceto tells how the lava made its way through the wall of Atlantis and my father and uncle rushed back to help. She talks about her delusional mother-in-law, my grandmother, throwing epithets and accusations her way. Then, the awful death of her husband and love. Here she stops, sinking into her chair. 17 years of time has done nothing to quell her emotions about these events. Ceto rises from her chair and crosses the room until she is nearer the table. After a brief moment of quiet, she turns to face us and continues her story.

"I was devastated and shocked beyond belief. My mother-in-law went completely insane and began accusing me of starting the lava flow. Sensing the threat that she was bringing about, Marisol – your mother and my dearest friend – took me by the wrist and together we made our way to the surface.

"But it was too late for me by then. If only Adrian and I had gotten away sooner, the change would not have been so advanced. But as it was, I found that I could not breathe once I broke the surface of the water. All I could do was wheeze and sputter. It was pitiful and devastating. Marisol had worked so hard getting us both to the surface and to safety that breathing was the only thing she could do. I looked into her eyes and I think we both knew what had to happen. She had to go to shore. I had to go back to the sea.

"My heart was breaking in so many ways that I couldn't say a word. I tried to convey all my love and pain and loss and life into a single look. And then I went back into the ocean." Ceto moves to the ottoman and takes Gwen by the hand.

Gwen is staring at Ceto with a look that I don't understand. It is somewhere between sympathy and irritation, like she can't decide how to feel about the woman in front of her. Even though I understand that Ceto is the enemy of Atlantis, she is still my aunt and I cannot help but feel sadness for her situation.

"What did you do once you went back into the ocean," I ask. "Where did you live and how did you survive?" I can tell that answering my question is something that Ceto is not excited about. Considering her life up to that point and where she is now, I can only imagine that life back in the ocean had not gone well for her at all. With a sigh, Ceto makes her way slowly back to her chair and sinks into its soft cushions while she speaks.

"I knew I had no other choice than to live in the sea forever. I had simply moved too quickly into my transformation to go back to the land. I don't know. Maybe I could have made it on land, lived with a wheeze for the rest of my life. Whatever my physical discomfort, I knew I wouldn't have lived for long. And I needed to live. You see, Evelyn, by the time Adrian and I were headed to live on the land, I was already with child."

Wow.

Just wow. My mouth dropped open and I was powerless to close it. Ceto was pregnant when my mom was pregnant with me. I am sure nobody in Atlantis even had a clue about this. I risk a glance at Gwen, but she is looking down, playing with the fringe on a nearby pillow. I look back at Ceto, questions pouring into my head. What happened next? Had she carried the baby full term? Had it lived after birth? Where was the child she had carried? All of these are questions I know would be out of place to ask. I shake my head to clear my thoughts.

"Oh Aunt Ceto. I had no idea." I reach my hand out to her in sympathy. She takes my hand gently in her own, looking into my eyes as she continues.

"For several months I tried to return to some kind of normal life. I tried to talk to Adrian's family, to tell them about the baby and how much I needed their support, but I received none. Your mother and father were already busy having a new baby of their own. They were the light of everyone's life. I was too much the opposite of what the family wanted and expected their son to marry. I don't think your parents ever even knew about my pregnancy."

That is true. I know my mom's sense of right would never have allowed her to abandon Ceto in her time of need. If only she had known.

"Your mother tried so many times to reach out to me from the land, but I couldn't face her. When the time came to deliver my baby, I went to an outcast sea nurse for help. We found a small cove with enough water and privacy that I could have my baby on land but still return to the sea as I needed. Breathing had become so difficult above water that it nearly killed me to give birth. But by an unseen power I was able to make it through the birth and had a healthy baby girl.

"I stayed in the cove and nursed her for a month. One month was all that I could stand before I knew my life was being drained out of me. The sea nurse who had helped me give birth attended to my needs while I recovered and cared for my child. But we could not keep on this way forever. Nobody from Atlantis would help two outcasts like us. We were completely alone and the meager living the sea nurse made was not enough to care for extra two-worlders.

"So, I did what I could and reached out to my half-sister, the one who told me when my father died. Though we had never been close, she was the least unkind of my family members. I had to trust that she would care for my baby and help her know about her mother, one day returning her to me in the sea."

I looked across at Gwen, but her expression surprises me. Her eyes are wide and she has a small smile on her face. It looks like she is trying to stifle a laugh. She seems to be amused by what Ceto is telling us about her past and her life. Maybe she just thinks Ceto is crazy. I don't think she understands there is another Ceto out there somewhere, someone we should be aware of and on the lookout for. I give her a single eyebrow, inquisitive look so she knows this isn't funny. She gives me one more half smile then looks back down at her pillow fringe.

As I turn toward Ceto, she is already looking at me intently. She isn't done talking and telling me what she needs to get out.

"Evelyn, you must understand this. Once I returned to the sea, I was shunned and outcast more than ever. I had lost my husband and my child – both within the same year. I was completely shunned by those who should have cared for me. I had to do something if I was going to survive. That's when my thoughts turned to the Atlantis power source."

"The Atlantis power source?" I ask, wanting instead to hear more about her baby, "I thought that was just a myth."

"No, my dear. It is very much real," she says. "It had been hidden for centuries but its power still gave life to all of Atlantis. I knew if I could harness that power that I would be able to force everyone to pay attention to me. I knew I could make them treat me with the respect I deserved. I was done being hated and tossed out of society. I was done losing all of my heart and love to the violent workings of land life. I knew I had to bring the balance of the ocean to the entire world. Then everyone would understand that they should never have underestimated me and judged me and condemned me. I was going to be a force that nobody could turn from ever again."

Her eyes are fervent and that reddish tint is creeping up her neck again and into her face. I feel an urgency in her voice. Gwen gets up from her seat as though she is bored with the conversation. I could not be more captivated. Ceto doesn't seem to notice Gwen's behavior. All of her attention is on me. She wants me to understand her. She wants me to accept her when nobody else will. I decide to see what else Ceto will tell me.

"What did you intend to do with the power source once you found it?" I ask.

Ceto leans back in her chair, dropping her hands on its arms. A smile plays at the corner of her mouth. She is satisfied that our conversation has led to this point. As she folds her hands together in her tentacle lap, she says, "I want to bring the ocean to the world, Evelyn. I want to cover the entire earth in water as it was meant to be."

Gwen, who has moved to the dining table at this point, actually lets out a laugh. Not anything long and resounding, but one loud and hard "Ha" as though she thinks the entire scheme is completely insane, which it is. But she is loud enough for Ceto to hear. Ceto focuses her attention on Gwen.

Rising from her chair, Ceto crosses the room to where Gwen is picking through some snacks on the table. Her movements frighten me and I stand from my seat to protect Gwen if I need to. But Gus is right by my side.

Do not upset yourself, Evelyn, he says. *Gwen be fine. This not first time she and Ceto disagree about this thing.*

Wait. What? What do you mean? Are you saying you have seen them together before?

I say no more, Evelyn. You just stay here and you watch.

Ceto takes Gwen by the arm and turns her body until they are facing each other. Gwen looks bored. She is risking her life by acting this way. How can she not see that? I cannot see Ceto's face, but the tone of her voice is anxious and pleading as she speaks to Gwen.

"Gwen. Gwen, my darling girl."

What. The. Heck.

"Gwen, I so want for you to understand. We have gone over this so many times. I didn't want to leave you. I was dying. I had no choice. To have brought you with me could have been death for you. We would have been cast out and who knows if your latent abilities would have even awakened so you could live in the sea?"

Gwen is Ceto's daughter. The one she sent to live with her half-sister. Gwen's upbringing was affectionless just like Ceto's and it was Ceto who put her there. With each new point she makes, Ceto shakes Gwen's shoulders ever so slightly. It is like she is trying to force understanding into her. Gwen raises her hands and shakes Ceto off.

"Look, *Mommy Dearest*, your stories may get thousands of your 'outcasts' to follow you, but they won't work for me. Look at Evelyn. You have her eating out of your hand." Gwen points to where I am standing by Gus and Ceto makes a quick glance in my direction, but I can see that she doesn't care about what I am thinking or doing. Her real purpose is to convince Gwen and she returns her gaze toward her daughter. *Her Daughter!*

"But *me*," Gwen continues, "You haven't convinced me. You will never convince me. You left me. You didn't care enough about me. You never reached out to me. You were hurting so you thought you could just sit in your ball of hurt and find some way to force everyone else to make *you* feel better. But you didn't care if I was hurting. You never reached outside of your own pain to lift the burden of your daughter." She turns from Ceto and goes to the other end of the table, her back to the rest of the room.

Ceto's shoulders sink with the weight of Gwen's words. It isn't the first time she has heard them. "In time, Gwen," Ceto says, "I hope you can forgive me. I hope you can understand. I hope you can come to love me."

As she utters those words, there is a commotion outside the door. A shark bursts in through the door the doctor eels left through.

"Your majesty, we are under attack," He says. "We have been discovered and the enemy is at our gates."

Ceto straightens and goes into commander and monarch mode.

"Get the city cleared," she commands. "We have prepared for this eventuality, Captain Slee. The people will know what to do."

Captain Slee swims out the door and starts barking orders to everyone he sees. 'Get Going!' 'Get to your posts!' 'This is just like our drills!' I hear his commands echoing down the hall, through the open door. Gwen stands at the end of the table, fear written across her face. Ceto has other places to be. She embraces Gwen around the shoulders, and though Gwen doesn't even respond, Ceto whispers a few words into her ear. To me she nods and says, "I hope we have time to finish our discussion later, Evelyn. I must see to the battle and the welfare of my people.

"Gus," she says. He stiffens at attention, "take these girls to the safety bunker next to my own. Make sure they have enough food and protection then join your comrades at your post." And with a flourish of tentacles, she swims out the door.

Chapter 27

I feel as shell-shocked as Gwen looks. I can hardly believe what is happening. I am a prisoner and my enemy is under attack. My enemy also happens to be my aunt and it turns out that my friend is also my cousin. Oh, and I am being guarded deeper into the fortress by an octopus. An octopus who is becoming a friend to me.

Gus is swimming hastily through the halls, a single tentacle around me and another around Gwen.

Where are you taking us, Gus?

A booming sound comes from just outside the hallway and the cave walls tremble.

Gus take you safe place.

Another blast. The people of Atlantis are here and very, very close. If I am ever going to get out of here, it has to be now.

Gus, I know you want to follow Ceto and take us where she asked, but if you let us go, we have the chance to be free and not be prisoners anymore.

You safe with Gus. You not safe in battle.

But, Gus, I am a trained soldier, remember? If you let us go at a safe place, we can get back to the Atlanteans on our own.

223

Ceto no be happy I let you go. And no be happy I let Gwen go. Gwen her daughter, Evelyn.

Yes, Gus, I know. But Gwen doesn't want to be here anymore than I do. She is Ceto's daughter, but she is also a prisoner.

More rattling of walls. We are nearing an opening that was blasted through the cave. Atlanteans are swimming toward the hole that leads into Ceto's palace. Gus pauses, unsure of what to do now that his path is blocked and his queen is being invaded by the enemy. He doesn't have the ability to think his way around that.

Gus, let us go here. Our people are coming and will not hurt us.

I feel the battle within him as he hovers, silently staring at the opening in the wall.

Gus, please. You have taken such good care of me, just like a friend would do. I think you are my friend, Gus. Don't you think you are my friend?

He swells with pride as he understands that I am calling him my friend. He has wanted that title ever since I first came to Ceto's fortress. I feel the tentacle around my waist slacken.

Oh Evie friend. You make Gus so happy. Yes I you friend. I let you go. But what I do when Ceto find me?

Gus, come with us. You can live with us in Atlantis. Together we can defeat Ceto and show how well all of the ocean can live together and be friends. Nobody needs to force anyone.

My guard considers this thought for a moment, but before he can answer, the first Atlanteans are through the opening in the palace wall. Gus is unprepared. This isn't his post. He is out of his element and training. He freezes where he is, his tentacles tightening around my waist again. As the first of the troops make their way through the door, they move straight toward us, shouting at Gus to let us go. He stays there, frozen. Gwen comes to her senses and pushes at Gus, trying to get free. When an Atlantean soldier grabs hold of my arm, it pulls Gus out from whatever trance he is in. He reacts instinctively, pulling me away and raising his tentacles to fight off the invaders. He pulls a sconce off of the cave wall and uses it as a weapon.

It is like watching slow-motion as he swings and swings at the invaders. I scream and scream at the invaders – my people, trying to get them to stop. Gus will not harm us. He will let us go. He is afraid and confused. But the sound of the battle is too much for my voice to reach the Atlanteans. More and more of them make their way through the blast in the hallway. Gus is forced back into the room from which we came. Once we reach the room, Gus tries closing the door, but he is overpowered. He tries so hard to hold on to Gwen and me, but there is too much going on. We slip out of his tentacles as he fights off the enemy Ceto gave him. I scream to him with my mind as loud and as strong as I can.

Please stop, Gus, my friend! They will overpower you and hurt you! Please, Gus! They will kill you if you don't stop fighting! Please stop!

Finally, Gus gets the message I am trying to send. He stops what he is doing and turns to face me. But he is too late. A huge mace – my weapon of choice – comes gliding through the water from an unseen hand and strikes Gus squarely on his bare head.

I don't need to look anymore. I know that Gus can't survive that kind of blow. His skull is so much softer than my own. He has no helmet. I know he is dead. As my head sinks down to my chest, I see his lifeless body sinking to the floor. My fellow Atlanteans have no idea that they have killed an innocent creature. Gus was only following Ceto because she reached him first. But I had reached his soul. He would have made a better choice if he had lived to do it.

The soldiers swim over his motionless body, some toward Gwen and me, some toward the large stone door. They are shouting to Gwen and me but I am reeling. Just as the door to this beautiful room opens, I sink to the floor and start to cry. Hands, fully human hands, reach out for me on the floor. I am carried in a pair of strong arms out to where the battle is raging. Gwen is swimming out on her own. She has no desire to follow in her mother's footsteps. She wants Atlantis.

I just watched a friend die. I am so lost in tears that I can hardly move. My mind is still calling out to Gus. I still receive only silence.

I am carried somewhere near the back of the battle. I hear voices shouting that I have been found. They are grateful. My tears slow as I take in the scene around me. What am I supposed to do? I am left in a sea-cart where I can be tended to by a nurse, but I don't have any wounds for her to heal. My pain is all internal. I look toward the battle at the walls of Ceto's home. The amazing fortress is quickly being overtaken by Atlanteans. But, to my surprise, the battle is slowing. Where are the fighters for the other side? I expect there to be defenses firing from the tops of the palace walls, but there is nothing. Several sharks, eels, stingrays, octopi, and others of Ceto's sea creatures are being rounded up by Atlanteans, prisoners of war. But for the most part, the palace is desolate.

James.

I forgot about James. What about the prisoners kept in Ceto's dungeon? Were they freed? I put my hurting for Gus in a little box and stow it away in my heart as I rise from the makeshift bed I have been sitting on. The nurse protests, but I assure her I am fine and I leave the cart.

I swim to where the prison entrance lies below Ceto's home. Atlanteans are conducting a thorough search of the hallways and cells, but it is completely empty.

"What happened? Where are all of the prisoners?" I ask of a soldier nearby. He is in full battle armor, with a club in one hand and a shield in the other.

"They had an evacuation plan ready. We were only able to save a handful of her prisoners before the rest were taken and hidden away with the rest of the city," he answers.

"But where are the ones we rescued being kept?" I ask.

"They are in the back of the company by now. I'm sure Lady Pescara has questions for them."

I thank the soldier and swim away again from the city walls, making my way toward the back of the company. My heart falls when I reach them. There couldn't have been more than a half dozen rescued Atlanteans. I search their faces but recognize none of them. Panic stricken, I ask each of them if they have seen James. I describe his features: his hazel eyes, light freckles and auburn hair. But nobody registers what I am asking of them. They are still too dazed from the battle.

I am getting ready to leave when one final Atlantean joins the group. His face is bruised and he has a large gash on his shoulder that hasn't been tended to properly. When I pelt him with my questions, his face registers understanding, then disgust.

"Oh, I saw that one alright," he says. "He led me to my cell. Told me if I knew what was best, I'd be a saint. But I wasn't a saint, see? I don't take orders from the enemy and that guy let me have it." I'm not sure I understand what the man is saying. I am beginning to think he is talking about someone else. He continues, "He made sure I got one good sock in the gut every day, right before dinner. Then he would take my plate away before I could finish eating. Said I had better start talking if I wanted to eat a decent meal. Said if I didn't show Sergeant James some humility, I wasn't going to get any kind of meal. I tell you I hate Ceto and everything she stands for. Her little fish army isn't so bad to deal with, but when her follower is a two-worlder, watch out! They aren't going to take any pity on you."

I watch silently as the man is taken to have his injuries treated. I cannot understand what he means. It is a mistake. I saw James in the prison as I was being taken to Ceto. He was surrounded by an octopus guard. Wasn't he? Was he inside the cell or outside of it? Was he a prisoner or a guard himself? I can't remember. I think about what he said to me months ago about a woman who was changing into a different creature. I assumed that he meant Lady Pescara with her mermaid tail, but maybe it was actually Ceto. I hadn't seen any other two-worlders than those living in the city below the palace. Ceto kept

228

only full sea creatures around her all the time. Is James the exception to that rule?

I am brought out of my thoughts when I notice another former prisoner being brought to the group. It is Kai. His black robe is missing and he is dazed and confused. His skin is grey, and where his legs should have been a gorgeous merman tail has taken their place. A triple-layered row of scales winds around his mid-section with a slight dip below his belly button. He wears no shirt and I see that his torso and arms are strong from years of swimming in the sea. His feet are the only thing on his lower body to look at all human. His toes are webbed, yes, and scales are creeping down the tops of his feet, but I can see that the skin on his feet is turning into a gauzy white, a precursor to the split fin they will become.

Once he reaches me, the guard holding him asks another soldier to get the nurse to him quickly and alert Lady Pescara. Kai raises his head and sees my face. His face is worn and worried and strained with years of stress and concern. But as our eyes meet, he sighs deeply and says, "Evelyn. Oh my Evelyn. You are safe," then he cries. When the guard looks at him, then at me, I see understanding dawning in his eyes. The nurse arrives at that moment with a small carrying cot for Kai.

"Could you help me get him into the cot, Evelyn," the guard asks. I cannot say no to him. Kai looks so weak and sad, how can I not help him. I come to his side, his guard still holding him on the left. I wrap my arm around his waist and put his arm around my shoulder. He is still crying softly and saying my name over and over.

It is like he is trapped in some kind of dream. The kind of dream where he can't wake up and he is trying to save somebody – me.

Chapter 28

It takes a week to get back to Atlantis. We travel at a slow pace as we have to accommodate the wounded as well as prisoners. Everyone is worn out from the strain of travel and battle. I learn that the battle I saw when I was captured lasted for nearly twenty hours. It wasn't until two days later, when the accounting of wounded and dead were being made, that anyone recognized I was missing. Pisces died before the battle ended. Nobody saw what happened to him because we were so far behind the fray. A heavy weight lives on my shoulders now as I feet guilt and responsibility for his death. When Jack realized that Pisces was dead and I was missing, he went directly to Lady Pescara. My abilities were too valuable to allow me to be captured, and all generals were employed in figuring out where I had gone and how to get me back. When the Atlanteans attacked Ceto's city, they weren't even sure I would be there. All they knew from their spies was that several others had been taken prisoner and were being held there. But everyone was relieved to discover that I was alive and well. That did very little to comfort me.

I have spent much of this traveling week sitting alongside Kai. Whatever he is to me, I cannot leave such a pitiful creature on his own when I have power to help him. For several days, he tosses and turns in his traveling cot with fitful dreams and nightmares. I hold his hand, rub his arm, and speak soothing words to his sleeping ears until he finally quiets down and returns to a peaceful rest. It is amazing how much you can come to care for a person you are serving. I do not yet accept him as my father, but I still feel protective of him and have started to feel more than general concern for his welfare.

The nurse tells me she is certain he was either drugged or under some kind of mind control. It was rumored that Ceto was using those methods to draw other of the less willing two-worlders to her cause. No one knows about the source of her power to control minds. Kai is the first two-worlder captured alive who can be of any use to us. But he is in such a state of confusion and healing that we have to wait for him to recover before we can get any kind of useful information from him. Once we make it back to Atlantis, I make sure Kai is safely settled in the hospital. He will be cared for there by the best sea doctors from all forms of sea life and two-worlder life, that is except for the smooth-skinned creatures like eels, sharks, and octopi. Once I have gotten Kai settled in, I am summoned by Lady Pescara for a debriefing.

It feels surreal to be back in my Atlantean home. I swim the streets only partially aware of where I am headed. Fortunately, Jack is with me or I would have gotten lost. We make our way, weaving through the city streets to the government building where Lady Pescara is waiting. Jack came to see me several times on the journey home to check on how I was doing. I still remember our final meeting and the feeling I had when he held me, but I am so consumed with the things that have happened that I can't give him much of my focus. This is the first time we've been together alone.

"What does Lady Pescara want from me?" I ask as we swim.

"It's just a regular debriefing, Evelyn. You were held captive by Ceto and had actual communication with her. Anything you have to share could be helpful to us as we continue to plan and strategize." Finally I am going to be useful. I wanted to spend as much time as I could with Ceto for this very reason. I wanted to gain something useful. I hope that what I did learn will be helpful to Atlantis.

When we arrive at the doors of the government building, Jack swings one open wide for me and allows me to go in first. He places his hand on the small of my back as I enter and he follows closely behind. I get a tingle up my spine from the contact. It is a feeling I have not felt for a long time. A fish guard – very similar to Pisces – announces us to Lady Pescara before we enter her office. I am suddenly saddened to see this fish here in this place and I long to be with my friend again. Lady Pescara greets us in a warm yet official fashion and invites us each to take a seat near her desk. She remains upright in front of her chair, using her large and fully developed mermaid fin to keep her aloft. I recognize the underwater map on the wall behind her desk. I saw it when I first came to Atlantis. But now it has several new markings in a dark brown ink. It takes me a moment to realize it is Ceto's fortress city. It was recently drawn in as it was discovered by the Atlanteans.

"I cannot tell you how pleased we all are to know that you are safely back with us, Evelyn," says Lady Pescara. "We feared for your life when we discovered Pisces." I shudder and can feel the color leave my face as she mentions Pisces. Lady Pescara notices my reaction and takes sympathy on me. "I am very sorry for your loss,

Evelyn. I know you were fond of Pisces and he was fond of you." A single tear escapes from the corner of my eye and enters the salty water we sit in. I nod my head, too choked up to speak. "Evelyn," she continues, "I know this must have been a terrible and difficult time for you. I know it is hard to go over such painful memories and talk about them. But I am going to have to ask you many questions. We are still at war with Ceto and any information you may have gained while her prisoner could be helpful to us. Do you think you are strong enough to talk with me? I know it is what Pisces would have wanted."

I know she is right. Pisces would never have allowed sentiment or difficulty to keep him from his duty. Besides, there are so many things I want to share that can change life under the sea forever. Like how Gus and the other octopi have no real allegiance to Ceto. Maybe if Atlanteans had reached out to them sooner, we could have avoided this war and all the pain that it has inflicted so far. Maybe Ceto would never have turned against her Atlantean home. Maybe. Maybe. Maybe. Maybe I can help find an end to this madness. So, I take a deep breath and tell Lady Pescara I am ready to help her in any way I can.

"Good," she says, "I'm glad to hear it. I know it must be painful, Evelyn, but I would like to start from the beginning. Can you tell me how you came to be captured and Pisces killed?"

I feel like I have just been sucker-punched. I am prepared to share all I know about Ceto, but I am not ready to talk about the events leading to my capture. I feel so much shame washing over me. I hadn't thought about it since becoming a prisoner. I wanted to protect myself, to protect Pisces. I must be pale because Lady Pescara tells me I can take all the time I need. I turn slowly to look at Jack, wanting to see that he still cares about me for a few more minutes before I completely disappoint him. I take a deep breath then straighten in my chair to begin my story.

I start with how I was given very clear orders and had been completely frustrated by them. I cry openly as I talk about how I tried to force Pisces to let me fight. I talk about how my arguing made us fall so far behind the army, open victims to the other side. I apologize over and over for being so stubborn and for disobeying a direct order. This is not what I was trained to do and my foolishness and pride got one of the best fighters in the Atlantean army killed. I pause in my account to calm my tears. Nobody will be able to understand me soon if I start to sob. Jack reaches his hand over to me and places it on my arm. How can he stand to touch me? I am so ashamed.

"Evelyn," Lady Pescara says, "though I appreciate your honesty, I don't want you to take the burden of Pisces' death upon yourself. Yes, you should have obeyed orders and stayed close to the army, but Pisces was your companion for a reason. He was there to protect you, even if it was from your own decisions. He knew the risks of being the companion to such a valuable asset and he was willing to take those risks. You would not have been attacked if you didn't have the link you do to Ceto and her past. If you want to blame someone for Pisces' death, let it be Ceto."

I can't help but think that Ceto's lifetime of being unloved and unaccepted may be the thing to blame, but this isn't the time to bring that up. I calm down so I can continue to share what happened that day.

"I would have been killed for sure," I explain, "had it not been for Gwen. She came to help me and Pisces when Ceto's soldiers were attacking us." Lady Pescara seems unaware of who I am talking about. I guess she didn't know the names of all of her recruits.

"Your Gwen?" Jack asks me. I feel guilt in my heart when he calls her *my* Gwen. We hadn't had that closeness for weeks. Now I know she is my cousin. She saved my life. I am indebted to her. Yes, she is *my* Gwen.

"Yes, Jack. My Gwen."

"I haven't seen her here," Jack says. "Are you sure she was with you? It was a battle. Maybe the person you saw just looked like Gwen."

"No. I saw her in Ceto's fortress as well."

Jack sits back in his chair, a look of confusion on his face.

"Evelyn," Lady Pescara says, "you actually saw this Gwen girl in Ceto's fortress? How do you know her:"

"Gwen is my roommate at FIU. She's actually the closest friend I have here." I blush as I think of why I have avoided her for so long. "I knew that she had become a two-worlder as I had, but we were both so busy and preoccupied with our lives that we never really saw each other long enough to talk about it. The day of the battle was the first day I saw her with the army of Atlantis."

Lady Pescara has a look of concern on her face as she turns to Jack. "Captain, you know this young lady as well?"

"Yes, Lady Pescara, I do," he says. "I can ask the other officers in our meeting this afternoon if she is one of their recruits. Evelyn what is her last name again?"

"Mizrahi is her last name. Is that helpful?"

Lady Pescara lets out a small gasp then addresses me.

"Evelyn, Mizrahi is Ceto's last name." This news doesn't shock me. I already knew that Gwen was Ceto's daughter. I guess Uncle Adrian's family didn't allow her to carry on the Marin name. I turn to Jack.

"You've got to find your other captains, Jack, and find out who trained her. I'm not surprised by Ceto's name," I say as I turn to Lady Pescara, "Gwen is Ceto's daughter by my Uncle Adrian. We are cousins."

Lady Pescara sinks into her chair. I understand her surprise. I don't think Gwen even knew who her mom was until she was captured. But she is on our side, so it must be a good thing. I explain our relationship, Uncle Adrian's and Ceto's secret marriage, the lava flow in Atlantis, Ceto leaving my mom and giving birth in a cove. It's such a sad story to retell. My heart is breaking for my Aunt and her daughter. They have missed so much together.

"Evelyn," Lady Pescara says, "I would have known if a Gwen Mizrahi were in our forces. That kind of last name isn't something any of us would have overlooked. She isn't an Atlantean."

Jack speaks up, "We do know that several two-worlders have actually entered the ocean only to head to Ceto and her army. Many from the regions of the Indian Ocean have been living in her city for years. Recently, several from the Gulf of Mexico area have been drawn to her. It is possible that she was on Ceto's side from the beginning. She *is* her daughter, after all."

Two-worlders coming from the Gulf of Mexico. That would explain James being at Ceto's palace – even as a guard, but it does nothing to convince me that Gwen is a traitor. But how can I convince them?

Chapter 29

"There has to be some kind of mistake," my mind is racing as I listen to Lady Pescara and Jack tell me Gwen isn't an Atlantean. "She was with us in the battle. She saved my life and protected me all the way to Ceto's fortress. She was a prisoner too!" I am getting worked up. Gwen saved me. I know there is something they are missing. How else could Gwen have been at the battle with us?

"Calm down, Evelyn," Jack puts his hand on my arm again. "We'll figure this out."

"Yes," agrees Lady Pescara, "We will look into it further. If indeed Gwen was an Atlantean, we will know by sundown." She takes a quill and seaweed parchment and scribbles a few notes. "Simmons," she addresses the guard by the door, "Please take this to General Levey immediately. Let him know he can report in tonight's council meeting." Simmons leaves his post by the door, gathers the note into a satchel around his neck, and swims out the door. Lady Pescara folds her hands on her desk and returns her attention to me.

"Now, Evelyn. Why don't we discuss your time in captivity with Ceto? What were your accommodations like? How many other prisoners did you see? How were you treated by the guards? Did you happen to overhear any kind of information, anything at all?"

I have helpful information. It was only a few weeks that I was in Ceto's custody, but I learned and experienced so much. I tell Jack and Lady Pescara about my first prison cell and interactions with Gus. My eyes tear up again as I think of his life so unnecessarily lost. I make it clear that he had no real allegiance to Ceto and that I think other neglected sea creatures could be accepted by Atlantis and joined to our cause. This news is a surprise to Lady Pescara and she makes some notes for herself.

Then I tell her about the several times I was with Ceto herself. Lady Pescara seems astonished that Ceto reached out to me, a prisoner of war. As far as either of us knows, there is no reason to suspect that Ceto knows about my abilities with the air lingering above the ocean. If she had, I don't think I would have been allowed to have such freedom of movement in her presence. I would have been shackled and imprisoned or escorted to my cell by Ceto herself. It's a trait she has been looking for in a follower for years. She never would have let me get away if she had known. Thankfully, I still have that secret from her. I learned so much about myself that Ceto knew but I did not. It is nice to have the upper hand in something.

It is difficult to talk about Gwen and the meeting we had with Ceto. I believe that Gwen is on our side. I don't doubt her. But I know Lady Pescara and Jack feel differently. I know they suspect the worst. All I can do is wait and hope the council is able to find evidence that will clear Gwen of any wrongdoing.

It is uncomfortable when I finally tell Jack and Lady Pescara about Kai. The idea that he claims to be my father (let alone if he actually IS my father) is still so new and strange to me. I haven't had the time to process my feelings on the subject. Lady Pescara listens intently as I tell her about my first visit with him, how he tried to help me, and how he has acted since his capture by Atlantis. She listens like she is completely enthralled by what I have to say. When I finally finish, she lets a moment of silence pass by before she responds. She lets out a long and slow breath into the water and raises out of her chair before she speaks.

"Evelyn, if there is any reason to believe that this man is indeed your father, we will be able to discover it." She moves to the front of her desk and rests on it, arms folded as she continues, "I'm sure that these allegations are very emotional for you and something that you will need time to work through. However, until we can fully determine the validity of his claims, I think it is best that this conversation stays between you and me and Captain Jack. Please don't mention it to anyone, not even your mother."

Mom. I haven't had a chance to send a note since my return to let her know that I am okay. That should have been the first thing I did. After the way we parted, she must have assumed that I was being emotional and angry with her. Ugh. Mom.

"I will keep this to myself," I assure Lady Pescara. "But I haven't spoken to my mother since before the battle began. She can't possibly have a clue about what has happened. I need to see hear, to speak to her, to let her know that I'm okay." I am filling with anxiety. "May I please take leave for the week so I can visit her?"

"Evelyn," Lady Pescara says as she rises again, "There will be no trips to Arizona for you." My heart beats a mile a minute as I realize I am being told no. I can't go see my mom. The best I'll be able to do is send a message. I can't call from Atlantis. I open my mouth to protest, to beg really, for Lady Pescara to reconsider. But she stops me before I can start. She holds up her hand to silence me.

"Evelyn," she says, "Your mother came to Atlantis to look for you after we left for battle. Unfortunately, we had already been out to sea for several days and she was not allowed to follow us. She resided in my home while we were away, every day asking the Atlantean Guard if they heard any word of your whereabouts or our battles. I have been told that she was quite persistent."

Yes, I am sure she was *persistent*. She came for me. My mom is in the ocean like a two-worlder. She *is* a two-worlder. I am surprised that she didn't defy orders and follow us out to sea. Of course, I am a rule breaker and look at where that has gotten me.

"Once she heard you were captured, she nearly went out of her mind. She tried to leave despite the order she was given to remain in Atlantis," (Way to go mom!), "but she was restrained. We had to keep her under a guard so she wouldn't do anything foolish that risked both her life and yours."

I smile at the thought of my mother yelling at the guard to let her go. I can imagine her scolding them for keeping her from going after her daughter. I am familiar with those guilt trips.

"Where is my mother now?" I ask. "When may I go to see her?'

"Your mother is being escorted here, Evelyn," Lady Pescara answers, "I expect her at any moment."

There is a knock at the door. Simmons enters and announces that my mother has arrived. Lady Pescara turns to me with a gentle, but warning eye, "Remember what we have discussed, Evelyn. Remember what you can and cannot share."

"I will, Lady Pescara." With a satisfied look, Lady Pescara tells Simmons to allow my mother in. Simmons disappears for a moment before the door to the room bursts open, my mom charging through like a woman on a mission. It is like watching slow motion. I haven't seen my mother in the ocean, not one single time in my whole life. I know how much she detests it. I haven't even imagined her here, it is so out of place. To see her here, in a place where she tried to convince me she didn't belong, is like watching a dream. Her gorgeous, dark hair moves like the wind as she advances toward me through the water. Even in the hazy light of Atlantis, I see the little shimmers of grey peeking out through her hair. She is wearing a white tunic and flowing pants. She is a blur of tan skin and white clothing as she rushes toward me. She looks like a sea angel. I rise from my own chair for the embrace I know is coming. My mother bowls into me like a bull after a cowboy and I am wrapped in her warm embrace. She is sobbing and saying my name over and over again.

"We will leave you two alone," offers Lady Pescara, "please feel free to use the room for as long as you need." With one more furtive glance in my direction, both Lady Pescara and Jack exit the room.

Once the door closes behind them, my mom pulls me out in front of her.

"Evelyn, I have been worried sick! I am so sorry for not telling you about your water abilities or mine. I should have trusted you to be able to handle that kind of information on your own. You are such a smart and capable girl. You're a young woman." And she pulls me into her embrace again with more tears and assurances of how much she loves me and has worried about me. I hug her back and tell her I love her. I am sorry I left my mom in anger and I want to be sure she knows it. Eventually her tears soften. We sit together and talk about what has happened in our lives for the past weeks.

I tell my mom about my capture and captivity and fears for Gwen and James. I answer all her questions until she is satisfied that Ceto hasn't done any lasting harm to me. If Ceto had really hurt me, there would be no need to have a war. My mom would have ended it with Ceto personally. I do as Lady Pescara asked, however, and don't mention Kai. This is for the best. My mom has enough to keep her mind and heart occupied. She asks me the same questions over and over, 'Were you hurt?' 'Are you sure you are okay?' 'Will you forgive me?' and tells me how much she loves me. It is nice to hear that my mom loves me so much. I know how lucky I am.

Once she is satisfied about my health and wellness, it is time for me to hear about what has been happening in her life. When I left her in the hotel room with all of those journals, she figured I needed some time to myself. She didn't want to crowd me or force me to do what she said. She figured I would come to my senses better if left alone. She went back to Arizona and let the letters I sent be our communication. Then she received a note from Uncle Russ telling her that the Atlantean army left for battle, and that I went with them. He assured her that I was in Pisces' care and would not come to any harm. But that was not enough for my mom. She came straight into the ocean and headed straight for Atlantis, demanding answers. We were too far gone by that time for her to follow so she waited very impatiently for our return. Once she heard of my capture, she really let the guards have it. "They locked me up like I was a lunatic," she says, "I railed on them continuously until word reached us that you were safe. I questioned if they were making their mother's proud by locking me up and keeping me from my baby girl." She looks a bit sheepish. "Maybe I did go a bit overboard. But I was worried SICK!!!"

We talk for several hours until there is a knock on the door. Jack peeks his head in.

"I'm sorry to bother the two of you, but I was wondering if I could escort you ladies to your quarters."

My mother gives me the *"don't you think he is a cute guy? You should date him"* look and smiles and nods to Jack. "Thank you, Captain, we would appreciate that." We get up and head arm-in-arm through the doorway behind Jack. He leads me to my quarters with the other trainees but continues ahead with my mom. She will be staying with Lady Pescara. As I enter my tent and turn to my hard and lumpy bunk, I remind myself that this is the life I have chosen and I lay down and fall into a deep sleep.

Chapter 30

I am soundly asleep, not even dreaming. My poor body and mind need a break. But I am awakened by a light tapping on my cheek and a tiny voice whispering in my ear.

"Miss Evelyn." Tap, tap. "Miss Evelyn."

I stretch and roll from my side to my back, blinking my eyes so they adjust to the darkness. I must have fallen asleep before dinner.

"Who's there?" I grumble, "What time is it?"

"Shhhh," whispers the voice, "Please, Miss Evelyn. We must be very careful to not wake anyone up."

I blink a few more times and can make out the shape of a little seahorse swimming by my head. But it is unlike any I have seen before. It is a little more than a foot long and has the head and long nose of a typical seahorse, but its body looks like it is growing out stems and leaves in all directions. If it hadn't been speaking to me, it would look like a plant.

"What in the world?!" but the little critter spits at me one more time.

"Miss Evelyn, you MUST keep quiet. I have an important message for you from Miss Gwen Mizrahi." All of my wonder at this little creature vanishes as I hear the name of my friend. I sit up straight in my bunk, tossing my blanket to the side.

"What message? What did she say? Where is she? Who is her Captain?" I do my best to whisper as I sit up on my bunk.

"She desires to meet with you. Please follow me and make your movements as quiet as possible."

"Wait," I whisper. "I can't just up and follow you. That has gotten me in plenty of trouble before. How do I know Gwen really sent you?"

The little seahorse parts his leafy arms and pulls out an octopus crystal. It is from Ceto's chandeliers and could only have come from Gwen.

"She said to remember your uncle," the seahorse says again.

I know Gwen wants me to remember our familial connection. She has never had positive family connections and now she has the chance to have that in me. I am nervous about leaving again, but I want her to know that I am family and I will come when she needs me.

"I'll come," I say to the seahorse and I hop down from my bunk. I grab my small pocket knife just to have some protection and I hide it in my clothes.

The creature swims out of the tent door and I follow as quickly and quietly as I can. My bunkmates are all in various deep-sleep poses, at least one of them snoring, so I am sure I haven't awakened them. I have to blink and rub my eyes when I exit the tent so I can see clearly enough to follow it. The creature is a yellowy-green color, glowing in the reflected light of the full moon in the sky over the ocean. It must be a cloudless night above sea; I can see almost everything with complete clarity. The little sea creature swims quickly down the row of tents with me close behind. He says nothing and neither do I. I don't want to risk waking up any others and having to explain where I am headed. Gwen isn't out of the clear yet.

Suddenly the little horse darts between two of the tents. I hear a guard coming and I follow the little seahorse, thinking that we are trying to avoid detection. But when I stop, I realize the creature is still swimming, just heading down another pathway that leads to the outer city wall. I continue to follow it, wondering where we are headed. Once we make it to the wall, we hide in the shadows quietly as two Atlantean guards swim above us, watching the open sea on their patrol. Once they moved far enough away from us, I follow the seahorse over the wall then sharply down the other side into more shadows. After a moment of pause and silence, it speaks to me in its regular voice. It sounds male, his voice oddly deep and raspy for such a small creature.

"I think we are safe now. As long as we stick to the shadows of the wall, we should not be detected. My name is Lachlan."

"Hello Lachlan. Where is Gwen? Can you tell me how far away she is? What is the message she has for me? Why do we have to sneak around at night to have this conversation?"

He continues in his deep bass, "Miss Gwen merely asked that I find you and bring you to her. What she wants to discuss with you is up to her." He turns around and swims away again, not turning to see if I will follow.

I pause for just a moment. I know Jack and Lady Pescara are wary of Gwen. But they don't know her like I do. But I still cannot help but doubt for a moment.

I do follow and eventually, wishing I had someone else with me. Jack maybe. I decide to not travel far beyond the borders of the city. Any further and Gwen will have to come to me. Lachlan and I come to a place in the wall where a landslide took place some time ago. I wonder if it is the landslide that took my uncle. Rock and debris mound over the wall on both sides, creating a small hill that has also swallowed up several houses. The surrounding area is lifeless and empty, abandoned by a people from long ago. An old fishing boat lays rusting and broken on the ocean floor as if it is trying to reach the city. Lachlan pauses near the hill, darting his head this way and that, checking to make sure the coast is clear. I'm not sure who we should be watching out for in an abandoned part of the city, but when Lachlan says the coast is clear, I follow him back over the wall and into the window of one of the abandoned houses.

This is the first dwelling besides a tent I have entered in Atlantis. The room we enter is dark but I can see that light is coming from a hallway. Together Lachlan and I swim to the hallway. I hear someone speaking. It is Gwen. Without giving it another thought, I swim by Lachlan and down the hall to the room where her voice is coming from. I enter a doorway on the left and find Gwen speaking to a room full of sea creatures. I see several more creatures like Lachlan in the front row, closest to Gwen and the doorway in which I am framed. There are other creatures, though, and their presence startles me. Several stingrays, eels, and octopi are listening to what Gwen is saying, and in the back of the room standing guard are two sharks.

I am nervous to see the group and I turn to swim back the way I came, but my route is blocked by a third shark that crept up behind me. I am about to scream when I hear Gwen addressing me, her voice calm and light.

"Evelyn! I am so glad you came to meet with me. You'll have to forgive Samuel. He is used to protecting me. That will be all, Samuel. Evelyn is not here to hurt me. We are safe with her here." The large shark relaxes his tightened jaw muscles, nods to me, and swims back down the hall. I turn to face Gwen and Lachlan darts in front of me.

"Announcing Miss Evelyn Marin, at your request," he says in his deep, gravelly voice.

"Yes, thank you Lachlan. I see that she is here." Gwen faces her audience in the room. "As I was saying, we have much to hope for and there is much to be done in the days and weeks ahead. May each sea creature do his part. Thank you for meeting here tonight. Your service is invaluable to our cause. This meeting is adjourned."

The room becomes a sea of voices as the creatures begin to move about the room, speaking to each other. Several of them look my way and turn to whisper to one another. I have never heard these kinds of sea creatures speaking before. I assume they are all two-worlders who have made a complete transformation into their sea life form. I feel awkward and uncomfortable, unaware of what I have entered into, when Gwen takes me by the hand and leads me into the hallway.

"I am so glad you have come. I have so much to tell you," she says.

I'm glad because I want to know everything she has to tell me. I want to know what she is doing here in this part of Atlantis. I also remember the conversation with Lady Pescara. I want to clarify some of Gwen's history so I can put those accusations to rest.

Gwen leads me to a great spiraling staircase so old that most of its steps are crumbling and gone. We swim upward to the top floor of the half-buried house. The entire floor is empty of any kind of furniture, walls, or doors. I see damaged outlines and burn marks of where those things once were, but they have been absent for many years. We move to a corner far from any windows where the hardened rock has overcome that portion of the room.

"Gwen, what is going on? Who are those sea creatures you were talking to?" She is beaming from ear to ear. She takes me by both hands as she speaks to me in excited tones.

"Oh, Evelyn! I am so pleased that you are here with me. I was afraid we would never get away from my mother." I feel satisfaction knowing that she wanted to get away as much as I did. I knew she couldn't have been involved in Ceto's plans.

"I have been playing a part to her for months, Evelyn! It was finally time to make my move."

I shake my head like there is air in my ears. "What do you mean *months?* What are you talking about? I thought you were captured in the battle when I was. Wasn't that the first time you actually met Ceto?" Gwen lets go of my hands and paces along the rock wall we are by. She turns to face me.

"Evelyn, I didn't enter the water when you did. I entered several years ago on a trip with my crazy aunt."

"I thought they didn't let you join them at the beach."

252

"They didn't. I snuck out at night just to get a feel for what they were all experiencing. I couldn't swim well. Nobody ever gave me lessons. The waves washed over my head again and again. I thought I was going to drown. Once I realized I could breathe in the waves, I got excited." I am reminded of my first encounter with water breathing: the fear and the excitement of it. Gwen keeps talking, "Each night I snuck out and went a little further until I reached the drop off area. That's when two sharks approached me. I would have been scared to death except they didn't try to attack me. One handed me a scroll for me to read.

"The scroll said that my mother had been waiting my entire life for me to enter the ocean to be with her. It explained who my mother was – the leader of an underwater seadom, destined to be the queen of all the ocean. She wanted me to go to her to train. But I was only 15 and this was the first I had ever heard of my mother. I told the sharks in no uncertain terms that I would come when I was ready. I left them there and didn't return until earlier this year when I entered FIU."

"Did Ceto try to reach out to you again?" I ask. "Did you have any kind of communication with her?"

"No," Gwen replies, "not a single word. She maintained the same radio silence she had for years. I was hurt and angry for a year or two, but then I started to come up with a plan of my own." Her eyes grow dark, any trace of a smile completely gone. She speaks in a low voice.

"I was determined to use my relationship with her to hurt her the way she hurt me. I was sure I could work my way into her home and find all I needed to in order to hurt her the most."

I can't believe what I am hearing. I know Gwen had a rough upbringing, but I have never known her to be vengeful or mean. She uses her experiences to drive her forward, to do amazing things despite her circumstances. This long-held hatred and plan for revenge aren't normal for her.

"It didn't take long for me to see that she was absolutely crazy," she says, "– that turning into an octopus bit by bit was really affecting her brain. You may have noticed that the octopi aren't the quickest set in the ocean." I nod, remembering how my own attempts at sea communication had only reached one octopus, Gus.

"She told me all about her crazy plan to rule the world by flooding it. She really thought that was the way to get people everywhere to care at all about what she did. But she could have had ME, Evelyn. She could have loved ME and I could have loved her. But it wasn't enough. She never really wanted love, Evelyn, all she wanted was power."

Gwen is so angry, and I get it. She feels she has been abandoned and betrayed her entire life. But I'm not sure what she is planning on doing about it.

"So," she continues, "once I fully understood her plans, I started making plans of my own. I started reaching out to some of the more vulnerable sea creatures in Ceto's city. I purposely sought out those who were outcasts; I knew they would be lonely and looking for acceptance. You saw some of them here tonight. I convinced them that together we could take over the entire ocean, both Atlantis and my mother's realm. I told them they could all be valued just like any other sea creature or two-worlder was."

"How are you planning on making that happen, Gwen?" Even though at first glance Gwen's mission sounds noble, I am beginning to understand the reality that she never was a part of Atlantis. I suspect that she was at the battle because she was fighting, not with Atlantis, but against it. Her protective embrace was actually a restraint to hold me until I was a prisoner. I guess that capturing me was "playing a part" to her mother. A pit enters my stomach as I realize I am speaking face-to-face with another enemy.

"Well, let's just say that my mother's plans, senile as they may seem, actually have some merit. Using the Atlantis power source could increase our own sea powers like never before. We could freeze oceans, melt ice caps, create tidal waves over entire continents. Everyone would have to accept us as the new order." Her plans sound exactly like Ceto's, except she wants the power all to herself.

"What would be the purpose in that, though? Would you try to flood the world? Think of all the people you would kill." Gwen narrows her eyes at me.

"What have people ever done for me, Evelyn? For years, I've had to watch people who should have cared about me trample me under their feet, while my 'friends' like you had all the love you ever needed." My face burns at her words. Yes, I have been loved, but I have also had hard things to deal with in my life. Everyone does. Gwen can only see her experiences. Her pain.

"Nobody escapes life without troubles and trials, Gwen. The point is to make good things out of it, not to let it turn you into something you weren't destined to be."

"What do you know about my destiny?" She retorts. "Maybe it is my destiny to rule the world underwater. Maybe it is my destiny to claim it all for myself and for the lowest of the low! Just think of the possibilities, Evelyn. Didn't you see us coming together in our meeting? Couldn't you hear the voices of those cast out sea creatures as they planned and worked together?" she asks.

"Yes, Gwen. I heard them."

"How do you think they were even able to speak? You know that their kind don't use words like you and I do."

"How is it possible, Gwen?"

"The stories of an Atlantis power source hidden in the Bermuda Triangle aren't just myths, Evelyn. I have found it. We are practically on top of it right now. That's how those sea creatures could speak. With the Atlantis power source, they have the power to do so many things. So do I. And so do you."

I'm getting goosebumps. Gwen is trying to lure me in with promises of power. It's alluring and it's frightening.

"How can you be certain, Gwen? Have you seen the power source? Has anyone else seen it? How do you know what it is capable of?"

"Oh, it can crush worlds, Evelyn," she says with incredible pride and pleasure. "Why do you think Atlantis even ended up at the bottom of the ocean? It was a large and thriving port town on the other side of the Atlantic ocean." She is pacing again excitedly. "The people didn't respect the power source or understand what it could do for them. It wasn't until the two-worlders started to appear that the power source made its move."

"You make it sound like it's a living thing," I say.

"Oh, it's a living thing alright. Alive as either you or I are. It thinks and breathes and lives and moves. When the ridiculous humans of the port town proved that they would not change, the power source took matters into its own hands. It created an energy explosion so powerful that it buried the city in the sea in a single day. Every single person was killed and Atlantis was finally in a world where it belonged."

"How did the city end up so close to North America, then?" I ask.

"For centuries the power source has been driving the city across the ocean floor. As more and more two-worlders began to come into the ocean on the American continent, it was like the power source was trying to get to them. It finally did, only to be ignored once again. Now, I am going to make sure that it is never ignored again, just like me."

Gwen is acting like I have never seen her before. I can't understand what is driving her to speak this way. It sounds like the Lord of the Rings and how nobody could resist the power of the ring. It had to be destroyed. I know I have to play my cards right if I am ever going to figure out Gwen's plans.

"Can I see the power source for myself?" I ask. Gwen looks at me with a hint of skepticism. She isn't so willing to put her secret in danger just yet.

"Not yet, Evelyn. It isn't time for the unveiling. Come back tomorrow night and I will take you." She pauses then turns to face me. "You could be a part of my new order, you know. If I can trust you, you can follow me anywhere." Gwen pauses and considers my face for a moment. She wants to tell me something more, but isn't sure if she should. I look her straight in the eyes, mentally willing her to speak to me.

"There's something else I think you should know," she finally says and I brace myself for more of her world domination speech. "There is someone else you know who is following me."

No. Please don't say it.

"James has been serving my cause since he arrived at FIU."

She said it. No. No. No. No. No.

"When he first began testing some of his abilities at Corpus Christi, some of my scouts reached out to him. The promise of something more was alluring to James so he came here to learn more and join my army. Of course, he intended to bring you with him, but you weren't ready yet."

Gwen clears her throat before continuing, "When you saw us that day…Well, you weren't paying attention to him…We were spending so much time together…" She clears her throat again. "I'm sorry about your relationship with James, Evelyn. You just ignored him so much and we were spending so much time together. I hope you will understand."

Understand? Understand that my former boyfriend has fallen for my favorite roommate? Understand that the allure of power was so great he didn't care about *us?* Understand that he is a jerk and she is losing her mind? Yes, I understand. And you can have him.

"Gwen," I say as I take her hand and look her in the eye, "I am happy for you. I really feel like you two are perfect together. You don't need to worry about me." *Because you are crazy and I don't want any part of it.*

Gwen squeezes my hand and lets it go before continuing to speak. "Well, I'm glad to hear it. Thank you *so* much, Evelyn. I hope we will all be able to work together."

"Thank you for telling me, Gwen."

"Well," she says, "I have several things I need to do, Evelyn. If you meet me back here again tomorrow, I will take you to the power source myself. Until then, think about this decision. Think of what we could do." She pauses and straightens her shoulders, her chin lifted with pride. "Lachlan will take you back to your quarters." She turns to leave and I follow. She stops and faces me. "Speak of this to no one, Evelyn. Your life and future depend on it." I nod my assent and follow her out the door until we make it to Lachlan who has been waiting at the bottom of the stairs.

"Take Miss Marin home, Lachlan. Make sure she is neither seen nor heard."

"Yes, My Queen." And the little creature bows to her.

Chapter 31

I follow Lachlan along the same path we took before. Once we are a good distance from Gwen's meeting house, Lachlan ducks beneath a tumbled down section of bridge. It is a detour from where I thought we should be heading and I follow him with hesitance.

"Why are we going this way," I ask.

"Because it is free from prying ears," he responds. Lachlan has something he wants to tell me. He stops in a shadowy area surrounded on three sides by wall and rock, looking hesitantly out the opening of the little cave. Then he turns to face me.

"I feel that I can trust you," he says, "There are not many trustworthy two-worlders in the sea, Miss Evelyn, but I was friends with your sentry at Ceto's palace, Gus." I am caught off guard by this revelation.

"I am so sorry, Lachlan," I say, "I wanted Gus to be safe. I tried to help him be safe."

"I'm sure you did," he replies, "Gus spent quite a bit of time telling me about you. I know you reached out to him with your mind. That is something that Ceto cannot do and that I have not told Miss Gwen that you can do. Her own sea talents are lacking. All she can do is control water temperature and currents, and even those she does not do very well.

"Gus told me that you were kind to him and that you had a good heart," Lachlan continues. "He may have been a bit slow in the head, but Gus was a good judge of character. He said he wanted to be your friend and that he felt he was close to becoming that. Friendship is something that sea creatures like us rarely have with two-worlders. We are treated as though we are second-class citizens incapable of making useful decisions or being a benefit to society. We are usually the grunt workers."

"I know and I am sorry Lachlan. I wish things were different," I say.

"I know how you feel," Lachlan replies, "it is evident in your reaching out to Gus and your deference to me when I awoke you in the night. You did not swat me away as most two-worlders would have done. Even Gwen thinks little of us. She speaks to us as though she is the brains and we will follow her because we are too stupid to choose otherwise. But she is wrong."

"Why are you telling me all of this, Lachlan?"

"Because of all the sides and plots and plans of all the leaders in all the ocean, I truly believe that your heart is the most pure. I believe you want to do what is right and I want to follow you."

I am humbled by his words, but I also feel inadequate and undeserving of them. "Lachlan, I appreciate your confidence in me, but I still don't have a firm plan of my own. Or any plan for that matter," I say. "I believe that both Ceto and Gwen need to be stopped and that Atlantis, even the entire ocean, needs to be changed, but I still don't know how to do it."

"You may not understand right now," Lachlan says, "but I have faith that you will come up with a plan. You have influence in many camps and a heritage that lends itself to the extraordinary. I believe you will find a plan and act on it and when you do, I will be there to help you in any way I can. *And* I have nearly a legion of sea creatures and two-worlders alike who feel exactly the same way. We are simply waiting for you to act."

I can hardly grasp what I am hearing. If Lachlan is correct, there are thousands of sea creatures and two-worlders prepared to make a difference. But why are they waiting for me? Why don't they just do it on their own?

"What is it that you are waiting for me to do? Certainly there is someone in the group willing to take a stand."

"Many are willing to take a stand, but none of us has the power you do. You hold five of the seven talents that can be held by two-worlders. You are the key to success to any side. Once you are ready, we will stand behind you."

Lachlan swims out of the little cave. I hurry after him into the lightening waters as the sun rises over the Atlantic Ocean. I have 24 hours until Gwen expects me to follow her. I have 24 hours to make a difference. What in the sea am I going to do?

Chapter 32

"Mom! Mom! Mom!" I am pounding on Lady Pescara's door, determined to wake everyone in the house if I have to. "Mom! I need to talk to you!"

A burly merman opens the door. I would have pushed to get by him, but his gigantic, muscular frame fills the entire doorway. He is groggy and tired-eyed as he looks over the person trying to enter his home at such an early hour.

"Who are you? What do you want?" he asks in a low tone that demands an answer.

"I...I...uh..." he is HUGE.

I can hear Lady Pescara's voice from somewhere behind him.

"Who is it Henry?" she asks in an equally tired tone.

"Lady Pescara! Lady Pescara!" I shout, hoping it will reach her ears. Within two seconds she is peeking out from under his arm which he has leaned on the doorframe.

"Evelyn. What in the seadom are you doing here?" Lady Pescara's hair is a disheveled mess, with crazy strands poking out all over the place. She is wearing a nightshirt. I know I have awakened them both.

"I'm so sorry Lady Pescara. It's important that I find my mother immediately."

"Your mother isn't here, Evelyn. I'm sorry. I thought you knew. She went to the hospital hours ago."

"What?!" I feel panic rising inside of me. "What happened to her? Why was she sent to the hospital?!"

"Evelyn, please try to calm yourself," Lady Pescara yawns as she speaks. "Nothing happened to your mother. She said she had to check on a patient. An old friend from her days in the sea. I'm sure she just got caught up in conversation."

Relief swells my heart. At least she is safe. "Thank you, Lady Pescara. Thank you so much." I take off as Lady Pescara nudges her husband. He had started to fall asleep on the doorpost. Together they go back inside the house as I head to the hospital.

As soon as I enter the doors of the hospital I run straight into the head nurse. She is rather a large merwoman with a full tail and a heavy figure. Her short grey hair is curly all over and her face reminds me of what I used to think Mrs. Claus looked like. She is flustered at first, but calms herself and asks me what the matter is.

"I'm so sorry," I say many times, "I was just in a hurry. I am trying to find my mom. I believe she came to visit a friend."

"And who is the friend?" she asks in a matronly voice.

"I'm not really sure, but my mom is Marisol Marin. Maybe she signed into a register?"

The nurse's eyes soften. "There's no need to check the register, love. I know where your mother is and I will take you to her." She turns and heads toward two double doors on the left. I follow and thank her.

I imagined that the entire hospital would be dank and grey and covered in moss. I am surprised that it is actually modern. The walls are grey as we are still in an ancient building, but everything is quiet. I don't see any debris on the floors or even floating through the corridors. I notice heavy, swirling fans in the ceiling above. They must be filtering the water to keep it clean.

I continue to follow the nurse down one corridor, then another. I see more and more modern medical equipment the further we go. Gleaming operating tools sit on tables in glassed-in rooms. Fluorescent lights hang in waterproof lanterns along the hallway.

Just as I am ready to ask the nurse what part of the hospital we are heading to, she stops in front of a door labeled, 'Psych Ward.' Who on earth is my mother visiting? The nurse turns to me as she opens the door.

"You must be calm as you are in this part of the hospital. The people here are quite out of their minds, you see, and any little excitement could really get them going." I nod and follow her into the room.

Several beds line both walls. Some of the beds are empty, others are not. The beds that hold patients have tightly tucked sheets to keep the patients in their proper place. There are probably straps hidden beneath the sheets to keep their prisoners still. I try not to think about it, but I cannot keep the image from my mind. In one bed, a woman I see has no need for straps. All she can do is stare at the ceiling, silent and stony-eyed. Two beds away a woman is holding still but singing a lullaby about a dead baby delivered by a stork. I feel so sorry for her. On the opposite side of the room a man is flailing wildly, two nurses at his side. He is shouting terrible things at them, but they don't say a word. There is a needle in the hand of one of the nurses aiming for his dark, outstretched arm and by the time we make it across the room, the man is calming down.

We reach a set of double doors on the other side of the room and enter a hallway lined with doors. These are the private rooms. I can only imagine who is being kept in these rooms. The nurse leads me to a door to the right. She turns to face me and holds her arm out to the door. "Here you are, sweetheart. Your mother is here."

I go to the door and peek in, afraid of who the occupant might be and what their ailment is. I see my mother first, still wearing the white outfit she had on earlier, her hair thrown up into a messy bun on the top of her head. She is sitting at the foot of a bed, holding a grey hand in hers, stroking it softly. The nurse leaves and I move past the curtain, quietly as I can so I don't bother my mom's friend. I reach a hand to touch my mother on the shoulder. She looks up at me in surprise, her eyes red and swollen from crying. I look to the hand she is holding and look at the face. The patient is Kai.

Chapter 33

It feels like I have been standing here frozen for hours, but it can't have been more than a moment or two. I become aware, somewhere in my consciousness, of my mom. She is saying my name, ever so softly. The hand which was holding onto Kai is now brushing my hair away from my face, her other hand touching my shoulder. I feel her whispering into my ear, telling me so many things I can hardly understand. I hear the words *miracle, wonderful,* and *blessed.* Tears are streaming from her eyes, her voice strained from crying countless tears over the hours. How long has she been here? How did she know to come? Her being here, eyes filled with emotion, voice strained from weeping – they say it all. They tell me the truth I have been trying so hard to fight against. Kai is my father.

The room is dizzying and blackness threatens to overtake me, but I remain upright. I don't give in to the natural urge to black out from shock. I don't speak, afraid the sound of my voice will break the spell I am under and force me to accept what I see. I don't turn to embrace my mother. I don't move at all. I remain silent. I don't want to give in. I won't.

Slowly, when my shocked mind is ready, I start to allow her words to enter into my ears.

"Evelyn, darling. Oh my sweet girl. We have been blessed with such a miracle. My darling girl, this is your father. Oh my darling, my darling," all spoken in the softest and tenderest of whispers. "My darling you must sit down. Please, my love. Come with me."

I cannot see another place to sit other than the end of the bed and I know I can't be there. I let my mother guide me to a chair in the corner of the room. She sets me down gently, speaking those same words over and over, unsure of whether or not they are registering in my brain.

I sit in that position for at least another hour. My mother eventually kisses my cheek softly and goes back to sit on the edge of the bed. I watch as she picks up his hand, Kai's hand, my father's hand, and continues to stroke it softly. She is speaking to him, telling him that I am there, telling him all of the wonderful things I have done and am doing and all of the wonderful things that make her so proud. She might as well be telling a stranger. This man cannot be my father. The man she told me for so long that loved me and gave up everything to provide a better life for us. That man would not have abandoned me for anything. Not for anything in the world.

Eventually the nurse comes back into the room. She glances my way and gives me a very small and sympathetic smile. Then she turns to my mother. I hear my mother whispering to the nurse about me. Words like *shock, she'll be okay,* and *worried.* Then she starts talking about my father. Words like *unresponsive, silent,* and *still.* How can she help both me and my father? Would she have enough strength if I broke down? I can't do that to her. I know I can't.

"Mom?"

"Oh my Evelyn," my mother gets up from her seat by my father's side and comes over to me. This time I stand as she comes to me and I bury my face into her shoulder and I cry. I cry and cry and cry. The nurse tends to my father, adjusting tubes and making marks on charts, while I hug my mom. My mom speaks so much love to me, assuring me that everything will be okay. She says she is sorry to have given me such a shock. She heard some of the recently returned soldiers talking about Kai Marin being found. She could not rest until she knew for sure. She knew the head nurse at the hospital and was able to gain access to my father's room. One look at him was all she needed to know it was her husband who had been missing for 15 years. She had been sitting by his bed for many, many hours waiting for him to wake up. He hadn't stirred. He hadn't stirred in days.

"Evelyn, do you think you would be able to speak to him?" she asks. "I was told he was with you almost non-stop on your journey back to Atlantis. Maybe the sound of your voice will awaken something in him." I cannot let my mother down. Still holding her hand, I make my way to Kai's bedside, my father's bedside.

"Kai," I whisper as I bend near to his ear. His eyes twitch just a bit. "Dad. Dad it's me. It's Evelyn." Suddenly his eyes fly wide open and he starts screaming.

"Evelyn! Evelyn! Evelyn it's a trap! Evelyn you know what you must do! Do what you must do! I have prepared you. EVELYN!!!!!!" he is in absolute hysterics. He grabs my shoulder to pull himself up to me. The nurse flies to his side and shoves a needle into his arm. "Evelyn! Evelyn! You must…" he lies back down on his bed, his hand slipping down my arm and he again falls fast asleep.

The nurse is calm as a summer's day, a reaction I think is extraordinary. My comatose father finally awakens and shouts a warning to me. My heart is racing a mile a minute. My mom keeps asking the nurse what this could mean and what is going to happen. The nurse tells her that my father needs his rest, he cannot be allowed to get worked up like that or he will do harm to himself or others. To me.

"We'll try a different medication tomorrow," she says. "One that will allow him to talk but not to be physically alert."

Tomorrow. I can't wait for that. Tomorrow I will be meeting with Gwen again and probably Lachlan. I need all the support I can get. I need my father. I scream at the nurse and tell her she CANNOT do that again. I need to speak to my father and he needs to speak to me! What other kinds of medicines does she have? What can she do to wake him up? I need him NOW! She tells me to calm down, but I don't have time to calm down. I don't have time for…

I feel a sharp jab of pain in my arm and look to see as the nurse withdraws another needle. She just gave me some drug to calm me down! I have enough life in me to see my mom's hand flying to her mouth in shock. Then, black.

More traveling through tunnels, more brightly lit rooms, more voices calling my name, my hand reaching out, no more breathing.

When I wake up, I am strapped to one of those stupid beds. My mother is beside me. A doctor is just leaving the room. I nearly have a panic attack when I realize I can't get out of the bed.

"Evelyn," my mom says, "sweetheart, are you okay?" I pull at the restraints and give her a pleading look. "I know you want to get up, but Nurse Nelson insisted it was for the best. She said you needed to let the shock wear off or you might hurt yourself or someone else. The doctor was just here and he said after a good night's rest you would be better prepared for an evaluation."

"Mom, what kind of evaluation are you talking about?"

Her eyes shift to my sheets, "a psychiatric evaluation, Honey. You've been through a lot. You need to be mentally rested and prepared before they will let you go back to your battalion." This is so unbelievable. I know I need to act and act fast.

"Mom, you have got to listen to me," I say to her. "So much has been going on that nobody else knows about. I have got to have your help to get out of here. I'm running out of time." I tell her about Gwen – all about Gwen – from her kissing James to her relationship to Ceto to her plans for the Atlantis power source to Lachlan pulling me aside with his new plans. But will she believe me? Her eyes look doubtful, like she thinks I really am mentally exhausted like the doctors are trying to tell her.

"She's telling you the truth, Marisol," my father's warm and deep and lovely voice speaks up from the bed next to mine. My mom and I both turn to see him sitting himself up. She races over to help him. Once he is more comfortable and alert, he continues.

"Marisol, I have been reaching out to Evelyn for years, trying to send her the message that the Atlantis power source wanted me to send."

"What on earth are you talking about?" my mom asks, "What power source? I thought that was just a myth."

"It isn't," my dad says. "When I was lost at sea, it wasn't because of a treasure hunt. I heard the power source speaking to me, calling to me to find it and free it." My mom's eyes are wide and worried. Her husband and daughter are both out of their minds. "My ship went down in the Bermuda triangle very near where the power source was hidden. It was such a rickety boat. I don't know why I thought it could be of any use to me." He coughs weakly before speaking again.

"I went down, I was so close to reaching the power source, but my foot was twisted in the ship's rigging. I was a tangled mess and stuck that way for three days. Just when I thought I was going to die without seeing your face again," he reaches up and touches my mother's cheek, "Ceto appeared. I was never so shocked to see anyone in my life. Nor so grateful," he pauses and looks at us both, "until now, that is.

"She and some of her followers helped me to get loose of the rigging. Stewart and John were both dead, crushed underneath the boat. Ceto's guard carried me for what seemed an eternity, nourishing me with food the entire way. When we finally reached her fortress, I was feeling like a human being.

"Again and again I told Ceto how grateful I was, but that I needed to go home to my family. They would be worried sick.

"Her eel doctors would come in. They would give me a physical and a shot then tell her I needed one more week. For weeks this went on. I finally had enough. I was going to leave no matter what they said. I snuck out one night and got a day's journey into the trip when my body seized up. My muscles were tensing and my stomach was in deep pain. I was suddenly shivering from head to toe and crying like a baby. I could hardly think straight.

"Ceto knew this would happen, her sharks were right behind me, ready to pick me up. Whatever her eels had been giving to me, it had a lasting effect and my body was going through withdrawals. Once I was back in her fortress, the eels gave me another shot. I struggled so hard against them, they must have poked me a dozen times trying to hit a vein. But I was destined to lose that battle." My father's eyes grow sad as he remembers the past.

"Ceto kept me drugged for several months. She had a sense of my abilities and my connection to the Atlantis power source and she wanted my strength for herself. I slowly began to lose my ability to think straight. I stayed until she convinced me that was how my life would be forever. I was convinced that your life would be better without me in it. Eventually I was moved to the treasury and was given more body and mind-altering drugs. I was so far from anyone else that I rarely had any interaction with other two-worlders. Only an occasional octopus or stingray would come to check on me.

"My days were completely monotonous, but my nights were filled with dreams. The Atlantis power source was practically screaming at me to come and get it and there was nothing I could do. Finally, I reached out to the source myself. I told it I was a complete and total prisoner. I needed help to escape if I was going to free it. Then I had the dream that you have been having for years, Evelyn. The power source reached out to me with a vision of its physical form. I was convinced that you could do what I was powerless to do. All that needed to happen was for you to touch the source and it would be freed. I started playing the dream and sending it to you while you slept. I was sending the dream to my little girl. It was all I could do."

My eyes sting with tears as I listen to his story.

"My life went on this way for years, until just a few weeks ago when Ceto brought my girl to me." He looks at me, his eyes swelling with tears. Tears are streaming from my own eyes as I looked at my father, really for the first time. He had loved me. He wasn't trying to keep away from me for unselfish reasons. He had been a prisoner to Ceto for 15 years. My dad really does love me.

Mom is speechless. Then, as is typical for her, she makes up her mind and gets into action. She stands up from my father's bedside, comes back to mine and starts undoing the restraints the doctors placed on me.

"If you are going to save this world, my love, we had better cut you loose."

Just as she undoes my last strap, we hear the gong reverberating through the windows. My mom races to the curtains and pulls them aside. The roads are coming to life with Atlanteans rushing to their arms. The gong sounds again. A battle is beginning.

Chapter 34

My mom races back to my side and continues undoing my restraints.

"Come, darling. We've got to get you out of here."

My body is still sluggish from the shot Nurse Nelson gave me, but fortunately my mind is with me.

"What are you and Dad going to do?" I ask. I desperately want them to come with me. I need their support.

"As soon as I get you out, I'll unlock your father and we will come with you." My heart feels so much relief I want to cry, but I know I have to keep my wits about me. Tears won't allow for that. Once I am freed from my shackles, I sit up as quickly as my recovering body can and swing my legs over the edge of the bed. As my mom works away at my father's single strap (he was comatose for days which rendered multiple straps unnecessary) the door to the room bursts open. I hear voices echoing through the halls outside of the room as Nurse Nelson stands in the doorway.

"What do you think you are doing?" She booms in a voice that makes Mom pause.

"Listen!" Mom replies urgently, "we have got to get them out of here. The battle is beginning and Evelyn is the only one with the power to stop it."

"Oh, I know EXACTLY what Evelyn is capable of," Nurse Nelson has a look of madness in her eyes. She pulls a long syringe from a pocket in her shirt and comes at me. But she isn't fast enough. My mom catapults across the room and body-slams Nurse Nelson. I move to my father's side to finish releasing him from his restraint. My mom is strong, but Nurse Nelson has a fully-developed tail to use to her advantage. She pumps it in the water until she is finally above my mother. She raises her needle high above her head and comes screaming down on top of my mother.

"MOM!!!!!" I can't get the words out of my mouth before the needle reaches my mother. She is still crouched on the floor and has her forearm held protectively over her head, using a metal medical tray as a shield. She blocks Nurse Nelson's attempt to inject her, the needle barely scraping against her bicep. Then she uses her legs to shoot herself upward through the water. Again, she slams Nurse Nelson and this time the old merlady drops her needle.

I move to the floor where the needle drops, scooping the drug-filled syringe into my hand. My mom and Nurse Nelson are in hand-to-hand combat now. Mom pushes off the ground with such force that Nurse Nelson hits the ceiling. Now Nurse Nelson is using the strength of her tail to pin mom down. They are caught mid-water as one kicks with all her might and the other flips her fin. Mom is holding onto Nurse Nelson with incredible strength, unwilling to let her go. Nurse Nelson tries using her other hand to reach into her pocket again. I swim as fast as I can to the battling duo and wrap my arm around Nurse Nelson's neck. Just as I am about to inject her with a dose of her own medicine, she pushes my mom away and turns to me. She grasps my arm holding the needle with tremendous strength and the needle drops to the floor. She flings me into the wall and comes at me with both hands outstretched.

As she reaches me, two dark hands, then arms, then a merman plow into her. It is the same merman who was wriggling in his sheets in the next room. He acts out his own mental anguish on the nurse who has been holding him captive.

While Nurse Nelson is distracted by her new attacker, my mom gets ahold of the needle on the ground and plows it into Nurse Nelson's neck. The merwoman goes slack within seconds of the drug entering her bloodstream. The dark merman who came to my rescue suddenly registers shock. He catches Nurse Nelson in his arms, carries her to the bed I had occupied, and sets her down. He reaches for the restraints and straps her in. He sits next to her and starts singing the same lullaby sung by the grieving woman down the hall.

I watch, disturbed by the merman's behavior. I am pulled out of my stupor by my mom when she swims by me. She grabs me by my arm and together we help my father finish coming free of his bed strap. We swim to the window of the room and my mother swings it open wide. We all swim through, first my mother, then me, then my father, leaving the singing man and Nurse Nelson behind.

The streets of Atlantis are teeming with people rushing in a state of organized chaos. We make our way through the water, slowly at first as my father and I are working the sedative out of our systems, then quicker as our bodies wake up. We make our way to the group who is gathering just outside the city walls, listening to Lady Pescara as she addresses them.

"With a power never seen before," Lady Pescara says, "Ceto has made her way across the ocean to us. We have learned from our spies that before our attack on her fortress she had already prepared a series of secret tunnels through which her entire city could escape. They passed under us, completely without our notice. We expect that they will be arriving at our gates within the hour."

I break ranks as I swim over Celia and Jack, heading straight to where Lady Pescara is addressing the Atlantean army. My mom and dad are swimming right behind me, hand in hand, ready to follow wherever I lead.

"Lady Pescara!" I shout, "Lady Pescara!" Her eyes lift to meet mine as I swim above everyone's heads to reach her. When she registers who it is, she looks irritated to have been interrupted, but then she sets her eyes on my mother and father, swimming behind me. That's when complete anger enters her eyes.

"Private Marin!" She barks, "I gave you explicit instructions not to reveal this man's condition to your mother!" I slow my pace as I reach my commander.

"Lady Pescara. I'm sorry to be breaking ranks. But I have to speak to you."

"Private Marin," Lady Pescara scolds, "You have done enough damage with your disobedience of rules. We don't have time for any rogue initiatives. I cannot trust you. Now," she raises her hand

and points to the back of the army. "Rejoin your group of 10, or so help me, I will have you shackled."

My mom and dad have reached us and I can tell that my mom is NOT going to listen to Lady Pescara. But I know I am running out of time. I know I am going to have to make a plan on my own and that plan is just beginning to form.

"Cornelia," my mother says to Lady Pescara, "you've got to take a minute…" but I cut her off.

"No, mom," I say as I put my arm in front of her, "we don't have time for this. I'll go to my place as Lady Pescara has asked of me," I give her a furtive look that says, *don't worry, I have a plan.* "You and dad wait for me back at the training fields," I glance at Lady Pescara who is still fuming in front of me, "you'll have a better view from there."

I swim away, heading to the back of the gathering crowd where my own group of 10 and 50 are waiting. My parents head quietly and resolutely to the training fields. Good. They are going to help. Once I reach my group of 50, I head straight to Jack. I hope he will listen to me.

"Jack!" I shout. "Captain Jack! Sir, I must speak with you." Jack looks up as I swim to his side. Unfortunately, Celia has heard me as well and is making her way to where Jack and I are talking. Being a second in command to Jack and my group leader, she has every right to be there. I know I can't escape her hearing what I have to say.

"I'm sorry for breaking protocol, Captain," I begin, "but Lady Pescara won't hear me and I must speak to someone."

"It's no wonder her ladyship won't hear you, Private Marin," Celia spits out, "with your behavior and total disregard for regulation, I'm surprised she hasn't had you locked in the brig yet." Jack rolls his eyes at Celia then turns to face me.

"Evelyn, we are in critical battle mode. Whatever you have to say, make it quick."

"Thank you, Captain," I don't bother addressing Celia at all. "I have learned information that puts the entire army of Atlantis, even the entire ocean, at risk. Gwen, Ceto's daughter, is working against both her mother and against us. I have reason to believe that the Atlantean army is operating under false assumptions. We have to find a way to reach the entire army to change our focus before it's too late." Celia huffs at my side, but I am focused on Jack.

"Private Marin. I appreciate your concern, but we cannot afford to change course at this point," Jack says, "the enemy is too far advanced upon us. We must proceed according to plan." My heart sinks. I thought if anyone was going to listen to me, it would be Jack. I guess I thought wrong.

"Private Marin, come with me," says Celia in an authoritative tone. I take one last look at Jack, his expression is unreadable. I leave them with my heart sinking even further. I act like I am heading back to my place in Celia's group of 10, but I skip my place in line and just keep going. I hear Celia calling after me, but I know she won't follow. She won't break ranks, she has a group to lead and she is going to lead perfectly. I am a blight on her record anyway.

I am like a fish swimming upstream as I make my way to the training grounds. All other two-worlders, merpeople, and sea creatures are headed into their battle formations, weaponry ready to go. I bump into several as I pass through the throng. The crowds begin to clear as I climb higher up the sloping city and finally reach the training fields which crest the top of Atlantean hill. I can see my parents waiting there for me, the only two-worlders in all the ocean who believe what I am telling them. I know they will stand with me, but will it be enough?

As I reached my parents, I hear a familiar voice by my side.

"Evelyn! Evelyn! Please wait for me." Lachlan is swimming up to me, breathless.

"Lachlan, what are you doing here?" I ask.

"I've been following you around for the last hour trying to figure out where to tell my troops to meet. Should I have them gather here in the training fields, then?"

I am grateful to see that Lachlan has faith in me. I nod my head and he swims away. I turn to face my parents.

"We don't have much time," I say, "Lady Pescara won't listen to me. I tried reaching out to Captain Jack, but he won't listen either. He is too caught up in everything else that is going on."

My mom clears her throat and nods behind me. I turn to see what she is motioning toward and see Jack swimming to where we are. Beautifully glorious and devastatingly handsome Jack. My heart skips a beat as we make eye contact.

"Evelyn," he says as he finally reaches my side, "I'm sorry about a moment ago. I didn't feel that I could trust Celia, so I acted like I wasn't interested in what you had to say. When she came and told me you had left her group of 10, I thought it was the perfect opportunity. I left her in charge of my group of 50 and took off after you like I was going to throw you in the brig or something." He chuckles and meets my eyes.

"I am very sorry," he continues, "but I am here now and ready to assist you with whatever you need." My heart is swelling, my mom is practically beaming, my dad looks irritated.

Lachlan comes back in a few moments, completely out of breath. "My followers are at your command, Lady Evelyn." I am embarrassed by being addressed with this title. But as I look up I am overwhelmed by what I see. Rising to the edge of the training field fences is a group of sea creatures like I have never seen before. Octopi, sharks, seahorses, even two-worlders are gathering behind Lachlan on the training field, spilling over the edge because there are so many. I recognize a few of the faces in the front row from Gwen's meeting last night. I am astounded by the sight and amazed by the group that has gathered to follow me. But I am not the only one who sees them. Looking down I see the collective faces of thousands of Atlanteans staring at the army I have assembled. I am in trouble.

Chapter 35

"Evelyn, we have got to get going," My mom and dad are by my side ready for the plan I have prepared. I am not yet sure how I am going to put those plans into place. And I have tens of thousands of eyes looking at me, waiting for my next move.

"Evelyn," it is the first time my father has addressed me since I acknowledged him as my dad. My heart yearns for his guidance. "We must get to the Atlantis power source. It is calling to me louder than ever. It will give us the strength we need."

I feel the pulling of the power source as well. It is like that old familiar voice calling to me in my dreams, drawing me to it. The feeling is stronger than I have ever felt before. In an instant, I know my father is right. I will follow my heart. It will lead me to the power source.

Raising both hands far above my head, I shout out to the gathering crowd – my army, "FOLLOW ME!!!!!!" and I turn, swimming with tremendous speed in the direction my heart is pulling. We cross the field, my parents on one side, Jack on the other, followed by an innumerable host of sea life. We swim over the other side of the training fields to where the training armory is waiting. Jack speeds away, returning with my mace, shield, and helmet. I have no time to put on additional armor. My helmet and shield will have to be enough to protect me, my mace enough to battle. Other two-worlders and sea life raid the training armory as well. The stockpiles are in battered shape from years of training, but it is better than going into war completely unprepared. I am grateful to have the supply.

The Atlanteans who have been watching from below are now moved to action. I have no idea what the Atlantean generals are telling their army, but they are all turned about and pursuing us. They may think I am a traitor and am helping Ceto. Fortunately for my band of followers, the Atlantean army has to do an about face. Their least trained recruits will meet my group first, their generals racing to catch up to the back of their lines. But nobody has reached my battalion yet.

We swim further and further along the housetops of Atlantis. The city center is below us and then behind us in a matter of only a minute or two. I have never moved so quickly in the water before. Then I realize that I am being pushed. Current control. My father has current control abilities. He is using them to push our army forward. I look to him with gratitude, amazed by the strength he is able to spare. When I see his eyes, I see that he is firm and focused, his mouth set in a hard line – a sign of his concentration. He is channeling the Atlantis power source. I wonder if anyone else in all of seadom is able to do what he is doing in harnessing that well of strength from the power source.

With my dad's help, our entire army blasts through the water at amazing speed. My dad is sending blasts of current into the faces of the Atlantean army as well, trying to slow them down. But they have several talented current controllers as well. Though they cannot match my father as he has a direct line to a greater power, they are nonetheless able to push through his contrary currents faster than I would have liked.

I press forward even harder with my army. We turn and head over the houses of the city until we reach the row of recruit tents and then the outer city wall. I am still being pulled toward the source with tremendous force. We sail over the wall and make a hard right, dipping below the top of the wall and following alongside it for several minutes. With our turns, the Atlantean army is able to make up the distance between us as they cut through the corners we create. A moment later their first soldiers are reaching the back of my group and the fighting begins. We can't stop. Those who are in the back stay to fight off the Atlantean army and to keep them at bay while the rest of us move ahead. Jack breaks away from the front to help lead the fighting in the rear. I know my group is in the best hands they can be in.

Onward we swim until we come to the same hilly landslide I saw last night when I followed Lachlan to Gwen's secret station. I brace myself to meet her. But we don't turn as we had the night I followed Lachlan. Instead, the directions in my heart take us over the top of the hill. I feel a strong, tight pull on my heart and I stop where I am. I hear several fighters running into one another as they skid to a stop behind me, unprepared to cease movement so quickly.

We are positioned over an enormous crack in the ocean floor, just below the bottom of the hillside. A few hundred yards to our left I see that rusted out old boat. It has moved maybe a hundred feet since I last saw it, edging ever closer to the crack in the sea floor. I realize with sudden clarity that it is the rickety, rusted out, rotting fishing boat my father sailed in 15 years ago. It is still being drawn to the Atlantis power source, its bow pointing the way to the giant crack.

I take a deep breath and look at my parents. My dad leaves my mom's side and comes to me. He holds my hand.

"Are you ready my girl?" he asks. In this moment all I want is to melt into him, to rest my head on his shoulder and cry. To cry for all the lost years of our lives, to cry for how much I missed him, to cry for the memories we could have made. I want to relive those years with my dad by my side loving me, encouraging me, and supporting me. But I know it cannot be. What is lost is lost. We only have the future now. And I know he will be a part of my life, however long it lasts.

"I'm ready, Dad." I feel the firmness of his grip as he holds me for the first time in years. His hand is rough and strong. Strong enough to see me through anything. We turn to face that point in the sea ahead of and below us that is screaming for us to come and get it. We squeeze one another's hand, then dive down, still linked together, my mom right behind us, with an army of support.

The Atlantean army is being held at bay for the time being but I am unprepared for what awaits me as we enter the tunnel. I see a golden light reflecting off the walls. It is the same color and pattern that I have seen in my dreams. I know we are close to the power source. My dad and I get only fifty feet or so into the gaping mouth of the cracked opening in the ocean floor, my army entering behind us, when we come face to face with Gwen. She is in full body armor, from head to toe. Her helmet comes to a perfect point between her eyebrows, scales carved into the steel plates. Her torso is hugged tightly by the steel armor, covered in scales that protect the most vital parts of her body. Her arms and legs are free from the heavier weight of the steel but are covered in a lighter mesh to still protect from injury. A gilt sword and shield are at her sides. She glitters in the golden light from behind her that is seeping out from the walls. If I weren't so uncertain of what she would do, I would have told her she looked beautiful.

"I was afraid something like this would happen, Evelyn," she says, "I tried to give you the benefit of the doubt and this is how you repay me." Her voice is filled with anger and she has a look of fury in her eyes, so unlike the Gwen that I know. "I see that you have come with some of *my* followers." She gives Lachlan a withering look as he swims up behind me.

"It doesn't have to be this way, Gwen," I say as I let go of my father's hand to face my friend and foe on my own. "You don't have to try to destroy everything to prove something to yourself or anyone else. We can end this here and now. Join us, Gwen. We can make a difference together."

In an instant, Gwen raises her sword into the air with one arm and lets out a yell that calls to her followers. The tunnels fill with them, all coming from deep inside the crack that led us here, all in glittering body armor and carrying jewel encrusted weapons. They must have raided Ceto's treasury to have access to such amazing tools and weaponry.

Gwen lets out another yell and comes shooting through the tunnel toward me. I am not interested in fighting her in these close quarters with my followers so close behind me, so I rocket upward to avoid her blow. In the twinkling of an eye, her soldiers are racing toward my soldiers, both those in the tunnel and those outside. They spill over one another like a wave on the shore. Gwen explodes after me into the water above. I lead her away from the tunnel, away from her troops – the battle in the tunnels exploding into the water. The sea walls created to make those tunnels can't stand up to the immense pressure of an active battle. Hundreds of soldiers swinging their weapons and pounding into one another only serve to broaden the crack in the ocean floor. Soon, they are all spilling out into the open water, Gwen and I still farther above.

I swim until I feel a knot within me forcing me to stop. I turn just in time to see Gwen barreling down on me with her sword. Time freezes and everything around me quiets as I focus on my enemy preparing to strike. I lift my shield just in time for her sword to come crashing down. The force of the impact jolts my shoulder and a searing pain shoots down my arm. Gwen skids by me as she deals the blow and is now behind me, turning back to attack again. I raise my mace and shield my torso as she comes careening through the water. This time I swing as she reaches me. My mace wraps around her sword, breaking it in two. Her face is furious when she sees her useless weapon. She drops her damaged sword and withdraws a small knife strapped to her ankle.

Just beyond where she is I see the Atlantean army gaining ground on my followers. More of my group are engaged in battle, unable to fight off two opponents at once. I reach out with my mind, begging the power source for help. We can't free it if we have to do it alone.

Suddenly I hear a loud explosion behind me and I turn to see what it is. A lava burst has broken through the surface of the ocean floor. It creates a rumble that sends shockwaves through the water. Gwen, who was ready to attack with her knife, is blown backward through the water. I manage to brace myself against a rock just before the current hits. I am able to hold my ground. But all of the fighters behind me have been similarly knocked backward.

As they rise up again, many of them shaking their heads to clear the ringing from the blast, I see a new terror rising above them. Ceto has arrived with her army. She is at their head, a huge smile spread across her face. We could not have played more perfectly into her hands. She shouts orders to her followers and I watch with fear as they descend upon the mass of fighters. Ceto heads straight for me.

Chapter 36

By the time she reaches me, my mace is raised, but Ceto isn't battle ready at all. Her hands are empty of either shield or weapon. Her body free of armor. She glides toward me with her hands outstretched as if she wants to hug me. I shrink back, unsure of what awaits me once we are face-to-face.

"Evelyn." She says my name calmly, a stark contrast to the battle sounds coming from behind her. "Evelyn I am so happy you are well." I stand frozen as she wraps her arms around me in a hug. She whispers in my ear, "Thank you so much, my dear, for leading me here. I don't know that I could ever have discovered the exact location of the Atlantis power source on my own."

"I don't understand," I say. "I didn't even know the power source was anywhere near here a few days ago. How could I possibly have led you here?"

"My dear, this has been my hope all along. I was fully aware that Gus was beginning to take a liking to you. When I left you in his care in my fortress, I knew that somehow you'd be able to find a way out. I made sure Kai was left as well. I knew that together you would lead me to where I wanted so desperately to be. And here I am. Thank you."

The knot in my stomach tightens as I register that I have been used by Ceto. It was a trap. She had no way of knowing everything I was going to do, but she gambled on letting me and my dad go and she won. Now she is going to claim the victory.

"Oh, I don't know that Evelyn is so special," I hear Gwen's voice behind her mother. "I found the power source completely on my own without her help at all." Ceto turns to face her daughter who still holds that small knife in her hand.

"Oh my Gwen." She moves to embrace her child, but is met with a defensive stance, knife raised defensively toward her. "Gwen, what are you doing? I thought we were going to do this together."

"Yes, you thought a lot of things, mother. But I am not going to be your puppet. Your dreams for me were not ever and are not now *my* dreams for me. I don't want to reign side-by-side with you. I have never been side-by-side with you. It would be completely unnatural."

"Gwen," Ceto says as she moves closer to her daughter, "please my darling girl. Listen to me. I don't want to rule if I cannot rule with you. There would be no purpose in that. Come with me and enjoy all the power that can be yours."

"I know what power can be mine!" Gwen says. "And I don't have to share it with you, *Mother!*" In a blinding flash, Gwen dives at her mother with her knife. Just as the tip makes contact with Ceto's flesh, Gwen's arm freezes. She screams in pain as ice crystals start to form along the entire length of her arm.

"Oh Gwen, dear," Ceto speaks softly, "I had hoped it wouldn't come to this. You see, I have always planned to have you by my side and have you by my side I shall." The ice that covers Gwen's arm moves upward to her shoulder, then her neck, Gwen's screams growing louder and more desperate as she is quickly and painfully freezing to death. "My darling girl, do you relent your designs? Will you change your mind and follow me willingly?" Ceto continues to speak with complete calm and peace in her voice. It is the most unnerving sound I have heard.

"Yes," Gwen screams, "Yes, I will!"

Ceto slows the freezing down just as it encrusts Gwen's chin. She reaches for her daughter who collapses into her arms, all the while whispering her love and affection in her ear. She is completely lost in her attention to Gwen. Ceto has forgotten I am here.

I swim upward and outward, heading to the edge of the continental shelf above me. I have to get away from them. I hear my name being called. I glance over my shoulder just quickly enough to see Ceto rising in the water toward me. But she is not the only one. Both of my parents are swimming after her shouting at me to swim faster. They will help me. I will not be alone in my battle with Ceto.

I reach the edge of the continental shelf in just a few minutes but I know I still have nearly 500 feet to go. I drop my shield and mace to allow myself more freedom of movement. In a few minutes more I breach the surface, taking in the first breaths of fresh air I've had in a long time. The effect is momentarily debilitating as I cough up water and gasp for air. As I regain my ability to breathe above water, I feel rain droplets pounding on my face. The waves above the sea are in just as much turmoil as the battlegrounds I left behind. The water is incredibly warm and getting warmer by the second. I wouldn't have expected the water to be so warm in November. It must be Ceto's work already starting in anticipation of finding the power source.

Rain feels warm against my skin. It isn't the refreshing kind of rain I grew up with in Arizona. This is laden with humidity so thick I can hardly breathe. That may be the point. I know that Ceto is creating the perfect conditions for a hurricane, and knowing her plans, I know it is not going to be a small one. My parents break the surface of the water to my left. My dad struggles for breath for only a moment before re-entering the sea. He has been so long without the air above water, he can no longer breathe it. He has to stay below the surface to survive.

My mom swims to my side. "We have to work together to stop her, Evelyn," She says as the rain pelts her face, "I can only talk to the air above the ocean and to sea creatures. What are your strengths?"

"I can do both of those too," I reply, "I can also control water temperature, waves, and tide." My mother lets out one, hard laugh.

"Well, then. I don't see how Ceto stands a chance," she says. "Your father is headed below to the power source. Ceto will be too distracted to fight us all off."

My mother and I clasp hands and turn our faces into the wind.

Please, I can feel us both speaking in unison to the air surrounding us. *We humbly seek your help.* The air molecules brush our cheeks, wanting to meet the two-worlders who are reaching out to them. I feel the air around my face cool in a collective gasp. Their unified mother voice speaks to us.

The Marin child has returned. We are so very pleased. We had begun to wonder where you had gone, Marin child. We had such a fine meeting the last time.

She has brought her mother with her. We have not heard from her mother since her father disappeared. It has been such a long time.

We both have missed you. My mother and I both reach out to the molecules with our minds, *we have been at war with Ceto. She is trying to destroy life on land. She has found the location of the Atlantis power source and plans to use it to carry out her plans. This hurricane is just the beginning of her designs.*

I feel sighs of worry and concern in the warm air around me. *Can you help us?*

Yes, of course we can, replies the mother-voice. *What do you need us to do?*

Would you please help us to cool the air? We ask. *We are trying to break the power she is growing in her hurricane.*

Of course we can. Though she has some already on her side.

Then to themselves, *Ladies. All you've got.*

The air begins to chill immediately. I am amazed by its iciness on my cheeks and nose. But I am grateful for the help. My mom and I send our gratitude to the air and I focus on the water temperature.

I'm grateful I had a Hurricane class this semester. It will come in handy for me now. Water needs to be 79 degrees in order for a hurricane to grow and maintain a steady pace. What I am swimming in is close to 90 degrees. I reach out with my water abilities, but I have only used this particular talent in small areas. I need a super-cooled ocean. I reach out as best as I can, draining my energy into the cooling of the ocean. I rapidly became aware of Ceto working against me to heat the water. She is so much more experienced with her water skills that I know I cannot win that part of the encounter with her. I am growing so tired it is difficult to stay above water, my body wants to sink down and go to sleep. Then, I hear the mother voices speaking to me.

Let go, Marin child. Let us take over this part for you. You'll be surprised by what we can do.

My mom swims to my side and takes hold of my hand. I let go of the water and let the air take over. As soon as I release my hold, the air starts blowing wind about us with tremendous force, causing havoc all around. The water stirs and circulates and cools as the lower elevations of cooler water are stirred to the top. I am aware of the mounting waves breaking on the shore. I know the kind of damage that can be inflicted by a storm surge. I need to use my skill with waves and tide to negate those effects as much as possible. But I am weak from my battle with the water temperature. The waves and tide refuse to listen to me.

Panic grows within me as I realize that I am powerless. My mother is comfortable working with the air. She has the ability to handle that on her own. All those hopes for my powers being the thing to save the ocean and the world are being dashed to pieces like the waves slamming against the shore. I am feeling desperate when I hear the power source reaching out to me again, this time with words that actually fill the air. Its voice sounds laced with gold. I know royalty is speaking to me.

"Evelyn," she says to me in a piercingly soft voice, "I need your help now. Your father cannot reach me on his own."

"But what do I do about the hurricane?" I ask. My mom rests her hand on my shoulder with a reassurance that she will stay.

"Your mother will stay and work with the air to end it," the voice says, "It will get worse before it gets better, Evelyn. But it will end up for the best. You must trust in me."

Every concern leaves my heart as I understand that I can fully trust the voice that is speaking to me. My mom wraps her arms around my shoulders and kisses my cheek.

"You can do this, Evelyn. I have faith in YOU." I answer her words with a kiss to her cheek and dive below the waves, leaving her to guard the world above on her own.

Chapter 37

Once I am back in the water, I see Ceto focusing all of her attention on the water's surface. Gwen is by her side, just as focused as her mother. Several two-worlders float in the water around them, eyes closed, as they join their collective forces to strengthen the hurricane. No wonder my efforts have been met with such difficulty. Ceto has so many resources at her disposal, I am never going to win head-to-head with her. Beneath Ceto and her band of helpers, the ocean floor is still covered with fighters. Very few are aware of the battle raging above them. I cannot tell who is on which side and who is fighting who. It is a scene of chaos.

I reach out with my mind to the power source, looking for guidance. I feel the familiar tug telling me where to go. I swim forward, battles raging all around me. I am aware at some point of Ceto and Gwen coming to their senses and looking for me, but I am too far gone to be stopped. I move silently and unnoticed through the water. Everyone is engaged in fighting off another combatant - no one has time to see me. As I reenter the tunnel through the gigantic hole that now threatens to swallow the lifeless old boat, I move with an absolute peace. I feel like I am in a trance or in one of the many dreams that I've had over the years. Though I am unprotected and vulnerable to attack, I am grateful to not be burdened by my mace and shield. I know I will not be needing them here.

I move down the hallway, feeling the pull of the power source growing ever stronger as I move closer to it. The hallway grows lighter and lighter the farther I move down its length. I see the familiar doors I have been dreaming of for years. I stop in front of the door I know I need to enter. I hover motionless in front of it for a moment or two, taking in the surreal nature of living in one of my dreams. Then I reach out and grasp the handle.

The door swings open gently at my touch and I enter the blindingly bright room. I blink until I can focus my eyes, raising my hand to shield them from the brilliance before me. As I lower my hand and look around the room, I see the same furnishings from my dreams. The same paintings hang on the walls. The same books cover the tables. Had I not seen it so many times before, I would be tempted to take the time to admire my surroundings. But I am already fully aware of this room and all it holds. I know I have just one thing to look for, and I cannot risk missing it.

In the center of the room, hovering a few feet above the floor, is the power source of Atlantis. She hovers angelically in the water before me. She is a large pearl, the kind you would see in some old painting of English or French aristocracy. The kind that divers spend their lives and fortunes searching for. She is the size of a small orange, but a completely perfect sphere of white. Her exterior shimmers and I can see worlds of color moving across her surface. Those same colors curl away from her, joining together to create the magnificent light that shines throughout the room. My heart skips a beat as it speaks within me again that this is not one of my dreams. This is finally happening. This is real.

The power source pearl speaks to me once more in her soft but firm tone. "Evelyn, I am so grateful you have come to me. It has been many years since I was able to see another two-worlder like myself."

"What do you mean?" I ask her.

"I was once as you are, Evelyn. I was a human being who lived on land and walked and ran and loved. But that was so long ago for me. I have been in this state for thousands of years, the slave of humans and two-worlders alike. They all wanted the same thing. They all wanted my power in one way or another to rule the world. I thought that by casting myself into the sea I would be able to escape that burden. But I was mistaken."

"I am so sorry," I say, amazed by what I am hearing. The power source is human, is a two-worlder. "Is there no way to free yourself?"

"There is a way, Evelyn, but I have never met someone willing to do the task." Her words move sadly, searchingly through me, making my spine tingle in anticipation. Whatever the task is, will I be prepared to do it? I know that this is what all of my dreams and urges were pushing me toward, but I also know I still have a choice.

"Take the bottom book from the table, Evelyn," she says.

I go to the side table I have seen so many times in my dreams, and pick up the book that has laid there for so long. The book is bound in red, with gold lettering almost burning its way out of the spine. _Atlantia_, it reads. A long, golden bookmark hangs from the pages and I open to the place it holds.

"Read it aloud, Evelyn. I want to be able to hear the words again."

My eyes move down the page to a passage that is underlined in black ink. As I read, the words evolve from some kind of Ancient Greek hieroglyphs to beautifully scripted English.

The one who lives as the stone once lived must one day give
her life.
She lives to die for such is fate and the ending of all strife.
The sea cannot see settled days until this offering,
Is laid before the silent stone as peace for all to bring.
But such a sacrifice indeed cannot be compelled,
For it is by choice that all is given and all law upheld.

I close the book and rest it on the table. The words are no surprise to me. I have known for years that I will die if I reach out to touch the glowing orb in front of me. She is silent once again, allowing me to feel all that she feels. I see her life in the glowing water before me. I see the baby girl born with magic living inside her. A powerful magic bestowed by a curse. I see her as a child, long and dark wavy hair bouncing on her back as she runs with her brother down a grassy hill, her white robe blowing in the wind. Then the picture changes to show her as a young woman wrapped tightly in the arms of the man she loves. She is kissing him fervently for she loves him with all of her heart. I feel it all.

Then I see the same young man betray her. He is pointing to her as he receives money from a purple-robed man who stands by his side. The source of so much power, so much potential for love and happiness, is chained and put on display. For years she is forced to give her power to several different owners. Until one day she sees an opportunity. She focuses inwardly, her eyes closed as she hums a tune she remembers from her youth. The melody fills the water around me. It is deep and moving, like the currents of ocean around me. I feel the music in the water, speaking to me.

I see the young woman humming her tune. Her hair catches fire, but she pays it no notice. Soon she is entirely engulfed in flames, still humming her tune to herself. She burns until she explodes in a radiant display of light. Then there she is, the glowing, magical sphere that I have come to know and recognize from my dreams. She is no longer chained, can no longer be touched by human hands.

I am silent for a moment as I take in her history. All of its pain and suffering. Her yearning for complete freedom. She finally speaks to me again.

"You see, Evelyn, the only way I can be freed is if you agree to give your life for mine. That is the only thing that can outweigh the suffering and loneliness I have endured. Several two-worlders have come to my home. They too had the ability and power that both you and I possess within, but they only wanted power. Greed, power, money. That is all they have ever wanted. Are those the things you want too, Evelyn?"

Of course those aren't the things I want. But I do want to live with my parents again. To have time with the father I have really never known. I want to live. But I know that if I don't do as she asks, I will be handing her over to the enemy. Ceto will take her power and ruin the world. My parents will be killed. So will countless others. I won't be able to live like that, knowing that I could have stopped her and saved all of those people. I know what I will choose.

I have already chosen it so many times.

Voices echo from down the hall. This time I can distinguish every single one of them. Ceto, Gwen, my father. They all burst into the room with an army of two-worlders right behind them. Ceto and Gwen scream at me to stop, but my hand is already on its way. My father hovers silently by them, watching me reach for my destiny. He knows what this means for me. He also knows why it has to happen. I see sadness in his eyes. But I also see something else. Pride. Pride in me.

"I love you, Evelyn." He whispers it, but it is the most penetrating thing that I could hear. I needed to hear it.

"I know. I love you too, Dad."

Gwen reaches out to grab my arm, but she is too late. My fingers brush the swirling ball of light in front of my face. She is warm and inviting. I reach further until the warmth turns into burning. So much screaming is in the room it is amazing how peaceful I feel about my decision. Then, with my arm raised up to the light, my fingers brush a cold and hard stone.

Light explodes into the room, pushing back everyone but me. My fingers wrap around the stone, the room grows silent, and for the last time in my life I cannot breathe.

End of book one.

Trapped, Book 2 in the "Called" Trilogy

Chapter 1

"Evelyn!" I hear my name fading in the distance, screamed out by half a dozen people in a battle undersea. The voices fade, my mind goes black and I struggle for breath.

Fire fills my lungs as I try to breathe. Breathing hasn't been such a painful chore before. It's sharp and stinging in my chest, and stabbing pains are striking at my sides. But air is coming in. It isn't the feeling I expected when I touched the Atlantis stone. In my dreams as I'd reached through the water to grasp what I felt was my destiny, I knew I could no longer breathe. But I thought that drowning would feel more like my chest caving in on itself. Like all the air was being burned out of me and I was collapsing from the inside. It wasn't ever _in_ my dreams; the actual drowning. But I had always imagined how it would be when it finally happened. I feel the burning I envisioned, but not the collapsing.

I also feel something different around me. The cool, swirling waters from the bottom of the Atlantic Ocean have been replaced by something warmer, dryer. I try to steady myself, slow down my thoughts for just a moment so I can look at what is now around me. I turn to look for my father whose proud and sad eyes were the last thing I registered before reaching out for the pearlescent Atlantean stone. But a large olive tree has taken his place. Its branches are wide and outstretched as though they want to wrap me in an embrace. A brief shudder tingles its way down my spine as I think of those scratchy arms cutting my body and clothing, trying to hold me close.

The water I was floating in is gone. Nothing is floating, groundless around me anymore. Everything is motionless but for the occasional breeze making everything sway as it moves across the dry earth.

My feet are planted firmly on the ground and I turn to survey the changed landscape. I feel something prickly on my feet. I look down to see that dried grass is scraping against the leather sandals which have replaced the underwater shoes I was wearing just moments ago. Instead of battle armor, I am dressed in light linen robes of some kind. My body is glistening with sweat as though I have been running. That must be why my lungs are burning and I am so out of breath.

"Pearl!" I hear a young voice call out and I turn to see where it is coming from. A very short distance from me, a young boy with dark, curly hair is staring straight at me. He is just down the hillside from me, standing, also breathless, in the long, golden grass. He is calling to someone I cannot see.

"Pearl!" He says again, "You're it. You've got to get me now!" My body remains still as my head swivels around from side to side to see who he might be speaking to. With a roll of his eyes, he jogs toward me. "Pearl," he grabs my arm and gives it a gentle shake, "are you okay? Do you need to take a break or something? Or are you just trying to get out of being the titan this time?" He gives a short chuckle like he knows he's caught me in some kind of sneaky act. When I don't answer, his eyes soften and his voice registers concern. "Hey, for real, Pearl. Are you okay?"

I blink several times, trying to understand what is going on. Why is this boy talking to me like he knows me? Why does he keep calling me Pearl? I look around, frantically trying to recognize anything in my surroundings that might help me understand what is happening. Nothing registers, nothing at all. Until…

I turn slowly to face the boy who is still holding my arm. He is only ten or twelve years old. His skin is golden brown and his eyes are a green/brown version of hazel. His hair is thick and full and his face is familiar. I know I've seen his face before. In fact, I Know I've seen this moment before. Only a short while ago I was seeing this same scene through the eyes of the Atlantean stone. The Atlantean Pearl.

I stumble backward a few steps, my head swirling with the impossibility of what is happening. As I look down at my own hands, I confirm for myself that they are changed. Rather than the rough skin and deep tan I have acquired over the past several months living so much in the ocean, my hands are now soft and small, similar in color to those of the boy in front of me. I reach my hand down to my stomach and run my fingers over my smaller waist and smaller chest. My hips are smaller, my legs are shorter, everything is different, more like it was when I was a preteen. I reach my hands up to my hair. Instead of the long, straight braid I had been wearing in the battle, I feel thick, soft curls. I pull a section forward in front of my eyes to

311

have a good look at what is growing out of the top of my head. It's black. My brown hair is now black.

I'm not myself anymore. I'm someone else.

I look up to meet the eyes of the boy in front of me. This is the boy I saw in the moment I touched the pearl. He, *this* is the first memory she showed me. "Pearl," he says again, his voice very gentle and a bit unsure, "I don't' think you're doing okay. We need to get you home." I slowly nod my head and let go of my hair. He reaches his hand out to me, and I take it, knowing instinctively that he is a safe place. As soon as our fingers touch, something registers within me. Brother. Twin. Domideus. Dom. This is the pearl's brother. Her twin. Pearl is who she is and what she became. Pearl is who I am now. As I followed dazedly behind him – my brother, focusing on putting one foot in front of the other, her voice enters my mind, filled with a search for freedom.

"You have come."

Acknowledgments

Here's a true story for you: you don't get through anything in life on your own – especially not the big stuff. Yes, there is A LOT to be said about perseverance and success despite difficult circumstances, but even in those instances, there are many who have a hand in helping us succeed. For me, there are several individuals who have made a huge difference in this self-publishing process. I want to take a moment to acknowledge and thank them here.

First of all, TJ Mackay. TJ is the owner of InD'Tale Magazine, a magazine dedicated to independent publishing and authors. She has a wealth of information and blessed me by her guidance throughout this process. She read my manuscripts several times and gave me the best advice each time. Thank you, TJ, for your time and devotion to this work.

As I learned about how to make this book happen, I sought advice and experience from others who have walked the path. Erin Huss, author of many novels and series, was SO KIND to give me loads of advice. She is *in* the business and was so generous with me. She gave me thorough and valuable advice and encouragement. Thank you, Erin, for taking the time to help a new author grow.

Kristen LePine was introduced to me by a friend. She is an author herself and is several steps ahead of me in the self-publishing world. She spent time with me on a long-distance phone call to share the things that have been most helpful to her. Thank you for your help, Kristen.

I LOVE grammar, punctuation, spelling, and a million other things that go along with good writing. I even pay my kids when they find printed grammatical errors. Fortunately for me, Penny Friday Baker of Baker Blooper Editing REALLY loves these things. She was AMAZING at catching everything that needed to be adjusted to make my novel spectacular. Thank you, Penny, for your dedication to the editing of my novel.

I LOVE MY COVER!!!!!!! I love it! I love it! I love it! But I love Mindee Thyrring of PostModernLaundry.com even more for designing it. Mindee's guidance and questions along the way helped me to convey what I was looking for in a cover. She realized my vision flawlessly while working within my budget. Thank you, Mindee. Here's to many more!

Kara J. Miller has been a HUGE lifesaver as I have worked on growing my business. She is a blogger and business owner herself and answered countless texts and questions from me. She understood my drive to make my vision happen and guided me through. Thank you, Kara, for your constant willingness to help a girl out.

Kirsi Kilpelainen is amazing. I sat and stared at my website for months with no idea how to make it happen. I finally hired Kirsi to help me get the job done and she did an amazing job. Kirsi knows her stuff and knew how to help me get the site I was dreaming of. Thank you, Kirsi, for teaching me and helping me make this thing work.

Now I get to be all teary-eyed over Erin Salvesen and Sarah Bleyl. These ladies are some of the best friends a girl could ask for. Not only did they both read my drafts and offer advice and helpful commentary, but they were so excited every step of the way, they made me feel so good. Whether it was texting their thoughts while reading or sending crazy GIFs to share their excitement, these helped keep me excited and proud. Thank you, Erin and Sarah. I love you. I love you. I love you. Thank you.

I have been blessed throughout this process by a loving Father in Heaven who guided me along the way. Without His love and Faith in me, I would not be where I am. Because it is important to me, it is important to Him. I am so grateful.

And, thank you, my beautiful readers, for picking up my book and reading it until the end. You are helping me make my dreams come true. I so love you.

About the Author

EJ Pay is a happily married mother of three. She lives on the central coast of California and loves her beach days almost as much as she loves her books. You can find out more about her and shop her store by visiting ej-pay.com. Connect on Instagram @ej_pay_author or EJ Pay on Facebook.

Coming Soon

Be on the lookout for

Trapped, Book 2 of the "Called" trilogy set to release in 2019

And Released, Book 3 of the "Called" trilogy set to release in late 2019 or early 2020